Uncoupling

Uncoupling

IRA SADOFF

HOUGHTON MIFFLIN COMPANY · BOSTON
1982

Library of Congress Cataloging in Publication Data

Sadoff, Ira.
Uncoupling.

I. Title.
PS3569.A26U5   813'.54   81-23963
ISBN 0-395-32136-0   AACR2

Printed in the United States of America

S 10 9 8 7 6 5 4 3 2 1

Parts of this novel have been published,
in significantly different form, in
Partisan Review and *Carleton Miscellany*.

To:

Tom Parker, always my best and toughest critic

Ronda Gomez, who made me do it

My wife, Dianne, who listened to and criticized
more versions of the book than anyone should
have to, always with that balance of patience,
support, and toughness which made me
want to get better and get finished

Anne Borchardt, for her continuing faith in my work

I

1

I'LL NEVER FORGET the episode of *Ozzie & Harriet* where a beautiful single woman moves in next door. One day when she's trimming the bushes in ski pants and a tight sweater, Ozzie takes a serious interest in gardening. A cunning Harriet bakes Ozzie a blueberry pie, leaves it steaming on the kitchen windowsill, and her husband's corralled back into the house. Most families I work with bear little resemblance to the Nelsons. The creased faces of my clients usually reveal their sufferings before they ever open their mouths. Some mothers are so timid their chins recede into their necks when the fathers speak; some fathers are so stern their eyebrows furrow when the word *no* is uttered. I'm no longer sure what my own father and mother look like together, since they haven't seen each other for twenty years. But the Carletons, referred to my office by three other family counselors they've been seeing over the past two years, look like the model couple. Both in their late thirties, both blond and blue-eyed, both impeccably and conservatively dressed. Mr. Carleton, with his short-cropped hair, slim build, and boyish, genial face, could pass for Ozzie Nelson's double. And all high-cheekboned Mrs. Carleton would have to do is change her hairdo from a shag cut to a pageboy and practice the cracking whine in her voice when she's exasperated by her husband, and she could qualify as Harriet.

The Carletons have been married for seventeen years. Mr. C. is a successful buyer for a hardware firm, and Mrs. C. has mothered two children into advanced stages of puberty; to all public appearances, their marriage could have been scripted for television. But then Mrs. C. went back to work to save some money for the children's college educations; as she became more and more involved with her job as programs director for the Board of Education, the Carletons began to fight and fight.

"She's never home when I get home from work," says Mr. C., covering old ground.

"Now he knows what an empty house feels like. I lived in one for fourteen years. It's his turn."

"My turn? My turn for what?"

"He's so easily threatened," says Mrs. C. Both address their grievances to me without looking at each other. A bad sign.

"What do you mean by 'threatened,' Mrs. Carleton?" I ask. "And let me be the therapist. I'll be in charge of the psychological jargon for now, all right?"

Mrs. C. pouts a little, then her face brightens. It's difficult to filter out what ideas they get from their friends, TV talk shows, how-to books, which conflicts they invent, and which are deeply felt. "He can't stand that I make more money than he does," she says.

"That's not true," responds Mr. C. "I appreciate it."

"Bull. And he's not too happy about the men I work with either."

"Like Milton Craven?" Mr. C. laughs. "Is she kidding?" He laughs again, then grows deadly earnest. "What are you saying now — that I don't trust you? Is that what you're saying?" Silence. Mr. C. decides to take up the slack. "She's so tired at night she doesn't even talk to me before we go to sleep."

"It takes two people to talk," she says.

"Sometimes three," Mr. C. mumbles in a defeated voice, looking up at me as if for divine inspiration.

"Mrs. Carleton," I say. "You seem so angry with your hus-

4

band. Do you know what makes you angriest? What triggers that feeling?"

"Isn't it obvious?" Mr. C. interrupts. "The family doesn't mean anything to her anymore. She wants something else. I don't know what it is."

"Let her speak for herself, Mr. Carleton."

"Guilt trip," she says, standing up and pointing a finger at her husband. "Guilt trip. No one said that to you when you worked nights and left me to raise the children by myself."

"I know," Mr. C. concedes. "I know all that. I'm not stupid. I've read *Ms.* magazine too."

"People change, Mr. Carleton," I say. "It's always hard when the terms of a relationship change. It's a time of enormous stress."

"I know that too," he sighs. "I'm afraid that's no help, Mr. Jarriman. No help at all."

"Well, then," I ask, "what is it exactly that you expect from your wife? That you're not getting." He turns to her for a moment, purses his lips, clenches his teeth. And says nothing.

"How about you, Mrs. Carleton?"

"I want him off my back."

"Is that what you want?" he asks, addressing her directly for the first time, raising his voice. "Because if that's what you really want, you'd better watch out. Because that's what you'll get."

"Look, this is getting us nowhere," I insist. "Think about that question carefully for next time. What you really want from each other. And let's save most of the arguments for our next session if we can."

Their hour is long since up. It is only in their anger that the Carletons seem to come alive, that I can take them seriously, as they should be taken. Because looking at them, listening to their borrowed arguments and speeches, it's difficult to believe that whatever problems they have, they can't be solved with a few fatherly fireside chats. The truth is, though, their lives weigh heavily on me. A labyrinthine history. Who

5

did what to whom? How can we untangle the guilt from the crime? Why do I sometimes confuse the Carletons with the Andrewses and the Parrishes? All day I sit behind my desk while the couples come marching in, tearful or stoical, offering their lives' stories and grievances. I counsel them all, or at least as many as I can fit into my case load. But the troubled families are overflowing. Having worked hard for my reputation as a competent and sympathetic counselor, I suppose I should be pleased that couple A recommends me to couple B and couple B to couple C, and so on. But why do I remain so professional that I refrain from becoming an advice giver, and why is there so little advice to give? I page through a textbook in search of the Carletons: case study number 648, *The New Family*, Harvard University Press. Woman goes back to work because she feels unfulfilled at home. Husband gets jealous. The relationship flounders. Text suggestion: provide clear role modeling. Suggestion neo-Freudian: woman should have another child; family should do things together, as a unit. Not threaten his masculinity. He should provide her the love and approval her job now offers. Structural solution, behavioral solution, not much better. So much for the casebooks. The text for my clients doesn't yet seem to have been written.

No sooner do I finish taking notes on the Carletons than my last client of the day appears and sits down. Mrs. Annette Eller comes in alone because Mr. Eller says, "We have no problems. *You* have a problem." Annette is a twenty-six-year-old secretary who works at Hertz Rent-a-Car while her husband, Larry, puts on dolls' heads at the Ideal toy factory in the South Bronx. Mrs. Eller is tall, blonde, pale, and zaftig. She has a round face and a slightly protruding chin, which she points in my direction whenever she feels most defensive. She sits as close to my desk as she can manage, propping up her head with her palms, her elbows firm on the desk top. This week I ask her to identify her lovers serially for the last three years, according to age. She sighs, and counts on her fingers: her boss, age forty-eight, two Massachusetts executives

6

who dropped off their Ford Fairmonts (one-way) and whom she serviced, ages about forty-five and forty, the produce manager of the local A&P, age fifty-six.

I interrupt her. "Do you see a pattern here?"

"I happen to like executives," she says.

"That's interesting too. But I mean their ages."

"So I like middle-aged executives. Do you think, Doctor," she says, fluttering her eyelids and leaning her chin in my direction, "that I might be a nymphomaniac?"

"Come on, Annette. You know I don't believe in that stuff. Why do you think this is so funny?"

"Because I see what you're getting at, Mr. Jarriman, and I don't buy it. Larry comes home from work, starts discussing his dolls' heads and how many of them fell off the assembly line, and it puts me to sleep. The people *I* sleep with are interesting."

"Then you don't think we ought to talk about fathers?"

"You have a problem with your father, Mr. Jarriman?"

"Sure," I say. "Doesn't everyone?"

"Okay, let's hear it, then," she says. "I've been through it all before. I want to sleep with my father and you want to get off on my mother. Now where does that get us? I mean honestly," she says, "you guys knock me out."

"All right," I say. "We don't have to talk about fathers if you don't think it's helpful. But tell me, if all these men are so interesting to you, why do you stay married to Larry?"

Suddenly Mrs. Eller frowns, takes her elbows off my desk. She puts her hand to her forehead and brushes back her hair. "Interesting question, Doc," she finally says. "Because it's easier than living alone? Because one man's as good as another? I don't know: you tell me."

"You know I can't tell you: it's different for everyone."

"Now that's what I call earning your pay. 'It's different for everyone,'" she mocks. "I think our hour's up for today, Doc. Maybe for longer than that." She stands up, straightens out her dress with a brush of her hand.

"You want my advice?" I say, rising from my chair. "Is that

7

what you want? I'd drag Larry in here by the hair and let him know how serious this is. I'd do that instead of wising off all afternoon. That's what I'd do. If you really want to save your marriage, Mrs. Eller."

"If I want to save my marriage," she sneers. "I'll tell you what, Doc. Next time we'll both make up lists of ten reasons why marriages *should* be saved and then we can compare notes. The person with the best reasons wins. How does that sound?"

"All right. If that's what you want." But before I'm sure that's what she wants she's out the door and gone. My last appointment. I sit back down, turn my chair around to face the window. Outside, it's just outside. It's November, the calendar says; the sky is gray and as I look down I see that the few trees that punctuate Lexington Avenue near Fifty-sixth Street have lost all their leaves. The last time I remember looking outside in the afternoon, the trees were just bruising into bud and Mrs. Eller had walked into my office for the first time. She was here, she said, to try to salvage her marriage. Progress made? Invisible. Why do people stay married? Why do they get divorced? Why am I being paid for all this? Why indeed.

2

I REMEMBER THE NEW YORK GIANTS' last ball game at the Polo Grounds, the only game I think my father ever took me to. This was a time when I ate, slept, and breathed baseball, and although I didn't really like the Giants (my father's team), I was excited at the prospect of seeing an important game with my father. "This isn't just a ball game," my father tells me, "it's history being made." Apparently my father has little interest in history, though, for after he dutifully explains what he knows of the rules of the game ("Three strikes and you're out, except for a foul tipper") he takes to reading his trade newspaper, *Variety*, circling in red ink whenever his name is mentioned as so-and-so's accompanist, or as an up-and-coming executive at NBC. My father comes from a show-business family, the only thing I know that distinguishes us from other suburbanites. He does buy me all the peanuts, hot dogs, and Cokes I can eat and drink, and when he takes out his wallet I notice a picture of a woman who looks like a movie star, a photograph taken with one of those fuzzed-up lenses — the kind they put in new wallets — but it's not made out of cheap paper, and I don't recognize the woman's face.

The Giants lose in a rout to the hapless Pirates, making errors at every opportunity, as if their minds were already preparing them for San Francisco. As soon as the game ends, fans rush onto the field, tearing up pieces of sod for souvenirs, fighting one another for possession of second base, ripping out grandstand seats with their bare hands. In this mayhem I ask my father to get me Frank Thomas's autograph (the Pirates' only decent ballplayer — today he owns a bar and grill in Queens). My father takes me by the hand and drags me to the first row of the third base line, elbowing his way through the crowd. "Thomas, hey Thomas," he yells out, "my kid wants your autograph." Thomas looks over to us and glares: he's just gone o-for-5 and has a look on his face that suggests, *Please Lord, let me be traded.* My father annoys him like a high fly in the sun field. I ask my father if we can please go, I'm dying of embarrassment, but my father is persistent. "Come on, for Christ's sake," he says, holding out my program, "give the kid a break."

As Thomas passes us on the way to the clubhouse, his red Irish face no more than inches away from my father's extended hand, he clears his throat, spits on the program, and continues walking. My father is speechless, stares at the program in disbelief while fans push past him to grab players' hats, uniforms, spiked shoes; then he grabs me by the hand again, hard, and leads me to the car. We sit silently in our '51 Chevy while other cars crawl out of the stadium in a massive traffic jam. My father honks the horn, sticks his head out the window, yells to the air, "Come on you sons of bitches, clear out of here." When we get home, my mother, cheerful and innocent, asks us how we enjoyed the game. My father runs upstairs to their bedroom and slams the door. "The Giants lost," I say, but I can hear my voice rising as if I were posing a question while my mother stands, puzzled, open-mouthed, by the stairway, looking up at the closed bedroom door.

Two weeks later my father takes me to his office at Rockefeller Plaza. It's the first and only time he's brought me to work with him — my memories of him are of the man who works past my bedtime, who often stays in midtown on weekends to take my mother to show-business parties, or stays out late working club dates by himself.

In the elevator he proudly introduces me to his colleagues.

And when he opens the door to his private office, there is a very attractive woman sitting on his desk, her legs crossed self-consciously like Bette Davis in a 1940s movie, her wavy dark hair covering one eye, her black dress sequined at the neckline, apparel obviously inappropriate for daytime wear. I know immediately this is the woman whose picture is in my father's wallet: she is his mistress.

"This is Lisa," my father says. "A good friend of mine."

Lisa lights off the desk and pats me on the top of the head. In a throaty voice she says, "Allie, he's so tall for his age." A lie: I'm short for a thirteen year old.

"You don't have any kids of your own, do you?" I ask.

"No, why?"

"I didn't think so."

My father kisses her on the forehead, a gesture of intimacy I try not to register on my face. At thirteen, I'm trying to learn how to be sophisticated, grown up. But all my hormones are working against me — I nestle against my father, wrapping his arm in mine. I know it's only a matter of time before he will leave my mother for this attractive young woman, this woman who holds some charm for him I do not yet understand. So I wonder if she'll like me, why this meeting has been arranged, whether they're thinking of taking me with them.

My father suggests we all go out for breakfast. Outside, it's an extraordinarily breezy autumn day, a man is chasing his Panama hat down the street, and the wind lifts Lisa's dress above her knees. She says, and I remember the exact words, "Oh, it's snowing down south," a remark I'd expect one of my classmates to make. From that moment on I resent her totally, although my mother must have said the same thing more than once.

In the restaurant, my father orders French toast and orange juice for me. I eat mechanically, but I eat. Lisa talks for a while about business (she's a theatrical agent — I imagine that's how they met) and my father tries to bring me into the conversation. "Tell Lisa why you like the Yankees better than the Giants," he says. "Tell her about that lovely girl you've been seeing. What you like about English class. Say something, for Christ's sake. I didn't raise you to be a mute." I speak, nervously and frenetically, about everything I can think of, gauging their facial expressions after every sentence, modifying my opinions when they seem to frown or pay little attention. The meeting, I am sure, does not go well, but I keep talking, hoping something I say will catch, will change their minds, live up to their expectations, whatever they are.

A month later my mother and I watch my father pack his suitcase, the silence punctuated by his practical remarks — that we should forward his mail to NBC, that he'd be in touch as soon as he got some practical considerations figured out. I remember my mother's face, her eyes narrowing in anger. I remember that she does not cry, that she watches each piece of clothing being folded into the suitcase. I remember her saying, "I want to know what's going on, Allie. What's going on?" She knows less about Lisa than I do, and I felt then, as I do now, that it was my duty to protect her from the terrible knowledge.

☆

It is 1968 and I'm about to get on the fifth-floor elevator of the NYU library. An attractive woman in her midtwenties, with long auburn hair parted in the middle and hazel eyes that seem to forbid entrance, stands in a corner of the elevator with her hands clasped tightly to her sides. I get in and Muzak starts playing (some unrecognizable tune with hundreds of violins), the tape moving so slowly the sound resembles a whine more than a melody. I notice the woman's hands seem to be trembling. "Is something wrong?"

"I can't tell whether this thing is going up or down. The floor lights don't seem to be working."

Sure enough, when the door closes and some time passes, I can't tell whether the car is moving or not. "I hope you brought your lunch," I say. "We could be here all night."

"Don't make jokes like that. I think I'm frightened."

"Here, take my hand," I say, moving toward her. And al-

12

though we are in the middle of the most suspicious city in the world and have never seen each other before, she does take my hand. A few moments later the elevator reaches the ground floor, the doors opening like an expansion of breath. "Are you all right now?"

"Much better, thank you."

"You ought to come see me. I just got my doctorate in psychology. I'm going into family counseling."

"That's a pretty decadent profession," she says.

"And what do you do? Work for CARE?"

"I'm finishing up my M.S.W. I'm going to reform the welfare system."

"Good luck. Hey, would you like to go out for dinner sometime? I mean now that I've held your hand."

She looks at me suspiciously.

"I'd settle for a cup of coffee. Honestly, I'm perfectly harmless."

"All right," she says with a smile, "but I've got to be home early to study for an exam."

We order two cups of coffee at Chock Full o'Nuts and I find talking to this stranger easy, as though I'd known her for years. I ask her how she got interested in welfare reform, and she tells me that she's always been political. Shyly she adds, "It's also a good way for me to get out and meet people."

"You must be the youngest child."

"Yes, I am. How did you know?"

"They're usually the shiest."

"And how did you get interested in psychology?"

"Personal therapy," I say, raising my eyebrows. "Actually, I like to talk and listen to people. I have a perverse interest in motives and personal histories."

"I can tell," she says.

"That's because of my family. My father left my mother and me when I was thirteen. I spent the next ten years thinking that because I thought I was happy, it really didn't matter. Now I plan to spend the next few years figuring out why I was wrong."

"Then what?"

"Then I'm going to forget about myself and save the world."

"You could save a lot of time if you just left out the middleman."

"The middleman?"

"Your father," she says. "We need good people like you out there. There's a lot of important work to do."

"I know. A lot of people are afraid of elevators. Do you have a lot of sexual anxiety?"

"Loads," she laughs. "I should always take the stairs."

Two years later, this strange woman whose hand I held before I ever knew her name, becomes my wife. And when I recall that first conversation, I think of how much we discovered that day of what was essential to and about us — what differences we'd have, what arguments, what we'd choose to hide or reveal to each other. And how our narrations of our life histories have been absorbed by intimacy, how we take in each other's pleasures and grievances with one ear while thinking about something else, the way most married couples do. Or the way people listen to each other when they first meet. To the point of distraction.

And although Evelyn has learned to "take the stairs," and though I can often put my family history out of my mind, those times when we argue most intensely, or when we all too often withdraw into privacy, I see in Evelyn's hazel eyes that same frightened look I saw in the elevator, and I'm sure she notices in my distracted gaze out the window the young boy watching his father's car pull out of the driveway and drive out of sight.

3

WALKING THE FEW DOORS between my office and apartment house I have the same feelings I've had for the last two years walking home in the dark. The streets seem more and more dangerous, each single face seems more and more threatening, each couple staring straight ahead seems on the verge of argument. Two weeks ago someone was stabbed and robbed in front of my office building. People apparently gathered around the victim and one brave person chased after the robber, who disappeared anonymously into Woolworth's. By the time I got downstairs the crowd had dispersed and there was only a trace of blood to prove the crime had actually occurred. I felt relieved that I'd been spared the ugly sight, the trauma of guilt and helplessness, just as I feel relieved when the doorman opens the door to our lobby and closes it behind me, shutting out the rest of the world and allowing me to make it home safely another night.

When I enter the bedroom Evelyn has a picnic-style Chinese take-out dinner spread out on the bed. She's sitting against the headboard, propped up on pillows in her bra and slip, watching the news. A familiar ritual. "Hi, hon," she says. "Sorry about dinner. I was just too pooped after work."

"You had one of those days too, huh?" I sit on the edge of the bed and take off my shoes. "Wednesdays. I hate Wednesdays. Between your late conferences and Mr. and Mrs. Carle-

15

ton, it's the one day I'm prone to having legitimate servant fantasies."

"There's no such thing as a legitimate servant fantasy."

"Of course, dear," I say, peering into one of the paper cartons. "Fried rice. Let me see if I can guess the rest: mushroom egg foo yung, two shrimp egg rolls, moo shoo pork. Am I right?"

"You did have a hard day. I can always tell when you're tired because your eyes are puffy. Should I get you some aspirin?"

I lean over to give her a kiss on the cheek. "No, that's all right. I didn't mean to be grumpy."

"I like moo shoo pork. And you do too."

"I know I do. It was a difficult day, though," I say, sticking a plastic fork in the egg foo yung and taking a bite. "Thirty East Broadway. I can tell with one bite: best egg foo yung in the city. So, what did you do today?"

"One second. I want to see this story on the budget cuts. Everyone in the office is absolutely panicked about their jobs." While Evelyn watches the news I catch up on the remainder of the Chinese food. Every so often she lets out a spontaneous "Shit," or "Bring back the soup lines." Finally she walks over to the set and pushes her palm hard into the on-off button. "Oh boy, we're really in for it."

"We are?"

"If you want to know what's doing me in, all you have to do is watch the news. Every cut increases my case load. The office today looked like Macy's bargain basement. All morning I ran around looking for Mrs. Washington, who's been borrowing kids from a neighbor so she can get AFDC. And we still can't find housing for Mrs. Foster, who may be the last living survivor of the Dresden section near the East River."

"I thought you found her an apartment last week."

"No," she says, throwing the empty carton of fried rice into the garbage can. "That was Mr. Craig. I'm tired of complaining, though. Tell me who's sleeping with whom and who has an inadequate self-image."

16

"Nothing very new. The Carletons are still into repetition compulsion, keeping seventeen-year scorecards on who did what to whom and when. I guess they didn't bother me as much as Mrs. Eller. She's got so much armor now she won't let herself be touched."

"The nymphomaniac?"

"Very sympathetic."

"I was only teasing. Let's not get into another one of our pointless discussions, Michael. I'm too tired. I just happen to feel that" — she pauses, reopening the carton of moo shoo pork and artistically spreading it on the thin pancake — "some of these people — she says for the thousandth time — are high on the self-indulgent decadent scale . . ."

"I know," I say. "What does one measly marriage mean in the face of the starving hoards?"

"You really do want to get into this argument again, don't you?"

"No, I really don't. We're both too tired to duel over such familiar territory — whose work is more useful, more important, who's had the harder day." Evelyn and I argue, like almost everyone else, for our own turf. For Moral Justice, which is abstract, disguised turf, a variation on the theme You Don't Value Me Enough, or Aren't I Someone Special? But tonight we truly are too tired to argue, so while Evelyn clears the cartons away in the kitchen I turn on the local news. In our household Evelyn keeps track of the arms deals, the international episodes, the unemployment and inflation rates, while I can't tell one treaty from the next. When a teen-ager pushes a little girl off a subway platform, though, or when a Hasid is captured with a briefcase of stolen jewels on Fifty-third Street, I perk up immediately. "Did you hear that, Evelyn?" I shout after her. "They've got some bonehead bleeding heart trying to explain the psychological ramifications of graffiti. Can you beat that?" I lean toward the kitchen. No answer. "Did you hear me?"

"I heard you."

"I'll wash the plastic forks," I say.

"Never mind," she calls in from the kitchen. "I did it already."

"Can we lay off the Chinese food for a while?" I ask, grabbing my stomach and rolling over on the bed. "I've got a bad case of MSG poisoning."

"Screw yourself, Michael," says the voice in the kitchen. "Next time, you take the subway to Chinatown. Then I can complain."

☆

After the news I join Evelyn in the living room, sitting next to her on the couch. "Now, what can we do to put a stop to this?" I ask, putting my arm around her. "How can we cheer each other up?"

"I don't know about me," she says, "but you'll be happy to know that before you got home I was looking through the *TV Guide*. Your uncle's on a rerun again."

"Uncle Burt? Great. That's the third time this month."

"I considered not telling you, but I knew if you found out later you'd kill me."

The first time I saw my uncle, earlier in the fall on *The Streets of San Francisco*, Evelyn thought I was crazy when I picked him out on the screen. After all, I hadn't seen him in twenty years. "Everybody on television looks like somebody in your father's family," she'd said.

"Just wait till the credits come on," I'd responded. "And see who the criminologist is. Unless he changed his name."

During the epilogue, the criminologist reappeared so Karl Malden could explain how only he knew where the murderer was. The criminologist, suggesting a crude gesture of awe, was amazed by Malden's superior psychological insight. And when the credits came on there was Burt Jarriman's name — fourth from the bottom, but there nonetheless.

"I wonder when he got back?" I'd asked Evelyn. "You know, last word I had from him he was going to England, into legitimate theater. He was an angry young playwright."

"I know. You've mentioned it before. I guess the lure of the bucks mellowed him out."

Tonight's episode of *Streets* is particularly banal, made in the show's last season, after Michael Douglas had left and the writers obviously ran out of ideas. They no longer worry about a criminal's motives nor gesture toward character. Every murderer is a psychopath, with a fetish for old ladies or long-legged blondes. In this episode Karl Malden and his new companion consult the police criminologist concerning the profile of a killer who stabs bus drivers. "A Vietnam vet," the criminologist says, placing two fingers on his chin, staring abstractedly out the window. "He associates the drivers with his military command. It's the uniforms. Looks to me as though he were suffering from fits of depression. He's what we call, in the profession, a 'paranoid schizophrenic.'" *In the profession*, I think. Very funny. Then the camera pans to a close-up of the criminologist: he's a man in his midfifties of average height, with a stocky build, wavy but thinning hair, sad brown eyes, and a nose that looks as if it's been flattened in a car accident. A low-pitched sensual voice. He speaks almost without moving his lips. Twenty years from now, if I break my nose, I could look like him. "I'm afraid," he adds, "he's extremely unpredictable. And dangerous."

After the show Evelyn says, "Given the insidious script, he's actually a pretty decent actor. Of course, with that lingo you've probably seen him at one of your professional meetings."

"It would be great if this were a continuing role," I say. "We'll have to look carefully through the *Guide* from now on."

"I suppose I just don't understand," Evelyn says, shaking her head, "your fascination for a man you haven't seen in twenty years. A stranger."

"He's my father's brother. He used to come over to our house. I suppose it's possible he just sold out, don't you think?" I say, getting out of bed to turn off the television, then the light on the end table.

"He didn't look too worried about it," she says, then turns

over on her side. In the dark I can't seem to take my mind off Uncle Burt. A face that made an impression on my childhood, a face I can't forget. For it was Uncle Burt, after one of my parents' many arguments, who first suggested they get divorced. He'd undoubtedly spoken out of genuine concern for this couple who seemed to cause each other endless suffering. Six months later, though, my father and Lisa took off with the family bank account and no forwarding address. My mother never forgave Burt: it was as though Burt's words had carried the power of persuasion, as though the mere mention of the word *divorce* had made my father leave my mother.

I remember Burt's coming to see us when I was thirteen, some eight or nine months after the separation. We were just sitting down to dinner when he arrived; I remember the meal as though it were still in front of my face: steaming potatoes, Salisbury steak soaked in gravy, green beans — what my mother would invariably call a balanced meal. I remember because I could not eat a bite of it. When Burt came into the kitchen, my mother acted as though he did not exist: she nervously served the meal and scurried back and forth between the kitchen and dining room, then began to eat quickly while standing up. Burt leaned up against the sideboard with his arms crossed. "Isn't this a little silly, Ruth?" When she didn't answer he added, "Shouldn't we act civilly to one another, like adults? Don't you think it was better for everyone that he left?"

"And I suppose it was better for everyone that he took the family's savings with him. What are we supposed to live on, 'what's better for everyone'?"

"And you blame me for that? He must have an explanation, but you've got to believe I had nothing to do with it. I'm sure he'll eventually get back in touch."

"It was your idea in the first place."

"Now, that's crazy."

"I don't want to talk about it."

"Do you want me to leave?"

"I don't throw anyone out of my house. Not even a stranger."

For the rest of the evening Burt sat in a living-room chair with his hands folded in his lap. My mother went about washing the dishes, straightening up the kitchen, then locked herself in the bedroom and turned on the television.

I was confused. For the first time in months there was a man in the house, a man who looked like my father. Suddenly it was as though my father's presence had returned: a man playing the piano, a man huddled over the desk shuffling papers. Everything in the house now reminded me of my father: the couch we had put on top of our station wagon when we moved from Stuyvesant Town to Long Island, the smell of cigarette tobacco, the raspy sound of a man's voice. Now, if I spoke to the man in the chair I'd be betraying my mother. Yet here was a man who had brought something with him, a message perhaps, some news from my father, or a gesture of friendship at least. I sat on the living-room floor, pretending to do my homework. Burt got up, put on his coat and hat, which was one of those old wide-brimmed felt hats you'd see in a Humphrey Bogart movie. "Michael," he said to me as he walked to the door, "your father is a grown man, he has a mind of his own. Someday, maybe a long time from now, this is all going to make sense to you. Believe me."

I buried my head in my book, but soon after he left I looked out the bay window and watched the lights from his car grow dimmer and dimmer until he disappeared. I have not seen him since.

Now, with the streetlights and reflections of headlights shining on the walls of our bedroom, I think of Burt again. I shake Evelyn by the arm, a violation of ritual, since when one of us is sleeping nothing short of fire gives permission to wake the other. "Honey, I'm afraid I can't sleep."

"Good," she moans. "Now neither of us can sleep. There's Valium in the medicine chest," she says, then turns away from me and puts a pillow over her head.

I sit straight up and stare out the window, wide awake.

"Your uncle Burt's got you all excited, huh?"

"I suppose it's stupid, but he brings back a lot of memories."

"Try reading. Catch up on your case load."

"I have to think of ten reasons why people stay married," I say. "But I can think of only three."

She turns on the light, looks at me, and shakes her head. "Do they have to be good reasons?"

"No, I don't think so," I say, reaching over her body to turn the light off again.

"Then you ought to be able to think of a hundred."

When I look at her again her eyes are closed, her breathing is slow and steady, she's far away from me in some dream I know nothing about.

4

THE CARLETONS ARE a thoroughly modern couple. In other words, hopeless. Articulate, college educated, interior minded, they've experienced several kinds of therapy, they've read several "major figures" in the field (as Mr. C. has told me several times), and have jargonized their emotions into oblivion. Mrs. C. accuses her husband of being "too defensive," Mr. C. says his wife's "on an ego trip." When Mrs. C. recently had an affair at Esalen, she claimed it "freed her up, changed her life." Mr. C. claimed the whole episode didn't bother him in the slightest, that whatever she chose to do outside their relationship was her business, it forced them both to "grow" and be "open to experience." I'm afraid he might murder his wife in his sleep. When, toward the end of our interview, Mr. C. says he "knows where she's coming from," I explode. "You two are really crazy," I tell them. "If you don't start talking like real people, there's nothing, absolutely nothing, I can do to help you. Do you understand?"

"But Mr. Jarriman," Mrs. C., on the edge of tears, says, "you've got to help us. You're our last hope. We've tried everything else."

When they leave the office I'm emotionally exhausted: I want to take a shower, burn their files, have a long talk with a member of the John Birch Society. Just before Mrs. Eller comes into the office I think of postponing our appointment, but there's a certain look in her eyes, liquid but not tearful, an availability, that changes my mind.

"You look tired," she says as she sits down. "Your hair's messed up. Hard day?"

"Pretty hard. Actually, very hard."

"It's almost a relief to see you slightly frumpy." She smiles. "It makes me think I don't have to be perfect."

"Now, that's progress."

"I made out my list of reasons," she says, pulling a piece of paper out of her purse. "I couldn't come up with ten, though."

"That's all right. Neither could I."

"I'm ready," she says, straightening up in her chair, looking around the room, "to talk about my father."

"What do you want to say about him?"

"I don't remember much about him."

"That's a start. Can I ask why this sudden change in attitude?"

"You mean talking about him? That's easy. I threatened to leave Larry this week. After I couldn't think of any reasons why we should stay together. I told him you asked me why we stayed married and I couldn't think of a single reason. I think he probably hates you."

"Hmm."

"I know it was cruel. The next day he came home early and told me he wanted to quit his job. He told me he couldn't stand putting on dolls' heads anymore, then he lay down and cried on my lap. There he was, falling apart, and I hated him for it. Now, isn't that sick?"

"And this has something to do with your father?"

"My father never would have fallen apart like that."

"So you do remember something."

"But I don't remember anything important. I'm sure he never made any advances toward me, he and my mother seemed happily enough married. I can't think of any important conversations."

"But that's important."

24

"I suppose. I don't want to be this way anymore, Mr. Jarriman. I want to stop hating Larry. You know, all the things we've been talking about. That's why I threatened to leave him."

"That's not your only choice, is it?"

"All this talk." She sighs. "I don't know where it's getting us. Me." She stands up, walks toward the window. My office is on the twenty-eighth floor, and the way she looks down at the street it's almost as if it were calling to her. "It all seems so petty and small. I had this dream where I was about three feet tall and getting smaller."

She tells me about her dream, about the little people and objects that inhabited it, and her face grows animated. All the while I'm looking at her face, this young woman who seems so brave to me, who makes herself so open to what causes her pain; I can almost see her, as she returns to her chair, as she moves restlessly about in it, trying to extract what she feels is ugly about herself and cast it out of her body. Then she looks me in the eye and actually smiles about it. That smile is enough to make me forget about the Carletons, to make me feel, for the moment, of some use. I want to remember the scene exactly, so when I get home and argue with Evelyn about the decadence of my profession, I'll have evidence to prove she's wrong, I'll be able to feel proud of what I do.

By the time Annette Eller finishes talking, her hour is long over. She looks at her watch, says, "Ooops," like a little girl, and rises to leave. I rise with her, look at her from across the desk, and walk over to hug her. Her body is soft and giving, yet her grasp is firm. I pull away, but she grabs me by the wrist. "Is this what you call a breakthrough?"

"It is, though that doesn't do it justice."

"My next project is to bring Larry in with me. I think I can do it. I think we can do it."

"I think you can too. Whatever *it* is."

"Oh my god! I didn't tell you about my father. And I didn't get to read the goddamn list."

"Next time."

"All right, but before I leave I have to tell you this one thing. I hope it doesn't hurt your feelings."

I nod, giving her permission.

"You've got to do something about the office. It's absolutely the ugliest room I've ever been in."

"It is?"

"Let's forget about the ugly paneling. There's not a single picture, no knickknacks, no draperies, no flowers. You haven't even put up your stupid degrees. It looks like a laboratory."

I look around the room, as if for the first time. Of course, though I've never given it a minute's thought, she's right. "I'll tell you what, Annette. By the next time I see you I guarantee this place will be all spruced up. I'll see an interior decorator. How does that sound?"

"Just get some plants or something. Make it look like someone's been in here for God's sake."

When she closes the door behind her I feel exhilarated, begin to pace around this barely furnished room. And I wonder how I've worked, all this time, in my little talking chamber, without a single concession, not even a picture of my wife, to the outside world. And it took a client to wake me up to that fact. I put on my overcoat, resolve that sometime this week I'll buy some plants, and perhaps, if my energy holds out, put up some prints or photographs.

5

EVELYN AND I are dressing for our biweekly dinner at her parents' Long Island home. The phone rings. It's Rick Chandler, a neighbor from down the hall. He tells me he's been looking through the newspaper and noticed there's a Burt Jarriman listed in the cast for an episode of *Barnaby Jones*, and he wonders if he's any relation.

"It's my uncle Burt," I say proudly. I cover the mouthpiece with my hand and whisper to Evelyn, "Uncle Burt's going to be on *Barnaby Jones*. Can you believe it?" She rolls her eyes and continues zipping up her dress.

"Listen," Rick says, "we're having a few people over to play cards tonight. Why don't you two join us? We can have an Uncle Burt festival."

"I don't know if we can. Is it a big role?"

"It says he's playing the bad guy. A jewel thief."

"Now that's a meaty part. Doesn't it start at nine?"

"Uh-huh. Are you a regular viewer?"

"Not on your life. I've never been able to sit through a single episode. I still think of Buddy Ebsen as Jed Clampett on *The Beverly Hillbillies*. We'll see you then." I hang up, excited about the thought of seeing Burt again.

Evelyn gives me a motherly smile. "You never let anyone escape his past, do you? Not even Buddy Ebsen."

"Nobody gets out alive," I say, beginning to untie my tie.

"What do you think you're doing?" she asks me. She's standing in front of the mirror, looking at my reflection while putting on an earring.

"I won't need a tie to go to Rick's."

"That's tonight? Michael, you're not serious. I'm sure my mother's already put up the meal."

"I think we could stay home just this once, Evelyn. By the time we get there and start eating, the show will be half over. I'm sure they'd understand."

"Don't be crazy. You can't just call them an hour before we're supposed to arrive. You know how much trouble they go to for these dinners."

"Yeah, I know. The way he kisses her on the cheek and holds her hand after dessert, the way they politely inquire about my job. The obligatory political discussions in which they're always on the correct side. It's right out of a Norman Rockwell painting. No, better yet, it's like *Father Knows Best.*"

"Listen: we're not breaking an engagement for a stupid television show, and that's all there is to it. And I don't think," she adds, lowering her voice, "you really believe that about my parents."

"You're damn right I believe it. I bet we're not out the door five minutes before they're at each other's throats about how the table was set."

"Like we are now?"

"Exactly. Because that's the way it is outside of storyland, Evelyn. That's the way it is."

Evelyn throws her earring down on the vanity, turns around, and makes fists with her hands at her side. "Oh yes, you couldn't stand it if they were really happy. If they really loved each other after all these years. It doesn't fit into your world view. You think everyone has to suffer," she says, putting her hand dramatically to her heart, "the way you suffered. Just like in the movies. Just like your artistic uncle Burt."

"That's right. That's exactly right, Evelyn; you've got me pegged. There's no need to discuss it any longer. I concede."

"I'm going to see my parents tonight. They'll be very disappointed, Michael, if you don't show up. No matter what you think, they like you very much."

"I'm going to the Chandlers to watch Uncle Burt. You can do whatever you want. You can stay there for all I care."

"Maybe I should," she says, her voice becoming suddenly calm. "Maybe I should stay there for a while."

Evelyn says nothing more, continues to fix her hair in the mirror. I sit on the bed and watch her, waiting for her to say something conciliatory, to give me a way to apologize for letting this issue get out of hand. I feel the childish rage my father must have felt when he slammed the bedroom door after Frank Thomas spit on his program. And there's nothing more to be said; nothing can be added or taken away. When she grabs her coat out of the foyer closet without so much as looking at me, I know there's been a serious breach in our relationship. The attack on her parents' marriage seemed to threaten our own future happiness.

I do my best to forget the episode and walk down the hall to interrupt the Chandlers' poker game. Rick is one of the few people I know in the apartment house; he works for an insurance firm, has written up policies for us, and seems genuinely friendly to almost everyone. His wife, Christa, is a West German he met while he was stationed in the army there. She is quiet, solicitous, and subservient, in the European female tradition. In other words, I never know what to say to her.

Rick turns on the television five minutes before *Barnaby Jones* is scheduled to go on the air. "Tell us about your uncle," he says, while Christa brings out a round of beers for everyone.

"I don't know what to say. I haven't seen him since I was thirteen."

"No kidding," one of the guests says. "You don't keep in touch?"

"No. Ever since my parents divorced I haven't seen anyone from my father's side of the family." There's a sudden quiet in the room: I sense my remark is too serious for the occasion. "Besides, Burt was always the Jarrimans' black sheep. Everyone always talked about him in a whisper. He was the 'artistic' one in the family; my father thought Burt was going to be the next Somerset Maugham. Then he disappeared after he went to England to become a serious actor and no one heard from him for years. There were rumors he was a homosexual. And this is long before it was fashionable."

"And years later he just pops up on television. What a life," Rick says, shaking his head. "You think it's the money?"

"That's what Evelyn and I were speculating. But who knows? My father's supposed to be out on the West Coast and my grandmother moved out there when Burt left. Maybe he was lonesome for his family."

"Fat chance," one of the guests says. His wife nudges him in the ribs.

The show comes on and Burt's name appears in the opening credits, right after Buddy Ebsen's and Lee Meriwether's. A good sign. We all applaud, and Christa, surprisingly, whistles through her teeth. "Top billing," she says. "Maybe that's why he came back."

In the episode, Burt plays a cultured jewel thief who uses his job as an art dealer for a cover. I think I detect a trace of British accent. He plays his role with dignity and aplomb, despite awful lines like "Mr. Jones, do you really think someone of my professional standing would dabble in merchandise as speculative as jewels? Stolen jewels at that?" and "I'm afraid we're going to have to eradicate him." Gradually Burt gets taken in by Lee Meriwether ("Don't trust her, don't trust her," we all say) when she poses as a contact to pass on the stolen jewels. When Burt's caught red-handed we hiss and boo; when the show ends with Burt saying to the show's star, "You haven't seen the last of me, Mr. Barnaby Jones," we madly applaud, hoping for Burt's prompt return.

"He was terrific," Rick says. "You know, now that I think of it, I'm sure I saw him on *Dallas* last season. He played a doctor who injected poison into people."

"I guess he always plays professionals," I say. "I can't imagine him playing a truck driver. Though given all those rumors about him, who knows, maybe he'd like truck drivers."

30

"Can I get everyone more beers?" Christa asks. "After all, this is an occasion of something, isn't it?"

"I'll say," Rick says, ignoring Christa's odd syntax. "The first meeting of the Uncle Burt Fan Club."

"What a great idea," I say. "I can give lectures: Memoirs of an Uncle Burt Watcher. I could mention the time Burt came to our house with another man when I was ten. My mother kept trying to get me to stay in my room. And who knows, maybe they were just friends?"

"Sure," Rick says. "As the capitalist representative in this crowd I think we ought to print up Uncle Burt T-shirts, membership cards, glossy photos. There could be a lot of bucks in this for all of us."

"Uncle Burt would never approve," I say. "He's not in this business for the money." Everyone laughs. But then I realize that this *is* my image of Burt from my childhood — a dark and brooding, principled man who took up acting in spite of convention, in spite of everyone's wishes. I imagine his own plays to be somber investigations into the darkest of psyches. "I really should be going," I say. "I'm afraid Evelyn wasn't too pleased I chose my uncle Burt over dinner at her parents' house. I'd like to get back upstairs before she gets home."

"You just exchanged one family for another." Christa returns to the room with the promised tray of beers. "She can't object to that. It's not daily your opportunity to see your uncle on the television."

"That's what I tried to tell her," I say. "But I'm afraid I wasn't too terribly mature about it."

When I get back to the apartment it's after ten-thirty, but Evelyn of course hasn't yet returned. By eleven-thirty I begin to worry about her: first, that she might have been in an accident, but then, as I undress, get into bed, and turn out the lights, I worry about what might have transpired at her parents' house in my absence. How she explained our argument away. How, when they're all together as a family, her parents might tell her what they really think of me, of her choice of a husband. "Childish," they'll tell her. "His obsession

31

with his past, with his father — at his age — it's a very bad sign." Perhaps they'll subtly suggest she should leave me for someone else. But now I'm sounding like my mother: the paranoia of abandonment.

I get up, turn on the light, and think of calling her parents' house to make sure she's all right. To ask her to come home. But instead I try to read, to catch up on my case load, as Evelyn suggested the last time I had trouble sleeping. The bedroom, too brightly lit, without Evelyn, seems almost like a motel room. Familiar objects — the bed, the vanity, the oversized lamp next to the valet — all seem out of place, as if someone else lived here.

Then I fantasize that Evelyn staged the entire argument as an excuse to get out of the house. Perhaps to see another man, although I have no idea who that man might be. I begin to fear the invisible. No amount of logic, reasoning (telling myself that I was the one who started the argument), can convince me otherwise. And that's the importance of Burt, the clue he offers me to myself. The connection with my father, the un-resolved fear of loss. And as I go into the kitchen for a glass of milk, as I look at my reflection in the kitchen window, it's not the middle-aged mustached man I see; it's the boy who was once left alone, who imagined it was somehow his fault, who really believed no one would come back.

When Evelyn does come home, some time after midnight, I'm lying awake with the lights off, pretending to be asleep. And when she reaches out for my hand, touches me with her cold fingers, I recoil, pull away, turn my back to her. I won't let her have this power over me again.

6

To DOORS DOWN from my office building is the recently opened Tendrils, Etc., an attractive little plant store with pine-paneled walls. I decide that now's as good a time as any to begin my interior decorating, so I walk in. The proprietress, standing with her back to me, is showing a plant to a customer, a middle-aged executive type with a gray glen-plaid suit and a tan that looks as though it's been imported recently from Bermuda. The executive speaks in a low murmur, but I can overhear snippets of conversation from the woman. "Now, this would work well in a bay window," and "No, thank you, I'm busy then." I pace around the store, examining various plants and the signs beneath them indicating genus, ideal soil conditions, light and water requirements. Each sign is hand-lettered in medieval-looking calligraphy. Picking up an asparagus fern, I try to imagine how its bright green spikes would look hanging in my window. Then I read the rest of the sign — "NOT FOR BEGINNERS: PRONE TO INSECTS" — and put the plant down.

Meanwhile the executive is in steamy pursuit, moving closer to her from behind, and then, pretending to be looking at the plant she's offered him, drops his chin on her shoulder. "Here," she says, turning around to face the two of us, "you can hold the cactus yourself. It won't bite." She recognizes my presence. "I'll be with you in a second," she says, and in the brief moment I see her face I know exactly why the executive is falling all over her. She's one of those intimidatingly beautiful women whom, if I'd seen her in college, I'd have been afraid to speak to, much less approach. Statuesque, with dark olive skin, sharp angular features, and black wavy hair flared out at her shoulders: she looks like something straight out of a pre-Raphaelite painting. She wears a plain white blouse and a pair of tight designer jeans. "No," she says again. The executive asks if he can see something else. "If you don't mind getting your hand off my ass," she says. He leaps backward, then moons, "Please," then takes a step forward, facing her, so close their shoulders almost touch. She squints, crosses her arms, and mutters, "For God's sake." That's when I step forward, before I know what I'm doing, and say, "Listen, sir, why don't you stop hassling my wife?"

The executive stares at me for a moment, looks me over, then takes a step back. "Come on, buddy, who are you trying to kid?" he says weakly. "Who are you trying to kid?"

"You're not my husband," she says.

Sabotaged. "Maybe not anymore. But that doesn't mean I'll stand for some menopausal computer expert pawing all over you."

"Pawing all over me?" She laughs, and this time the executive does withdraw, discouraged, his head down as he leaves the store. "And next time you want a plant, mister," she calls after him, "you can try the Botanical Gardens."

"You blew my cover," I tell her. "I was only trying to help."

"I thought I was really doing well for myself," she says. "He hardly laid a hand on me."

"Sometimes I'm ashamed of my own gender. So desperate," I say, shaking my head. "If only they could see themselves."

"You're not one of 'them'?" she asks, tilting her head.

"Not one of *them*. Certainly not."

"And so little imagination," she says. "They're not all like that, fortunately. Just enough so I've had to learn how to take care of myself. It's a jungle out there."

"And in here, too," I say, making a corny gesture toward

34

the plants. "I came in here to look at something for my office. I have to warn you, straight off, I know nothing about plants — which ones are poisonous, require injections. All I know is one of my clients told me my office is incredibly ugly and that it needed some plants."

"Sounds like a good idea. You're not a dentist, are you?"

"Thankfully not. In fact, I think I'm insulted. Do I look like a dentist?"

"It's just that dentists should have really durable plants, since most of their offices have insufficient light and plenty of little brats to pull out the leaves. And they like to call their patients clients."

"Well, I have plenty of light in my office."

"Let's see what we can do," she says, putting her second finger to her chin, walking around the store. "We should start with something fairly large but that would require minimum care. Say, watering every other week." She picks out a flowering cactus, a large and shiny jade plant, and a fern whose name I can't pronounce. She says, though, it requires mostly misting and direct sunlight and is easy to care for.

"No bugs?"

"No bugs."

"Can you hold these till tomorrow? I wasn't planning to go back to my office now, and I doubt that I could carry them all. I don't mind paying for them."

"Where's your office?"

"Just a few doors up the block."

"Then we're neighbors. We *can* deliver, you know. My name's Laurie Reid, by the way."

"I'm Michael Jarriman," I say. "I'm sorry if I overstepped my bounds before. I suppose I have an instinctive anger about involuntary flirting."

"The voluntary kind's all right, I presume." She smiles. "MasterCharge?"

I nod.

"Good. Means you won't immediately feel the pain. You'll have your plants in the morning."

"Guaranteed?"

"Of course, guaranteed. Tendrils, Etc., is a class operation. We have several months of bona fide experience. Thanks, ex-hubby, for your help. A shame we couldn't have worked things out."

I walk briskly out the door with my receipt, a satisfied customer. The streets are no longer crowded, I'm an hour and a half late for dinner, and the episode in the plant store has capped off my best day in weeks. When I walk in the door Evelyn greets me with a peck on the cheek. "You're late," she says. "What's that smile on your face?" And returning her kiss, humming some tune cheerfully to myself, I realize I have no intention of telling her.

7

————

Aᴡᴛᴇʀ ᴛʜᴇ *Barnaby Jones* episode, Evelyn and I argue very little. On the other hand, we don't talk to each other much either. One night I don't turn on the television, and when Evelyn comes home and into the bedroom to change from her work clothes, she notices the blank screen but says nothing. "I got pastrami sandwiches from the Carnegie Deli," I tell her. "Some Doctor Brown's Cel-Ray, and as a special treat, because you've been working so hard, strawberry cheesecake."

"That sounds good," she says, putting her dress on a hanger and into the closet, then putting on her robe and sitting on the edge of the bed. "It's better than the pizza you've been getting."

"It's the best uptown pizza. *New York* magazine rated it the best."

"Well, it must be the best if *New York* says so."

"My, we're cranky tonight."

"Just consumed, that's all. A flood of paperwork. The usual. My back hurts," she says, sitting up straight and placing her hands at the base of her spine.

"You want to hear what my day's been like?"

"Something unusual happen?"

"No, I guess not." The strain of trying to find something to say without the support of television white noise seems now like cruel and unusual punishment. The pressure of a first

37

date. We eat quietly; Evelyn lifts the piece of rye bread off the top of her sandwich and says that they're not making pastrami as lean as they used to. I apologize for it, tell her I gave them the usual instructions but they never listen to me.

"I wasn't blaming you. I'm sorry. I just don't feel like talking about work tonight. Sometimes I just want to leave it all back there in the office. What's on tonight?"

"It's Wednesday, so there are *Streets* reruns. Burt's not listed in the *Guide* tonight, but one of my clients said they saw him in another episode earlier this season as the criminologist. So it might be a recurring role."

"That's thrilling," she says, taking a bite of her sandwich and leaning back against the headboard.

I resist the temptation to turn on the set. "God, you look tired. Maybe you ought to take vacation time early. How about at least a weekend in the Berkshires? Did I ever tell you about the vacation Burt suggested to my parents to help them repair their relationship?"

"Only about a million times in the last month," she says, shaking her head. "Michael, Michael, Michael. You should hear yourself. The same stories, over and over again. A broken record. You're becoming a bore, an intolerable bore."

"If you want to know the truth," I say, "Burt's the most interesting thing that's happened to our marriage in years."

"I see," she says, making an *O* with her mouth. She gets off the bed to turn on the set, but I rise too and stand in front of it, blocking her way.

"God damn it, Evelyn, I purposely left this monstrosity off tonight so we could talk to each other for a change, but you've got a chip on your shoulder that would sink a battleship."

She walks back to the bed but says nothing.

"I don't like this, Evelyn. I don't like what's happening to us. You're still mad because I didn't go with you to your parents' last week, aren't you?"

"You're damn right I'm still mad. Lately you've been totally obsessed with the image of your uncle on that screen. You're impossible to reach."

"Let's not blame all of this on the television. It couldn't have started with the television."

"Then what is it?" she says, leafing through the pages of the *TV Guide*. She looks up at me. "Boredom?"

"Boredom?" The mention of the word, the admission of a problem, quickens my pulse. But the word also diminishes my anger: I'm like the calm at the center of the storm. "Boredom? I don't think that could be it."

"Then what?" she asks. "You're supposed to be the expert in these matters."

"Thanks a lot. I think we're not spending very much real time together. I think we're working too hard."

"*Real* time? Now you're beginning to *sound* like your uncle Burt."

"Well, maybe I don't know what it is any more than you do. But I know it's serious, Evelyn. I know you're a million miles away from me."

"I think," she says, enunciating each word slowly and deliberately, "I think you're unconsciously trying to sabotage our relationship. The whole thing with Burt is a diversionary tactic. It's driving me crazy."

"You know what the obsession with Burt's about. It's about my father. It brings up all the unresolved issues of my father's leaving."

"Don't you see, Michael, that's what's so crazy about it. If you're determined to relive your past, you're going about it the wrong way. Maybe you really ought to go back into therapy. I mean it."

"I know you think it's crazy for a grown man to think about his past. But there are lessons to be learned from it. Your great hero Karl Marx says that about history. In some ways we're still the same people we were as children. All your knowledge about modeling comes from your parents, for God's sake. It's as plain as day."

"That's not true," she says. "The point is, the thing with Burt diminishes your life. It's as though all you ever think about is your fantasy life or your wounded feelings."

39

"You know what this fight's about, don't you? It's just another way of telling me you don't respect my work. You don't respect my work? My God," I say, slapping my forehead with my palm, "I'm beginning to sound like the Carletons. This *is* serious. Maybe I ought to go into therapy. What are we going to do, Evelyn, what are we going to do?"

"I don't know," she says. But she reaches over the bed to hug me. I lie down in her lap and she caresses my forehead, but her caress is neither intimate nor comforting. It's the caress of a remorseful mother who's just punished her child. "But I know we have to do something."

8

Within a week of my visit to Tendrils, Etc., in the snapping December cold, I've gone out to buy reproductions of two Stieglitz photographs of urban scenes, a macramé wall hanging from Bloomingdale's, and a Sierra Club desk calendar. I've even contemplated, then rejected, the idea of putting up my license and advanced degrees. But still no plants. I decide to call up Laurie Reid.

"Hello. This is Michael Jarriman. I don't know if you remember me, but last week I bought some plants you said you were going to deliver."

"Mr. Jarriman, I'm glad you called. I wrote down the plants you wanted on that card you gave me, but then I lost the card. I didn't know how to reach you."

I give her the address, adding, "It's just that the client who complained about the office is scheduled to come in this afternoon and I'd really like her to see the change."

"Well, listen," she says. "If you'll put your fate in my hands I'll select a few plants and bring them up during my lunch hour. I remember there was the jade . . ."

"You can bring whatever you like. But I'd appreciate it if you'd also give me copies of the instruction cards."

"And as a bonus I'll throw in a misting bottle. Because you've been so patient."

An hour later she does indeed appear at my office door

41

with a box of plants on a dolly. She's dressed in a red-checked flannel shirt, dungarees, and a wool flannel hat. A female lumberjack. "I didn't know you were a shrink," she says, looking at the sign on the door. "It's probably unhealthy for these plants to be around neurotics. I should have brought up a coleus."

"Then thinking I was a dentist wasn't necessarily an insult," I say.

"Far from it. Dentists take care of their plants. It probably helps them feel less guilty about tearing up people's mouths day after day." She wheels the dolly into the office, refusing my help, examines the windows, and then, with some authority, lifts the heavy jade plant out of the box and tries it in each corner of the room. "You really do need an interior decorator. This place looks like an accountant's office."

"You should have seen it before I put the photographs up."

"What do you do all day, pull down the shades and look at people's brain waves?"

"You sound like my wife. She's always complaining about the life of the mind."

"There," she says, after placing the last plant on the windowsill. "You could actually do with another flowering plant. One on your desk, for example. Now," she says, lifting a plastic bottle from the dolly, "this is what we call a misting bottle. A couple of these should be sprayed every couple of days and watered once a week. The jade needs even less care than that. It says so right on the cards, and I made a little drawing of what the leaves look like so you wouldn't get confused."

"Plants for idiots. Perfect," I say, looking over her shoulder as she makes a notation on the jade plant card. "This is exactly what I need. Thanks an awful lot. Have you eaten lunch yet?"

"No," she says with a sigh, "I haven't. What happened to the Puritan who'd flog all the flirters?"

"I just asked you to lunch," I protest, feeling the blood rush to my head. "I didn't want to show you my etchings. A harmless gesture, really." I can see she doesn't believe me. "Look, you weren't in my office a minute before I told you I was married. Just wanted to show my appreciation."

"I noticed," she says. "No need to be defensive: I was only teasing. I do have to be back in forty-five minutes."

"And I in less time than that," I say, but I'm already putting on my coat, and in a few minutes we're walking east in a light, cold rain, toward Third Avenue, with Laurie and her dolly in the lead.

Despite my mild protests, Laurie takes me to a vegetarian restaurant nearby. "It doesn't taste like vegetarian food," she says. "Besides, it's quiet here." In fact, the decor of the restaurant, which is a converted and remodeled basement, is very attractive, with wicker chairs, butcher-block tables, and old-fashioned electric fans everywhere. "Lots of nice plants, too," I say.

"That's why they call it The Greenery. I did their plants for them." When we sit down she says, "Let me order for you. So I can prove vegetarian food doesn't have to taste like canned dirt." When the waiter comes over she orders hummus, braised mushrooms, a green salad, and lentil soup with chestnuts. "It's their specialty. Should I order a carafe of wine?"

"You're doing the ordering."

"The red's better than the white," she tells the waiter, who returns in record time with two glasses and the carafe.

It doesn't take long for Laurie to open up about herself either. Before the first glasses of wine have been drunk, she's told me she's thirty-two, has never been married, though she just broke up with an architect who traveled too much and wanted her to trek around with him all over the country ("What was I supposed to do with myself all that time?"). She loves the outdoors, cross-country skiing, hiking in Vermont. She got into the plant business to support her pottery habit. "The pots I make for myself," she says, gesturing with her arms in a big circle. "Pre-Columbian is the biggest influence. You know what pre-Columbian looks like?"

"I think so," I say, but I'm not sure.

43

"So how did you get into the shrinking business?"

"It's a long story. It started out as personal therapy, which is common enough, but now I want to be useful. I think the world makes it difficult to stay sane."

"People might be a lot saner if you sent them out cross-country skiing every once in a while. They'd be too exhausted to think about themselves."

"I'd like to see them try that on the Lower East Side."

"No, I'm serious," she says, motioning to the waiter and lifting up our empty wine carafe when the food arrives. "Haven't you read about how jogging can work as an antidepressant?"

"I've read about it. Sounds very California to me. I prefer self-knowledge, myself. You can do it at home and it doesn't destroy your cartilage." Following Laurie as a model, I swoop up some hummus with a wedge of pita bread. "Say, this is pretty good," I say. "You were right."

"See, you should listen to me more often."

"I took your advice about the plants, didn't I? What more could you ask?" She asks more and more. We talk and talk and talk. I become woozy from drinking so much wine. She asks me if I think men and women can be friends and I say, without thinking, "Of course they can. My wife and I are friends. Good friends."

"That's not what I mean. But what's she like?"

I draw a blank. "It's difficult to describe someone you've been living with so long. It's almost second nature."

"Well, what does she do? What does she look like?"

"She works for the Welfare Department. She's very devoted. Very pretty, I think. Very smart." I think about our last argument on the bed. "Very strong-willed. Enormous amounts of integrity and drive. She won't let you get away with any obliquity."

"Obliquity." Laurie smiles, reaches across the table, and puts her hand, for the briefest moment, on top of my hand. The heat of her fingers on my hand, though the slightest gesture of intimacy, seems to burn right through the table.

44

"Is that funny? Cute? Did I sound too businesslike, professional?"

"Well, it was kind of abstract. I'm afraid," she says, almost in a whisper, "you sound more like a proud father than a husband."

"We have sex several times a week," I protest. "Several."

Laurie blushes. "That's not what I meant."

"Good. I was lying."

"You don't have children."

"No."

"And don't want any?"

"I don't think so," I say. I pick up my fork and play with it, looking through the prongs as I hold it up to the light. "We've talked about it, that's for sure. But we're both very involved in our work. It's an enormous responsibility."

"I'm sure," she says.

"You don't believe me. Well, it's complicated. I didn't have the most stable childhood. I'd want to be the best possible parent."

Laurie looks at her watch. "Oh, my God. We're an hour late. I have to open the shop."

"Shit," I say. "I've just missed an appointment." Laurie gestures for the check, signs for it ("Don't worry about it," she says, "they're working off my plant bill"). My cheeks are flushed from the wine. "It doesn't seem as cold as I remember it," I say when we get outside. "Of course, I don't remember it very well. Should I walk you to the store?"

"Nope. I don't kiss on the first date."

"Please," I say, "my clients are waiting."

"I think it's cold," she says, wrapping her arm in mine. We walk the three blocks back very quickly, without speaking. Although I might ordinarily feel incredibly anxious about missing an appointment, I can't help thinking that I'm holding on to a beautiful, vivacious woman while walking the city streets. We're close enough so I can smell whatever fragrance she's put on her body this morning: something musky, mossy, outdoorsy.

45

"See," I say, "I walked you to the door anyway. I couldn't help it, you were on the way. Thanks a lot for lunch."

"Thank you," she says, extending her hand. "We just passed the first test. Maybe men and women can be friends after all."

"And maybe not."

When I get back to the office, I'm still slightly drunk, slightly dizzy. Three clients are waiting in the outer office, a single man and a couple. They're all looking down at their shoes. This is one of the few times I regret my decision not to keep a secretary, though I like working alone and the answering machine serves my needs perfectly well. I'm immediately depressed by the thought that the rest of the day will be spent listening to my clients' problems. "Sorry I'm so late," I say, as casually as I can manage. "Some trouble at home."

I open the door to the inner office, which, with the new plants and photographs, looks like it belongs to someone else. I fight off the urge to apologize for intruding on this strange space. My clients are patient with me, say nothing about my being late. The single man sits down, slumps in the chair, almost knocking over a plant with his arm, and before I've had a chance to sit at my desk begins to tell me how he's been thinking about suicide again this week. I take notes furiously, but except for a few leading textbook questions, say little. I don't look up when he leaves, I don't want to look him in the eye to see if he can tell the difference, if he feels cheated.

The rest of the afternoon passes slowly until Annette Eller, who changed the date of this week's appointment because she feels as though she's in trouble. She can't get Larry to go into counseling with her yet; they've been working hard on their relationship, but it means so many arguments, so little sleep. I give her as much encouragement as I can, but I can't tell what registers and what doesn't. It's a painful session. Needless to say, she says nothing about the new decorations, the plants that, from a certain angle, make the room look like a tropical forest.

When I get home an hour behind schedule, Evelyn meets

me at the door, smiles broadly, and gives me a hug. She gestures to the dining room with an open palm. "Ta-da," she trumpets. "At last. Mr. Jarriman, dinner for two. I took off from work this afternoon to make it."

"Lasagna. My favorite," I say, lifting up the top of the casserole. "And a good bottle of Bordeaux." She lights two candles on the table and brings in a large bowl of salad from the kitchen. "What's the occasion?"

"I just thought we deserved a real sit-down dinner for a change."

I sit down, pour wine into the glasses, and stare across the table at her.

"Besides, don't you remember? You're leaving for Los Angeles tomorrow."

"Leaving? I'm leaving?" After only one sip of wine I feel the blood rush to my head.

"The American Psychological Association. You're delivering a paper there in a few days. Don't tell me you forgot."

"No, I didn't forget. But I'd like to." I lift my fork, then put it down. I place my napkin in my lap, put some salad on my plate. Everything requires so much effort. "I wrote it so long ago. The last thing in the world I want to do is fly cross-country on the red-eye. And listen to my colleagues."

Evelyn gets up from her chair, stands behind me, and silently massages my neck. "I have the vague feeling that you don't want to go," she says. "It's a good paper, though. You'll knock those idiots out."

Although I'm not hungry, although my mind is racing a mile a minute, although I want to curl up in bed and go to sleep, I eat as much as I can, I compliment my wife on the delicious food. When she asks me how my day went, what Mrs. Eller thought of the new plants, I want to cry. "She never mentioned them." I sigh. "It turned out not to be such a big deal after all."

In the bedroom, we don't turn on the television. Not for principle, but for the sake of ritual. The evening before one

47

of us goes away we have always reserved for intimacy, for making love. The practice has never been spoken of and we make no production of it — rather it's one of the few rituals in our lives that has unconsciously and spontaneously evolved and kept us together. Tonight begins no differently. Evelyn undresses first, neatly hangs her clothes on the valet, then slides into bed. She sits up and pulls up the sheets, half covering her breasts. She waits, shyly, expectantly, like a teenager, without looking at me. She makes me nervous, though, precisely because of her pose: I don't know what she expects from me. And she's not the only woman I'm thinking of. I take my time folding shirts, slacks, socks, and underwear into my suitcase. I take the necessary toiletries from the medicine chest. I pack my papers and case-load files. Finally she says, "How long are you going to be gone? Three years?" I apologize, undress quickly, and get under the covers with her. As usual, we leave the light on. We kiss, touch one another, but something's wrong, something's missing. When I reach for Evelyn's arm I feel like the wounded soldier touching the lost limb of his body: I remember it, but feel no response. We touch for a long time, I look at Evelyn's closed eyes, but I can't tell how she feels, if she feels the same way I do. Another night we might have told each other we weren't interested and it would have been all right, but tonight I know I'm going away. I try harder and harder to excite myself. I even think of Laurie for a moment, think of what it would be like to be inside her, the most common deceit. When I finally do enter Evelyn, when I'm leaning over her body with my full weight, I look at her face carefully, the way I would read a map. Her head is turned to the side; with each of my thrusts I see her nostrils flare — I can't tell whether from pleasure or pain. And then I think I see it, that look of distraction, that look, though her eyes are closed, of being far away, of thinking of someone else. But no, it's not distraction I see in her face, it's pain, in the inching down of her mouth to a frown, it's the gritting of her teeth. Or perhaps it's my own face I see in hers. Or perhaps, or perhaps, it's the rhythm of our sex tonight. Neither of us is brought to climax. I withdraw, she turns out the lights, we say nothing. Although we are lying on our sides, I pull her body close to me, so she won't drift any further away. And then, as I tighten my grip to her body, as my own body tumbles into sleep, I have to admit what I can't bring to speech: I'm lost.

9

THE APA CONVENTION. Downtown Los Angeles. It's December, seventy degrees, and everything else in the city makes that kind of sense. Downtown, it turns out, hardly resembles a city at all: the contemporary stone buildings, the attempts at skyscrapers, those shiny glass constructions without character, seem like they've all been constructed specifically for our convention. Enough artifice to make me wonder if there's anything behind the façades, or are they merely painted wooden shells supported by nothing but beams and crossbars?

The Hilton, one of the convention hotels, however, looks like all Hiltons, like everyone's convention — though the bellboys and desk clerks are Latin, Chicano or Mexican, instead of black, as they would be in New York. Once I'm in the elevator, which is packed with academics and practicing psychologists, it seems as though I'm not in the world at all. Pipe-packing men wearing tweed sport coats with cigarette burns on the lapels, the odor of the unwashed, briefcases that bear an uncomfortable resemblance to those our mothers made us carry in fifth and sixth grades. There is a woman on the elevator, only one, but she wears her own version of tweed — a bow tie, a dark suit, and the wire-rimmed glasses of the intellectual (my guess is she's either a graduate of Stanford or has come here from the East Coast); she is the exception who's not really an exception. I'm sure, nonetheless, the conservatives of the profession will be delivering papers about how these professional women suffer from castration anxiety. I'm grateful Evelyn won't be submitted to them, nor them to ner. we all give each other the once-over, and then, as the packed elevator rises to the fortieth floor, the jokes begin. "I hope no one has claustrophobia," one man says. "I had a dream about an elevator like this," another says, and from the back of the elevator, "I guess French Freud is still with us this year." "The complaint of a genuine rat-runner," another man says with no small degree of anger and animation in his voice.

When the elevator stops to let me off at the twentieth floor, I push my way through the stacks of bodies with considerable relief. Such a self-conscious group of human beings I've never seen before. The elevator becomes self-referential, the occasion of the nervous joke (cf. Freud, *Jokes and the Unconscious*), people who can't really communicate with one another or at least keep quiet. If I were an academic, the genuine article, I'd have made notations for a study concerning the motivations of these characters: What drew them to the profession? My hypothesis? My guess? They'd all been irreparably damaged as children, excluded from the comforting rituals of family, from the social subcultures in schools and human friendships. But I'm far from the real thing, as any of them would be glad to tell me: I don't sufficiently keep up with the scholarly research. The study's probably been done, my guess easily proven statistically incorrect. For the theoreticians are the elect, the truly brilliant in the field, and those of us who practice, who see actual clients, are the bastards of the profession, the popularizers who dirty their hands with the masses, the inarticulate. I have Evelyn to thank, partially, for this jaundiced and ungenerous view of my profession — she came with me to my very first convention and left two days early, her face etched in a permanent sneer, making me promise I'd never drag her to one of these fêtes again. Our cynical view is made possible only because we know so few of these people personally, because we've been spared their interior lives.

But that insight, as I open the door to my hotel room, seems too humane and abstract to make sense. The room has undoubtedly been inhabited by thousands of conventioneers before me: salesmen, doctors, mathematicians, funeral directors, and the like. They've all come and gone without leaving a trace. There are two single beds, one print of a Degas ballet dancer, a photograph of the ocean, and several sanitized glasses, which for some reason have been placed in the empty closet. So far from home, so uprooted do I feel, that a bellboy could knock on the door, tell me I'm not registered at this hotel, they have no record of my existence, and I would gladly pick up my suitcase and leave. My first impulse, after unpacking, is to turn on the television, to sit and stare at it for hours — they must have the same shows here as in New York — and not attend a single seminar. That's how removed I feel and want to be; that's how much like my colleagues, living high above this city, I'm afraid I am.

I decide to leaf through the convention program, circling the two or three seminars I might want to attend. My paper's not scheduled until the last day, so skipping out early is out of the question. I pull open the curtains, and across the way I see another hotel where several other psychologists are opening their curtains, airing out their rooms. It's as though I were presented with an enormous mirror; I sit on the heater looking out the window for a long time, watching people unpack, write notes on their tiny desks, try out their beds and television sets. Suddenly I fear the whole world is an APA convention, that I could walk the perimeter of the city without running into a single native Californian. If there were some conspiracy to round us up and lock us away, it would be an easy mission to accomplish: just look for the sport coats, briefcases, and pipes, the distracted looks of dislocated men, tap them on the shoulders and send them away in a U-Haul truck. The Invasion of the Psyche Snatchers. I change my clothes, put on a pair of dungarees and a loud polyester shirt with an oceanic design (I'm quite proud of the shirt — it took me hours of shopping in midtown Manhattan to find it, but it's just right for the occasion): perhaps now I can walk outside without being recognized as a member of my profession.

In the elevator on the way down to the mezzanine, I draw the condescending looks I'd hoped for, overhear the same jokes and snide remarks, then walk into the conference room where a seminar on "Recent Research on the Breakdown of the Nuclear Family" is about to begin. The topic is closely enough related to my own so I feel that I really should attend. This particular seminar, given by several prominent people in the field, is really an argument about narcissism, for and against. We're too narcissistic a culture, we're not narcissistic enough. We're too self-concerned, we've lost our image of the self. The family requires strong imaging, requires the absence of repressive modeling. The papers seem surprisingly passionate and intelligent, few people leave the session, I find myself taking notes on the back of my program, trying to figure out where my loyalties lie. In the middle of the last paper, though, a bellboy carrying two pitchers of ice water, balancing them on a tray, walks up the center aisle and unselfconsciously places the pitchers on the seminar table. The panel members don't recognize his presence, but I can't keep my eyes off the brown-skinned teen-age boy who's obviously listening to the speech on his way out. His eyebrows furrow, for a moment he seems lost, as if he'd brought the water to the wrong room. As he walks out the door he shrugs his shoulders emphatically, dismissing the problem. And when I try to come back to the talk, to remember what's been said, the spell's been broken: I can hear only the sounds of the words, the multisyllabic jargon that made sense to me only a few moments before. Now they seem like clouds of words disappearing in the air, little cartoons of human conversation.

The speaker finishes with a tirade of regrets: We've lost the nuclear family, the extended family is archaic and inapplicable to a highly technological culture. His eyes become liquid; I fear for a moment he'll break out in tears. He tells an anecdote, what he calls a case study, of an eighty-year-old grandmother who loses all contact with reality when she's placed in a nursing home. She calls out for members of her family who have died many years before; it's a perfect metaphor for his talk. He moves his audience. But this is not a real grandmother he's talking about, I soon realize, it's a grandmother several times removed, in an anthology he's read by another scholar whose research assistants may or may not have interviewed the staff of the nursing home where this alleged grandmother stayed. The image of pulling open the curtains in my hotel room, of seeing a world of psychologists in their rooms, involuntarily comes to mind. It's a grotesque scene, looking at these psychologists talking to other psychologists, talking to themselves, in a hotel in Los Angeles that is as far from anyone's grandmother as can be. As soon as there's a break, as soon as I hear the applause for his speech, before the question-and-answer session, I walk quickly out of the seminar room and downstairs into the lobby, my head spinning.

In the lobby there's still a flurry of activity. People registering and paying their bills, a labyrinth of doors and passageways. When I can't find my way out and pass the phone booths for the second time, I stop, pull out a local phone directory. I look for my grandmother, whom I haven't seen since I was a child, but who I believe lives in this very city. I want real evidence of her presence, of a real grandmother in a world of fictional grandmothers. And there is her name, Eva Jarriman, 384 Gardner, West Hollywood. So she is still alive and she is here. Then I look for my uncle Burt above her name, but he's not listed. I imagine he lives in Bel Air with the real movie stars, but it's just as possible he has an unlisted number. Finally I look up my own father's name, Alvin, Allie, and of course he's not listed either. Still, there is something exciting about seeing my own family name, my own grandmother, listed in a book of total strangers some three thousand miles from my own home. I write the address on my program, and after asking directions from someone at the information desk, I'm prepared for a ten-mile walk. I make my way out of the hotel and into the street. The walk away from my colleagues,

54

from my compatriots of the couch and the college, to some clue to my past, some piece of my origin, will be more than worth it. I feel as though I'm walking to some place that's real, to Gardner Street or Avenue, to a definite location, where my grandmother lives, and where my childhood, while it can't be recovered, might possibly have ended up.

☆

I follow the directions down Sunset Boulevard, and despite the increasingly gaudy billboards of rock and movie stars, the massage parlors and seedy storefronts, the farther I get from downtown L.A. the better I feel. Every so often I sit at a bus stop and watch the traffic, human as well as auto, pass me by. Real people going about their everyday business. None of them, I'm sure, needs a shrink.

The boulevard is incredibly long, and for a while I feel as though I'm walking through some endless, characterless suburb of gas stations, fast-food chains, muffler shops. But as I get closer to West Hollywood the neighborhood changes. Meaning, there is a neighborhood. Sid's Carpet Shop, an actual luncheonette, and on one of the side streets, a kosher butcher shop, a bakery. A real neighborhood, two-story attached brick houses with tiny yards and metal fences bordering them. Flower boxes in the windows. A chalk hopscotch board drawn on the sidewalk, and several old couples out for an early afternoon stroll, some walking their dogs, others chattering over fences. The faces of these strangers, the faces of transplanted Jews from the East, seem strangely familiar to me. An old man is watering the sidewalk with a hose, a woman in a quilted housecoat picks up the newspaper from her front steps. This is a tropical Brooklyn not so different from the Brooklyn where I was born, where my grandmother used to live and entertain my parents and me for Sunday brunches. She brought it with her.

I walk down Gardner, a short street where occasional palm trees instead of elms grow out of the sidewalk. I pass by my grandmother's duplex: Jarriman, the name's on the mailbox.

55

My heart beats a little more quickly now, I pause in front of the gate, then decide to keep moving. If I knocked on the door she of course wouldn't recognize me, and even if she did she'd be bound to protect my father from me, she wouldn't tell me where he was. Without fully realizing it, though, I've stepped into an irrevocable situation: there's no way I'll leave this neighborhood without knocking on my grandmother's door. It's an opportunity I may never have again.

I can almost hear Evelyn's critical voice asking me what I am doing, do I know what I'm doing? and I know it's a question I must answer. The impulsive escape from the APA convention has suddenly become serious. I think of one of our many arguments about Burt, about how Burt is a misdirected way of seeking out my father. And what now, after so many years, do I hope to accomplish by seeking him out?

At the end of the block there's a Sambo's restaurant: I decide to eat lunch and think everything over. I order a cup of coffee and a cheese omelette with onions, the only meal my father could cook for us. A Sunday morning ritual. I watch the old couples at the counters and in the booths, somehow still together after all these years, after traveling the plains of Russia and across the United States. The last survivors of the last century. They drink their cups of tea, converse in some mixture of Russian, Yiddish, and English. I hear fragments, arguments. Someone shouldn't have spent so much on a tablecloth, can you believe what the Congress is doing to Social Security, I can't stand how dirty the neighborhood's getting. Who's moving in, who's moving out. What they're going to do today, what they're going to do in the spring. I try to imagine Evelyn and me making plans at that age, staying together. I can't. And I'm devastated by the thought. I know what it felt like to have lunch with another woman, with Laurie. It was too exciting. And what I want to know from my father now is: What price do you pay to leave your family? And the question I can't imagine asking: Does he miss me at all, does he have any regrets?

I begin to vaguely believe that talking to Uncle Burt might clear up some of these questions with a minimum of pain: he would know if my father is doing well or not, if he's started another family, if he has any interest in seeing me again. If he doesn't, I can exorcise these phantoms, put the past behind me where it belongs. And if I find out nothing from Uncle Burt, what have I really lost? My curiosity will be satisfied. I'll be able to tell Evelyn, once and for all, that I've taken steps, that I'm facing the problem directly — I'm no longer wrestling with an image on a television screen, but I'm talking to a real person, a member of my family. I take my last sip of coffee, drop a tip on the counter, pay the check, and walk out into the arid city air, determined to knock on my grandmother's door.

An elderly woman answers, peers out of the crack in the door. The door is still chained, I can see only half her face, but I recognize her immediately. Her hair is died ebony and tied back in a bun, but she has the same gaunt face, almost skeletal in its severity. She does not look so different at all — she must have tried everything to retard the aging process (how many face-lifts, how many nights in front of the vanity with skin conditioners?), and by the glimpse I have of her now it seems as if she's succeeded.

"Excuse me," I say. "I'm looking for Burt."

"I'm sorry, there's no Burt here," she says, looking me over. "Just who are you?"

"I'm talking about your son Burt. Burt Jarriman."

"And I said there was no Burt here."

She won't budge. I wasn't prepared for this. "My name is Marvin Rutledge and I'm from Warner Brothers. I was told I could reach him here. It's concerning a part."

"And who said you could find him here?" Her voice still has the same Brooklyn inflection. "You should call his agent."

"I saw him in an episode of *Barnaby Jones* and I thought he'd be just right for the lead in a TV movie I'm producing. CBS gave me this address."

"They wouldn't. How did you get my name?"

"I just told you. Really, Mrs. Jarriman, this could be very important to your son's career."

"If it's so important you should get a hold of his agent at William Morris. I don't know who gave you my address, but I want to file a complaint." She looks fearful and angry, almost angry enough to strike out at me. "And never, never disturb me at my house again. You have no right," she says. "You people have no right." And she closes the door in my face.

William Morris, I think to myself. The adrenalin is pumping from the confrontation. From my grandmother's ferocity. But now I have a clue about how to reach him. I feel as though I'm a TV detective. Burt is a fugitive who must be brought to justice. I begin the long walk back to my hotel, and if I decide not to go through with this, nothing's lost. I haven't risked anything. I've just taken a look at my grandmother's face, a face I haven't seen in I don't know how many years.

10

BY THE TIME I get back to the Hilton it's almost four. Psychologists are wandering en masse in the lobby, examining one another's name tags, shaking hands with old friends, or drinking in the bar. There are lines at the house phones and conspiratorial gatherings of graduate students in corduroy jackets. There's no place I'd rather not be. My head aches from the noise. I take the crowded elevator up to my room, lock the door behind me, and collapse on the bed. My feet seem to be pulsing with ache from the walk. I stare at the television, which I have not yet turned on, roll over to the vanity, and pick up the local phone book. I look up William Morris, write the number on the desk pad, take a deep breath, and call the number. The switchboard answers: I give them my Marvin Rutledge story again, say I'm looking for a client of theirs, and is it possible to speak to his agent. It takes a number of interoffice calls to track the man down ("Don't you have the specific agent's name?"), and when I am connected, he doesn't recognize Burt by name. It occurs to me that Burt is probably one of a hundred file cards he thumbs through every day, a list of character actors who can play hit men, store owners, atmospheres of every type. "He recently appeared in *Barnaby Jones* as a jewel thief," I say. "And I think he's done a couple of *Streets of San Francisco*."

"Let's see, *Barnaby Jones*. That means he went into production six months ago. I think I know who he is."

"Listen," I say, "I'm his nephew . . . I haven't seen him in twenty years."

The agent's voice changes, as though I'm hearing him now from the other end of a long tunnel. "I don't handle personal calls," he says.

I begin to talk more quickly, sensing he might hang up on me. "Look, this is important. Can't you just give me a number where he can be reached? It's a family matter. Personal. He'd want to see me."

"Look, I'm very busy. I can't give out my clients' numbers to anyone who asks. They're entitled to their privacy just like everyone else."

"It's not as though he were Robert Redford and people were knocking down his door, for Christ's sake. I'm his nephew. A minute ago you didn't even know who he was."

"I'm sorry, I can't give out his number. That's all there is to it."

"All right, all right. Do me this one favor then: Call him and leave a message with my number at the downtown Hilton with him. It's listed in the book. This is a personal matter, tell him, of real importance to our family. I'll be waiting in my room for his return call, but I'll only be in town two more days. Then I have to go home. Please."

He hesitates. "I'll leave the message. But don't expect to hear from him: I don't even know if he's in town."

"Thanks. Thanks very much. It means a lot to me. To us."

When I hang up, I'm surprised by my determination and persistence, how caught up I am in the pursuit. As if something snapped when my grandmother refused to tell me Burt's whereabouts. Some thread of anger. But this sudden energy, this panic, makes me feel *this is right*, I'm listening to what my instincts tell me, this is what I want to do.

☆

For the next two days I live, essentially, in my hotel room. I wake up at eight, do sets of push-ups and sit-ups as a substitute for exercise, shower, pull open the curtains and watch other psychologists do the same. I eat breakfast in the hotel coffee shop, pick up a newspaper, then return to my room to wait for Burt's call. First I check out the television section of the paper to see if Burt's listed in any of the evening shows. He isn't. Then I read "Dear Abby": it crosses my mind that perhaps I should compose a letter to her.

Dear Abby,
    I'm obsessed by a man I haven't seen in twenty years. My uncle is destroying my marriage, coming between me and my wife. Now I have a chance to meet him and find out what he means to me — should I back out and apologize to my wife, should I seek professional help? He may be a homosexual.

Signed,
Hopeless in Hollywood

Evelyn would not think it was funny. I skip over the first section of the paper, "World News and International Events" (Evelyn's territory), and read a feature article on Duke Snider, former Dodgers star. He now grows avocados in California. He's a political conservative. My father and I never liked him — he was a Dodger, that was enough — and this article confirms my suspicions: he's an unabashed capitalist. I clip it out of the paper: here's something Evelyn, my father, and I could all agree about. I go to a meeting, leaving a message at the front desk with instructions to retrieve me — using the excuse that a neurotic client needs my attention — just in case Burt calls.

Most of the time, though, with the television turned to the station that features old movies and used-car ads, I sit at the desk in my room. I revise my talk a little bit, cross out or add sentences I hope will keep the panel awake, finish writing my reports on Mrs. Eller and the Carletons as well as the rest of my case load. Their manila folders, filled with questions and snippets of our dialogue, are like conversations with old friends. The reminders of their presence in this strange city anchor me. One client, Geoffrey Barchas, is scheduled, shortly after my return to New York, for his final appointment. I've seen Geoffrey Barchas through the breakup of his marriage, his total collapse, the loss of his job, the hospitalization that followed, and his lengthy but eventual full recovery. He's finally met a woman he thinks he can love, a warm and nurturing woman who cares deeply about his survival. He's brought her into the office several times, as much out of pride as out of the necessity of working things through with her. We've spent a number of important hours together, Mr. Barchas and I, and although I've never seen him outside my office (I'm always shocked when I see one of my clients in a supermarket or a movie theater, and am not sure how to greet them), I will certainly miss him, feel the loss of him. But he will do well, I'm sure, he'll more than survive; and his gratitude for my work with him, the help I've given him, is more than gratifying enough.

By late afternoon the hotel room's a mess. Room-service lunch plates on the dresser, the newspaper spread over the bed, file cards all over the desk, my clothes piled in a corner. I look out the window at the now empty rooms across the street; the psychologists are out doing their business. When I look down I see them milling around the front of their hotels, scurrying from one meeting to the next; I feel safe so far above it all. The phone rings, it fills me with panic, I almost choose not to answer it; but when I pick up the receiver and find out it's Leonard Ronowitz of Columbia, the director of my panel, I'm deeply disappointed. Leonard wants to make sure I've arrived safely, he hasn't seen me at any of the meetings, he wants to remind me about the time and place of our seminar. Because I've spoken to no one, really, since I've been here, because I expected Leonard to be Uncle Burt, I find myself withdrawing, answering his questions "yes" or "no," and finally cutting him short, telling him, "I'm in the middle of reworking my paper now." When I hang up I feel awful about my response to him, or rather my lack of response. Leonard, who's been a friend since graduate school, could have, I know, picked a more distinguished colleague for his panel: I'm sure he thinks he's done me a favor, extended himself in a gesture of friendship. Our relationship still means something to him, even though it's lost intensity over the years; though we live in the same city we've hardly seen each other since I went into private practice. Which explains why he wrongly thought he was doing me a favor, but doesn't explain my removal, my coldness on the phone.

Finally, on the second night of my visit to L.A., while I'm watching Ursula Andress in *The Sensuous Nurse* on pay TV, the phone call I've been waiting for arrives. "This is Burt Jarriman," he says, unnecessarily, since I recognize his voice from television. "Is this Michael, Allie's boy?"

"Yes, the very same."

"Is something wrong? I have this message . . ."

"Oh, that. It was the only way I knew how to reach you. Your agent wouldn't give me your number. Nothing's really wrong. But it's been exciting, seeing you on TV after all these years. It's brought back memories. I've really enjoyed watching you. Anyway, I have some business in the area, but I'm only going to be here for a couple of days."

"You scared me half to death," he says. "You'll excuse me if I think this is a bit odd. I mean I haven't seen you . . ."

"Oh, I know that. It's just that I thought you were in England all these years — then when you popped up in *The Streets of San Francisco* it got me thinking." No response. "One lunch wouldn't cause much harm, would it?"

"Well, I'm quite busy: I have a tight shooting schedule."

"I don't know when I'll get out to California again. I could come to the studio if you like. Only for an hour or so."

"All right," he says, "tomorrow's as good a time as any." He gives me the address of Paramount Studios, tells me he'll leave a guest pass at gate number two with the security guard, that he'll be shooting off the lot in *B. J. and the Bear*, so we'll have to meet at the commissary. "You'll have to look for me, because I won't recognize you, of course."

"Of course. *B. J. and the Bear*, huh? You playing a forest ranger?"

"As a matter of fact, a veterinarian."

"Another professional job, eh?"

"We'll see you then, Michael. I look forward to meeting you," he says, then hangs up the phone. Not exactly the picture of warmth. Nevertheless, listening to the dial tone I can't believe I've really spoken to him, that this conversation didn't take place on some soap opera set (the missing nephew returns). I turn the volume back up on the television and try to return to the movie. That's when I know our conversation was real: our dialogue was so much more awkward, less dramatic than the movies, and the man I've spoken to is my actual uncle, not a jewel thief, not a criminologist, not a veterinarian.

After the phone call I'm too excited to sit down. I straighten out the room, put my dishes next to the bathroom sink, pack my clothes into my suitcase. I open the window to feel the crisp evening breeze. I sit at the desk and try to read my paper once through, but I can't concentrate. Looking at the empty bed, I wish I had someone to share this experience with. Which is when it occurs to me that I haven't spoken to Evelyn since I left New York: I promised I'd call as soon as I arrived. It's after eleven P.M. there; I'll probably be waking her up, but not calling, after all this time, would probably be worse. Besides, I have important news to tell her. The phone rings several times before I hear Evelyn's drawn-out and soft-spoken "hello."

"Hello from Hollywood," I say. "Did I wake you?"

"You certainly did. What time is it?"

"I'm sorry I didn't call earlier. It's a madhouse here. I had to wait for an important phone call and I couldn't tie up the lines."

"That's all right," she says. Then, after a pause, she asks, "How is the conference going?"

"You're lucky not to be here. You'd find it more disgusting than I do."

"That's a healthy sign," she yawns.

"Listen to this: there's another healthy sign I have to tell you about. Are you alert yet?" No answer. "You remember all our arguments about Uncle Burt, don't you? The whole TV business, the oblique way of returning to my childhood?"

"How could I forget?"

"Well, I've been thinking it over, a lot, and I'm convinced you're right."

"You're going back into therapy."

"No. Not yet at least. I've gotten in touch with Burt. I'm going to ask him about my father. He set up a lunch appointment with me at the studio." For a long time I hear nothing from the other end of the phone. Then I hear footsteps. "Evelyn, honey, this is long distance."

"God damn it, Michael, I think you've gone off your rocker. A certified crazy person. Do you know what you could be in for? Do you have any idea? Isn't your life complicated enough now as it is?"

"But Burt's bound to know where he is. And if he doesn't, nothing's really lost: he can show me around the studio, I'll meet some celebrities and that will be that."

"Celebrities? Why are you behaving like such a child? I don't understand it. I just don't understand it."

"It's far from childish, Evelyn. I've decided to face up to this specter once and for all. It's something I have to face. You should be happy for me."

"Happy for you? That you're living in some dream world? That you want to go back to being thirteen again? Michael, it's over. Your father left twenty years ago. There's nothing you can do about it. Can't you get that through your head?"

"You don't understand anything, do you? What were those footsteps? Is there someone there with you?"

"I'm pacing around the room, that's all. I can't believe this. I've had it with you, Michael. You're hopeless. You're deceiving yourself."

"You'll see how everything will fit together when I get home. I'll prove it to you, you'll see."

"I don't want to hear another word about it. Tell it to a psychiatrist. Tell it to Uncle Burt."

"I miss you," I say, too late, for she's already hung up. I'm shocked by the intensity of her anger, I'm angered by it. How could she not be more sympathetic? Perhaps she was just cranky because I woke her up. Because I forgot to call earlier. Because of our last night together. I lie down on the bed, the receiver still in my hand, buzzing, then whining at a high pitch. I turn the set back on, watch it through every sign-off as I hear the conversations of the psychologists returning to their rooms. They are drunk enough to forget how loud a speaking voice can be. Footsteps. Then "The Star-Spangled Banner" and the evening benediction, then silence and the gray screen, until the first morning light pours startlingly into my room.

11

M<small>Y PAPER IS TO BE DELIVERED</small> in the Olympia Room at eight-thirty in the morning. I get off the elevator at the mezzanine, walk into the nearly empty room where the chairs are set up in neat rows of ten, and shake hands with Leonard. He seems genuinely pleased to see me — or perhaps he wasn't sure I'd show up. He introduces me to my fellow panelists: blah-blah from the University of California at Berkeley, blah-blah from the Cornell University Medical School, and blah-blah from the graduate faculty at the University of Chicago. Despite the geographical differences, after a sleepless night they all look alike to me. "I think we're in for a lively debate," one of them says. A thought that never crossed my mind. After Leonard's lengthy introduction of the cast of characters, the panelist from Berkeley is ready to begin his talk to a two-thirds empty room (by this time in the conference, after two nights away from home, after drinking with long lost or newly found friends, most of my colleagues put DO NOT DISTURB signs on their doors and awaken in midafternoon). He talks about the application of Laplanche to structured family relationships. He uses terms like *anaclitic* and *signifier*, a familiar-enough language that makes no sense to me. The professor from Cornell, ready to pick a fight, departs from his text to attack Laplanche and the French Freudians as fatalists who would destroy the nuclear family. He takes on the New Marxists, the Network Therapists, everyone in sight. Those few alert souls in the audience move to the edges of their seats, poised like animals ready to spring on their prey. The man from Chicago defends the humanist tradition, he wants to bring back the methods of Carl Rogers, whom he studied with at the University of Illinois.

When I rise to take my turn at the podium, I realize my talk hasn't taken into consideration any of the other papers; what I have to say will make little sense to my fellow panelists. I try to begin with a transition: "I'm afraid most of my clients remain relatively unconcerned about Laplanche and the French Freudians, or Carl Rogers or the Network Therapists. Most of them are uncertain where the money will come from to pay me, and not a few have considered strangling their mates to end it all." I look at the audience: one or two sneers, but mostly faceless expressions from the three rows of professionals. "The fact is, though I haven't kept up with all the research, this theoretical discussion is not easily applied to the families I work with each week. And my thesis is," I pause, with a slight sense of theater, "that we've lost a sense of audience in our profession, that in seminars like these we're only talking to one another, and when I get back to my practice all these abstractions go out the window. The family's changing at such a fast rate, the culture's become so stressful and full of change, no brilliant conception of the ego or id seems sufficient to the task, to the general and real breakdown of rules. Of any *a priori* law." I use, as examples, the Carletons, whom I call Mr. and Mrs. C., "who know everything and are still miserable as hell. They've seen the structuralists, they've been Rolfed, they've seen behaviorists, they've read all the literature — they know nothing about what they want or how they should treat each other." The French Freudian on my left is madly taking notes: he makes me nervous; I think for a moment of spilling my water glass accidentally over his papers. I continue, I don't look up from my text very often, I conclude by saying, "I hope not everyone will view this talk as hopelessly reactionary. My years of practice convince me that counseling is far from an exact science and should limit its aspirations in that direction. And we can start by bringing more academics into real practice, and bringing more clinicians into the classroom. Thank you."

I suffer through the mild applause, the moment of ritualized reverential silence, and then the hands go up for questions. For the next fifteen minutes my three colleagues are asked polite and naive questions, most requesting amplifications of certain positions. Not one question is directed toward me. But then, I suppose to include me, or perhaps to make use of the voluminous notes he took during my talk, the French Freudian stands up, and without facing me, says, "I don't mean to belabor the obvious, and I don't mean for us to take Mr. Jarriman's advice too lightly, but I must say I'm quite disturbed by the anti-intellectual tenor of his talk. Is he really suggesting, as a nineteenth-century romantic — I almost believe he should have worn some Baudelairean cape and cane to his talk — that we abandon all theoretical bases in dealing with our clients? That we should labor under the trial-and-error method of counseling?"

"That's almost what I'm saying." A few snickers are heard.

"We're talking about serious matters here, Mr. Jarriman, where a strategic error could cause the end of a marriage, a nervous breakdown, or worse."

"I see clients with those problems every day. I doubt that you could say that about Mr. Laplanche."

The word *Laplanche* strikes an ugly chord in the audience. The hands go up ferociously. I'm attacked as a bohunk who hasn't done his homework, a "nostalgic butterball," "a supreme example of why counseling is in such a chaotic state today." I feel self-righteous. I think of what Evelyn might say if she were here. I decide I wouldn't go into therapy if my life depended on it, much less my marriage. I meekly respond that my colleagues should take a walk around the city, leave

69

the cocoon of the hotel mezzanine, and speak to some actual human beings. The worst possible response. When a psychologist is attacked he becomes like the rats he studies. Cornered, he uses all his powers of manipulation and articulation to attack. One young man who looks as if he's fresh out of graduate school stands up and points his finger at me. "So you think you're the only person at the convention who's ever seen a client? Where do you get off? I think what we're seeing here, gentlemen," he says, gesturing with his hand, raising it in the air as if he were holding the torch that would burn the Frankenstein monster, "what we're seeing here is the kind of solipsism we've been criticizing this entire meeting. That's what I think."

"Frankly, Monsieur," I say, paraphrasing Rhett Butler, "I don't give a damn what you think."

"Well, I'm sorry our time is just about up," Leonard says. "Thank you all for contributing to such a lively and heated discussion." People rise reluctantly, then circle my fellow panelists. "I'm sorry, Michael," Leonard says, shaking his head. "I had no idea I'd be throwing you to the wolves this morning."

"That's all right. You had no idea what my talk would be like."

"That's true," he says. "I didn't."

I walk out of the seminar room, drop my paper into the first wastepaper basket I see. So much for deaf ears, I think. Maybe they have a Resignation Desk for those members of the profession who believe they've made a terrible mistake. But it's after ten-thirty, time to put the convention out of my mind. I want to shower before I see Burt, but I'm too hungry for real life, even Hollywood style. I stand in front of the hotel, surrounded by psychologists, waiting for the doorman to hail me a cab. "Paramount Studios," I say proudly to the driver as I get in.

"Say," he asks me, "you got some kind of convention going on there?"

"How did you know?"

"What a bunch of weirdos. I've been doing runs to the massage parlors day and night. You'd think no one had to make a living out here: they tip like a bunch of schoolteachers."

"It must be some kind of experiment," I say, calculating what a twenty percent tip might be, wishing I were wearing my polyester shirt. "They *are* a bunch of schoolteachers. That's exactly what they are."

12

WHEN THE CABDRIVER lets me off at the studio gate, I'm afraid suddenly that the security guard will never have heard of me, that Burt agreed to meet me only as a way of getting me off his back. The guard looks through a stack of file cards, though, and eventually comes up with one with my name on it. He reads the attached note and asks me if I know where the commissary is. When I shake my head no, he gives me directions. "First trip to movieland," he says and smiles, with the look of a neighborhood Irish cop of the 1940s movies. I nod and am on my way, in awe of the various sets I walk past: the model of New York's Sixty-third Street, where they used to film Cagney movies and Abbott and Costello shows. A block of the Old West, false-front saloons and hotels where *Gunsmoke* could have been filmed. All the shows from my childhood are here: a papier-mâché medieval castle, two parking lots, then a block of the suburbs. *Leave It to Beaver*, I think. *Ozzie & Harriet*. Mr. and Mrs. Carleton's next house. In the next lot I see my first movie star, John Cassavetes, speaking animatedly to someone I don't recognize. He's shorter than I thought, and his hair, worn in an old-fashioned brush-cut, is steel gray. Oh, the illusions are breaking down fast, southern California. I love it.

Walking into the commissary, an informal dining room with tables set up like a college cafeteria (differentiated only by different-colored tablecloths), I expect Burt to be sitting next to a movie star, an agent, or perhaps even, the thought occurs to me for the first time, with my father. But when I'm shown to his table he's sitting by himself, sipping a glass of white wine. He looks thinner than he did on television, and his face reveals his age, which I judge to be somewhere in his late fifties. He wears a European sport coat with padded shoulders and, incongruously, a maroon plaid shirt, buttoned all the way up. His face is covered with a grotesque orange pancake make-up, almost thick enough to make a second skin. Of course he doesn't recognize me, but he greets me with a polite hand-shake, stands up, and bows slightly. "Michael, it's so good to see you," he says, and again I hear that slight British accent, an exaggerated clarity of diction and enunciation. It's possible he picked it up in England, but it's just as possible it's an affectation. He gestures for me to sit.

"I wish I had time to show you around," he says, "but as I mentioned on the phone, my schedule is very tight. Even when I'm not working a scene I'm still required to be on the set from seven in the morning until six at night. On television everything's very rushed."

"Unlike the theater," I say. Then I panic, fearing that after this long prelude, this introduction by fantasy, I have nothing to say to him after all. "I appreciate the time. My wife and I have been watching you in several shows this year. You're quite good. Much better than most of them."

"Thank you," Burt says, bowing his head slightly again, this time to his wine glass. "So you're married now. Last time I saw you you couldn't have been more than twelve."

"Thirteen. My wife's name is Evelyn. She works for the Welfare Department. We've been married for ten years now. And you?"

"Married? No, no," he smiles. "I'm not."

"The last I heard of you you were doing legitimate theater in England. But that was a long time ago."

"Yes. I spent several years in England."

"What made you come back?"

73

"I got tired of it," he says, looking thoughtful, staring some-where abstractedly, far away. "That, and other things."

Other things, he says, and I wonder what they are. Was it money, did he leave a floundering love affair? With a man, a woman? Did he suffer from unaccountable depression? Whatever it is, he's not the least bit forthcoming about it. We order, a cheese sandwich for me and a garden salad for him: cottage cheese on a plate of romaine lettuce. "I've got to watch my weight," he says. "At my age it's hard enough to find a part even if you're in perfect condition. This is a young man's business, I'm afraid."

"You look fine to me. I suppose everyone looks heavier on television."

Looking me in the eyes for the first time, with some delib-eration, he asks, "Have you been in touch with anyone else in the family?"

"You mean on my father's side? No, not yet. Just you."

Burt nods, almost winces.

"I suppose you find that a little bizarre."

"A little. It's none of my business, of course."

"Have you seen much of my father?" I ask. The distracted look returns: I've breached one of the rules of decorum.

"Every once in a while."

"And he seems all right. He seems to be doing all right?"

"The last time I saw him he seemed fine," Burt says, but adds nothing more. He offers not a single clue: not where he is, if he's still married to the woman he ran off with, if he'd be willing to see me. Burt is the nondirective interviewer type, a strategy I recognize: it's a tactic I've used myself. He asks me what I'm doing in L.A., about my job, about whether Evelyn and I have any children, about where in the city do we live. About himself, he offers nothing that is not directly asked. I begin to worry that he passes judgment on every piece of information I give him: Is he pleased about my marriage, my line of work, the way I speak or dress? "How does that sound to you?" I ask. "Just fine, just fine," he says, nodding, as though he were mentally recording each detail, perhaps to pass it all on to my father without my knowledge.

"And what about your mother, Michael?" he asks. "Does she still live in New York? Has she married again? Is she getting on all right financially? I worry about her."

"She hasn't worked since her heart attack," I say, but then I answer the rest of his questions "Fine," "Yes," "No," "Thank you." About himself and his side of the family he says nothing. I begin to resent it. I'm being taken advantage of, I will find nothing out. Evelyn, in her cynical way, has turned out to be exactly right: I've made myself vulnerable to the point of foolishness.

Burt does talk freely about his life in Hollywood, about how tiresome it is. How the layman is given the wrong impression by the media. How he's had to go into other less glamorous parts of the business to earn a decent living. Burt is giving interview answers to a gossip magazine; he's not talking to his nephew, to his brother's son. In the middle of one of his sentences I blurt out, "Does he ever ask about me? Does he wonder how I'm doing?"

"Your father?" Burt says, putting down his fork. "Aren't you asking the wrong person?"

"What the hell does that mean?"

"I think you know what I mean."

"That I should seek *him* out? He's had plenty of opportunities . . ."

"Life's more complicated than you allow, Michael. You might be right. On the other hand, I'm not the person you should be talking to."

"On the other hand, my ass. What kind of clichéd crap are you trying to pull on me, Burt? This isn't television: you're my uncle."

"I'm not pulling anything on you," he says. "I wasn't the one who initiated this little get-together, if you remember."

"I remember all too well," I say, getting up from the table. "And you took every possible advantage of that fact, didn't

75

you?" I walk away from the table, my last foolish act of pride. Was this my family reunion, the entrance to my past? And how could I have ever expected it to be more? As I walk out the commissary door, I take one quick look back: Burt has put his napkin to his lips, in a gesture not of emotion but of cleanliness. And as I walk back to the studio gate, past the rows of centuries, which I pass in a matter of minutes, my legs feel rubbery, my anger is palpable and dizzying. I won't be able to tell Evelyn a single thing about my meeting with Burt. Good-bye to the Uncle Burt Fan Club, I think in the taxi on the way to the hotel. Good-bye to remedying my first thirteen years, I think as I pack my suitcases full of useless papers and wait for the bus to take me to the airport.

And as I walk to the counter to purchase my return ticket, as I look up at the television monitor listing the endless names of cities, destinations, as I'm caught and brushed into in the blur of human traffic at the airport, I hesitate before asking for the ticket to New York. I feel for the first time that I might have glimpsed, if only for a moment, my father's mind, hurt and confused, as he left his family. As he felt compelled to bury every unpleasant episode of his past. But when I say to the agent, "One way to Kennedy, please," the moment passes, as all moments do, and in a little while I am safely on the plane, looking down at the layers of smog, the rainbows of soot and strange symmetries below. The cars moving endlessly in all directions, and the people passing out of view.

13

BECAUSE MY FLIGHT arrives in New York after midnight, because the lights are off in our apartment when the taxi drops me off, and because I'm afraid to face Evelyn after the fiasco with Uncle Burt, I decide to walk to my office and sleep on my studio couch. The office is chilly and dark. My plants are alive, but droopy, so I mist them. Although I'm totally drained and exhausted (my bones ache from tension and from being cramped in an airplane seat for several hours), when I lie down, covered by my sport coat for warmth, I find I can't sleep. Sleeping alone in a hotel is one thing, sleeping alone in your office when your wife is sleeping a stone's throw away is another. As is sleeping on a couch where so many of my clients have spilled their fears and crimes: How could I not expect that some of it would rub off on me? Listening to all their troubles, how could I not be aware of the frailty of relationships, of how people hurt one another in seeking out their own happiness, or how, against their wills, people destroy the possibility of happiness. I'm one of many. I move to my chair, put my feet up on the desk, feeling slightly more comfortable in the controlling position — and just as the chilled winter sun comes up over the buildings, I do doze off, into a restless, discomforting sleep.

I'm awakened by a knock on the door; Geoffrey Barchas sticks his head in, offers a shy "Hello." My first appointment of the day, his last. "You look terrible," he says. "What's wrong?"

"I just got back from a convention late last night. I didn't want to disturb my wife. But I'm afraid I didn't get much sleep myself."

"Should I come back later?" he asks, looking down at the couch. I shake my head, no, and watch this man light up a cigarette and sit, remembering the first time he came into my office trying to light a cigarette, his hand shaking. It took fifteen minutes to get a complete sentence out of him. Now, after five years, Geoffrey Barchas, first with his wife and then without her, has learned, or relearned, the pose of confidence. He sits on the couch, his legs stretched out wide, his arms hanging over the length of the back of it. He's wearing a navy three-piece suit with a club tie, the costume of the successful. And as I look in the reflecting glass of the Stieglitz photograph, looking at the two of us, me unshaven and unshorn, dark circles under my eyes, I'm surprised our positions in the room aren't reversed: I should be coming to him for advice.

"I found a place on East Sixty-seventh this week," he says. "I negotiated with the landlord, an old lady; I lied — I'm surprised it wasn't with an agency — and said Mary Anne and I were already married. I didn't want to lose the place. I got her to lower the deposit a couple of hundred dollars. You would have been proud of me."

"I am. You know I am. When I was looking over your folder the other day, I couldn't believe you're the same person who came into my office all those years ago."

"Well, the body repairs and, eventually, the mind."

"With some luck and a lot of hard work."

"A lot of hard work," he says, nodding, giving the matter serious consideration. "I'm very grateful to you. You've been patient, very patient with me."

"The rewards are mutual, Geoff. I hope you won't lose touch: I'll want to know how you're doing."

"For free?"

"Of course for free. Next time you come in I'll buy you a drink."

"You'll have to buy me a lot of drinks to make up for all the loot I've dropped in here," he says, smiling. The joke. Another encouraging sign. He speaks with genuine confidence, brings up possible problem areas, what might happen if he and Mary Anne argue, how it will bring up old fears, what happens when he runs into his ex-wife, what happens when the pressures of his job increase. I bring up a few questions, the issues move effortlessly from mouth to mouth, we're having a conversation in overdrive. I want to freeze-frame this hour with Geoffrey Barchas; I want to remember him as someone who can be brought back to the safe bounds of health, a model of hopefulness. And when he leaves the office I'm filled with the loss of him, I shake his hand for a very long time, I almost want to ask him for a letter of recommendation to give to my wife. Not too long after he leaves I get up the courage to call her, but of course she's at work; when I call her office one of her office-mates tells me she's out on a case. It will be too long before I see her again.

I manage the rest of the morning with a minimum of effort, and during my lunch hour I return to the apartment to shower and shave, to change my clothes. When I open the door light is pouring in the living-room window, a few particles of dust float in the air, but the apartment is impeccably clean. Dusted, vacuumed. Magazines stacked neatly on the cocktail table, the dishes in the kitchen cabinets, the bed made compulsively, army style, hotel style. As I undress before the mirror in the bathroom, I think, so this is how Evelyn lives without me. I begin to understand how much of a burden I and my problems must be for her. Therapy: perhaps I should reconsider. There must be someone decent out there, some trustworthy soul who's less of a misfit than I am. I'll tell all. A self-improver, that's what I want to be.

Before I leave the apartment I write Evelyn a note, explaining how I've been trying to reach her, and that when I get home from work we should go out for dinner. The convention was tolerable, barely, I write. I'll save the rest for later. I return to the office with a little energy, some resolve, ready to face the remainder of the afternoon.

What I have not counted on, though, is my appointment with Annette Eller, who for the first time has managed to drag her husband, Larry, into therapy. Larry is a shy man, balding on top, about two inches shorter than Annette. He wears a black nylon jacket with a map of Vietnam embroidered on the back. He wears dungarees and black, shiny shoes. His handshake is firm, but he doesn't look me in the eye. Annette sits on the couch and Larry sits next to her, their bodies almost touching.

"I've told Larry everything," she says. "The lovers, the feelings of restlessness, everything. He doesn't know if he can live with it." Larry looks off to the side at the jade plant, pressing a leaf between his thumb and forefinger with so much force I'm afraid it will catch on fire.

"That must have been very difficult for you, Larry," I say.

"No shit."

"You want to talk about the last couple of weeks? How you feel about it?"

"His response has been very sane," Annette says, jutting out her chin. "He slapped me once and then went into the kitchen to look for a butcher's knife for my boss." Larry cringes, but says nothing. "I would have done exactly the same thing."

"Well, how would you have felt," Larry says, "if *your* wife was porking every guy who rented a car from her? Green stamps," he says, turning to her, "you should have given them goddamn green stamps."

"His anger's totally justified," Annette says, shrugging.

"Have you made a commitment to stop, Annette?" I ask. "As a commitment to Larry?"

"That was the first thing I did."

"Do you trust her, Larry?" I ask. No response. "Not at all?"

"No. Would you?"

"You can tell the truth, Doc," Annette says. "I can take it."

80

"It would be very hard. But bringing you here wasn't easy for her. It's a first step. It will require great patience."

"I don't know." He shakes his head. "My first idea was to go on a jag and screw the first ten women in my path. That was my second idea, too."

"He could have done it. I would have understood," Annette says.

"Then you could have felt less guilty, right?" I ask, then I put my finger to my lips, motioning for her to be quiet.

Larry squirms on the couch, crosses his legs in several different positions. "I don't see what this is going to accomplish," he says. "What's been done is done. I've been stabbed in the back. I'm bleeding," he says, and begins to cry. "I'm fucking bleeding."

There's much uncomfortable silence, then somehow they talk to each other, they raise their voices, Larry comes close to striking her, he cries, she cries. Once she takes hold of his hand. He lets her hold it for a moment before he pulls away. So much pain, the room is a wave of sighs, pain held back and pain released. I don't see how they're going to make it. I say nothing about it, it's not my place; but I don't understand why they don't walk out of each other's lives and try to start over as if their marriage never happened. The only solution I can see for them is a severe case of amnesia. My stomach is tight, my jaw hurts from clenching my teeth. It's an impossible hour. Then, at five o'clock, on the nose, there's a knock on the door. I rise to open it, and there's Evelyn, carrying her briefcase from work, dressed in her brown tweed suit. Her eyes are lined with red, she looks slightly disheveled, the way I must have looked this morning. "This is Evelyn, my wife," I say to the Ellers. "Honey, it's good to see you. I've been trying to call you all day." I reach out to hug her; her body stiffens, like that first day on the elevator. She clings to her briefcase, does not return my kiss.

"I didn't realize you were still with clients," she says. "I'm sorry to interrupt."

Then I notice, as I release my grip on her, that there's a

man standing behind her — a tall, thin, angularly handsome blond with horn-rimmed glasses and a black pinstripe suit. He stands stiff and erect. My body freezes too, my hands are at my sides, in military attention, as if awaiting orders. "We'll wait outside," she says, "until you're finished."

"That was my wife," I say again to the Ellers when I sit back down. Larry looks at the door, as if Evelyn were still standing there. Annette gives me a pathetic look of sympathy. We're all speechless. "I'm afraid our time is up," I say, taking a deep breath, looking at my watch. "It's a start. A start. And if something important comes up, some impasse, I'd appreciate it if you'd call me. We can set up an additional appointment. Take care of yourself, Larry," I say, getting up to shake his hand. "You too, Annette."

"You too, Mr. Jarriman," Larry says.

Annette Eller leans over and kisses me on the cheek. "Good luck, Doc," she says. "It looks like you'll need it."

14

As soon as the Ellers walk out of my office, Evelyn and her friend, the mortician, walk in. He has his hand on the small of her back, guiding her into the room. "This is Ross MacLean, Michael. My" — and here she hesitates, looks at him for encouragement — "my lawyer." They sit, simultaneously, on the couch.

"God. For a second there I thought you were going to say your *lover*." They glance at each other for the briefest moment, then stare straight ahead. "I think I'd better sit down," I say.

"Michael," Evelyn proclaims, with the genuine determination of someone who's prepared a speech that cannot bear interruption, "I want a separation. I've given this serious consideration, and given the way things have been going lately, frankly I can see no other solution." The mortician says nothing, but leans over to tie his shoelaces.

"Just like that?" I ask. "I can't believe it. The subject's never come up. You sound like the decision's already been made."

"It has been made. And if you remember the night you stayed home to watch your uncle Burt, the subject did come up. Seriously."

"That's not what I call a discussion. That's what I call an argument. Jesus Christ," I say, pacing around my desk, "I don't believe this. And why's the mortician here? We don't need a lawyer, we need a counselor."

"Ross has been doing some political work with me at the department. I told you about him before."

"I've never heard a word about him."

"That says something, doesn't it? I brought him here to make things as simple as possible. I want to leave your office with a signed agreement in hand. I've made up my mind."

"Listen, Evelyn, I know I've screwed up lately. The Uncle Burt thing brought a whole bunch of issues to the surface and I couldn't deal with them. But I agree with you: I've already decided to go back into therapy. I'm committed to working this out."

"Oh, Michael, it's not just your uncle Burt. The whole last few years — "

"No one ever said marriage was supposed to be paradise."

"Eventually I want to have a family."

"We can have a family."

"It won't work, Michael. You've always said children and adults have nothing in common. You're such a little boy yourself in so many ways." She shakes her head.

"That's not fair. Just when I've decided to let everything go."

"There's so many things," she says. "All our arguments about work . . ."

"But there's so much about work that we share. Where else are you going to find that, Evelyn?"

"I don't want to argue about it, Michael. If I weren't absolutely convinced it had to be done, do you think I'd put you through this?"

I turn away from her, walk over to the window, and stare down at the street. Early January, it's snowing here, gray flecks of ash on the sidewalk, the whole sky seems ashen, just as L.A. had when the rings of smoke enveloped the city. Here it's just visible at a lower level. "Ten years out the window," I mutter.

"Now, Ross has helped me work up an agreement. It's very simple. Ross," she says, "can you get it out?"

"Can you get *him* out of here? Before I sign anything I want him out. I have no intention of signing my life away in front of this vulture."

"My son and I have been through this process ourselves, Mr. Jarriman. It's even worse when you have a family," he says. "I think I know how you feel."

"How would you like to know how it feels to go feet first through the window, asshole? Now, did you hear what I said? Get out."

"Lower your voice," Evelyn says, when, unbelievably, there's a knock on the door.

"Now see what you've done?" I say. "All this shouting's brought the neighbors in. I want him out. O-U-T out."

I open the door and there's Laurie Reid in her lumberjack plaid jacket, holding a large flowering plant in front of her face. "Here's your bonus plant," she says cheerfully, tilting her head to the side so I can see her face. "Just like I promised — only a little bit late." She takes a step inside, looks around for a place for her plant; Ross and Evelyn stare at the intruder, first in disbelief, then in anger. "Uh-oh," she says. "I'm sorry."

My hand is still on the doorknob. "Could you come back a little later? I'm going through a divorce right now. That's my wife sitting next to her mortician."

Laurie smiles at Evelyn, does an about-face, and quietly walks out the door with her plant. Looking at her from behind, I'm tempted to reach for her shoulder, tell her I could use all the help I can get. "Now, if you'll only follow," I gesture to him, "we could get something accomplished around here." Evelyn nods at Ross, giving her assent; he picks up his brief-case, hands Evelyn some papers, and walks out the door, which I quickly close behind him.

"Where'd you pick him up?" I ask her. "Loitering in front of the Yale Club? This is wonderful, just wonderful. It's advertising for my practice, too. Now I can talk about people's problems from experience."

"Don't do this, Michael. You're only making it more difficult."

"You know what bothers me most? What bothers me most

is you're so calm, so collected, as though we were deciding who to insure our possessions with."

Evelyn bursts into tears. "You know how many times I've gone over in my head what I'd say to you when you got back? From the moment we got off the phone . . . I knew if I cried like this it would make it worse, ten times worse. For both of us."

Ross sticks his head in the door. "Are you all right?" he asks.

"I'm all right," she says, and he closes the door again, but now she cannot control her sobs. Each inhale of breath a small struggle. I sit down next to her on the couch, hold her hand, which is ice cold. I take off my jacket and put it around her shoulders. "I'm not the same woman you found in the elevator, Michael. I'm strong and productive, and I want to make a life for myself. For whatever reason, you're not ready to do that now."

"You're still the same person. You were always strong and 'productive,' whatever that means." Evelyn says nothing, and won't look at me. "Then your mind is made up. It doesn't matter what I say, no matter how I promise to change, it won't make any difference."

Evelyn shakes her head. "The time is past, Michael. You should have been seeing someone years ago."

"*I* should have. Not *we* should have?"

"You know I don't believe in it. For me."

"Okay, what do you want me to sign," I say, feeling my body grow cold, as if Evelyn's hands were contagious.

"I have a decent job," she says. "I certainly don't want any money. It's not fair for you to have to move. My clothes are already out of the apartment, and I'll call you before I come back to gather a few cartons of utensils and things. It's not that I don't still love you."

"Please," I say, grabbing the papers out of her hands, "that's not what I need to hear."

"It has to be signed in triplicate," she says, and her crying begins to escalate again. Ross sticks his head in the door;

Evelyn shoos him away with her hands. I sign, in triplicate, and ask her to "Please go away. I need some time to myself." She takes the papers from me, follows me to the window, and kisses me on the cheek. "Here's a number where I can be reached," she says, putting a piece of paper on my desk. "If you need me. For anything."

If I need her. I can't look at her. The door closes, I hear some mumbling on the other side of the door, then there's absolute silence. I've never heard the city so quiet. It's getting darker out. Heavy, wet flakes of snow are falling. The traffic is still backed up, bumper to bumper along the Avenue. What I feared most, I think, I brought on myself. I close my eyes and make a resolution: I can't, I won't, go back to the apartment tonight.

15

I'M NOT SURE how much time passes before I gain the presence of mind to cancel my appointments for the rest of the week. There's been a death in the family, an illness, an emergency consultation. Anything but the truth. I think of Geoff Barchas, how during his first three appointments he sat staring at his knees, mumbling, how he'd been seeing me for almost a month before he got up the courage to tell me his wife had left him. And now, for the first time, really, I understand why. If not so long ago I feared the dullness of marriage, I realize I underestimated how much worse it could become.

My conscious urges are to be sensible, to avoid self-pity, to figure out what just happened in my office. But I'm drawn to the moment of her leaving, of my unraveling, leaning my forehead against the cold glass of my office window, watching the two of them hail a cab uptown. I thought of following them, then rejected it; instead I sat in my chair and faced the door, waiting for it to open, for her to return and admit she'd been too hasty, that we still had time to change. The efficient finality of her voice, though, which I can still hear echoing in the dark office, makes me realize that possibility is a foolish daydream.

So what is there to figure out? What post-mortems need to be said? I draw a blank. Whatever it is, I know I can't do it now, by myself. I try to think of someone I could seek out, some friend I could trust. But Evelyn's and my time was so equally divided between the bedroom and the office, was so exclusive, I can't think of who to go to: Rick Chandler, insurance agent, whose most intimate act is a friendly Christmas card? Leonard Ronowitz, whom I've so recently embarrassed? Certainly not. My only remedy is to remove myself from the scene of the crime, to avoid all physical reminders, to get out of the office, the think tank, the emotional goldfish bowl.

Outside it's dark, past dinnertime; there's an oppressively low ceiling of clouds — more snow is on the way. The rush-hour traffic has not diminished, slush is building and freezing over on the sidewalks. I walk and walk — past all the strangers' faces, the couples coming back from dinner, certain they can see the shame and fear on my face. I walk with my hands in my pockets, past the small shops and the steam of sewage, the prostitutes just beginning their workday, the greasy windows of the department stores; past the idle garment district, the book-carrying students walking home from evening classes, the old-fashioned luncheonettes with their plastic Coca-Cola signs hanging beneath the canopies like pawn-shop insignias. In the window of one candy store just north of SoHo I see a young boy standing in front of the magazine rack reading a *Spider Man* comic. I'm taken back twenty years, to a sunny Sunday in October when I went out for breakfast with my father to Junior's Luncheonette. It was the only time I remember his confiding in me. The walk was a special privilege: I felt like a thirteen-year-old man, walking side by side with my handsome father, who seemed six feet tall with his graceful gait, his seersucker sport coat, silk shirt, and linen pants. He says he has a secret he wants to tell me, man to man — something so private I can't even mention it to my mother. But after that day in his office I know it's not going to be much of a secret. He and my mother have been arguing, he says, he doesn't know if they're going to be able to stay together. They've been trying their best, but it just might not work out. He wants me to know, he says, stopping for a moment to rest his hand on my shoulder, that it has nothing to do with me. That he loves me very much. Do I understand that? Do I understand that? I nod, of course I understand, although I don't know what I'm nodding about, to what I'm giving my assent.

We're all going on a vacation in the Berkshires in a few weeks, to give it one more try. If he fails, if that fails, he wants me to know he gave the marriage all he could. It just didn't work out. I remember asking him why, why they couldn't talk about it, work things out rationally (*rationally* was my mother's word, a word as foreign to her then as it is to me now). And I remember he did answer me, abstractly I think, but I can't recall for sure. I remember his lips moving and the glare of sunlight, but his words escaped me. We sat down at the luncheonette counter and my father said I could have whatever I wanted, but I ate what he ate. A bagel with cream cheese, and a cup of coffee, light. And then we talked as if nothing had transpired, about moving from Little League to the Babe Ruth League, how throwing the curve might hurt my arm. We talked about school, how proud he was of my grades. But walking back into our house that afternoon, facing my mother while trying to keep my face emptied of expression, our family had been irrevocably changed. That night, and the nights that followed, I watched television: *Father Knows Best*, *The Stu Erwin Show*, *Leave It to Beaver*, *I Love Lucy*. How did they stay together, why were those parents so full of sage advice? When nothing, naturally, changed during our Berkshire vacation, when I tried to mediate one of their arguments in the hotel room and they ended up screaming at each other loud enough so I feared the manager would barge in and interrupt them, the failed marriage seemed mine and not theirs. The first failure I remember. And I knew, when my father walked out of the room, slamming the door behind him, to go to the bar by himself, he was thinking of the lovely lady in the black dress and had already put all thoughts of my mother and me far behind him.

Now, in my evening trance, I find myself walking toward Evelyn's working neighborhood, past the rows of drunks with their limp bodies leaning against stoops and storefronts; reminded of my wife, I'm nonetheless totally out of my element. And I think I want to start a fight, to have someone pull a broken bottle on me, to push me into a hallway and rip the wallet out of my pants pocket. To watch that man's avenging face as he pushes me into a row of mailboxes. For in spite of my arguments with Evelyn about her zeal for the dispossessed, I never want to forget what they might say to me, or the looks on their desperate faces.

II

16

I'M A MAN WITHOUT A HOBBY. So if idle hands do the devil's work, I should expect to get a lot of ugly work done. Oddly enough, I do. If it's true for the first few weeks after Evelyn leaves I can't get used to sleeping by myself and don't drift off until three in the morning, it's also true that I can't wait to get up at seven, get out of the house, and go to work. And while at first I'm deathly afraid any client's anger or grief will send me into a tailspin, just the opposite occurs. I sit in my chair and stare quite objectively at the couples posed in front of me: I listen to their tales, their versions of their stories, with a new understanding of what they don't understand. Could you speak up? I ask them, as if they were talking from another room. So Mrs. Parrish thinks that her husband suffocates her with love; her husband claims she's afraid of sex. I ask them if they would recreate one of their lovemaking sessions for me. Mrs. Parrish sits straight up in her chair; Mr. Parrish stares at the jade plant, freshly misted. This couple is fifty years old, the thought occurs to me that neither of them has probably touched another naked body below the waist. With some prodding, Mrs. Parrish introduces me to their routine. That's her word, and it's appropriate. Sunday mornings, before he goes out for the paper, "as soon as he opens his eyes," she says, "his hand's on my thigh."

"Then she turns on her side away from me," he says.

"I don't," she says.

"And she pretends she's still sleeping," he says.

I have a clear picture of them, lying beside each other in bed. I see his awkward hands gather on her body, her eyes open wide, facing the wall. I see how they make each other suffer, how they're afraid to tell each other what they want. "And that's exactly how he acts when he gets home from work. As if he could just plug me in." Progress is made. Thanks to my training, my recovered clinical detachment. My clients will answer any question I ask and I'm not afraid now to ask them anything.

There's a new twist, a perverse curiosity, to my question, "Why do people stay married?" And to my clients' answers. Mrs. Eller, by this time, has thought a lot about it. What she likes about her balding husband is that he knows what he wants. He doesn't find many other women attractive. He knows what movies he wants to see. What teams to root for on television. What he wants for dinner. What positions he likes her to adopt in sex. She admires that. It's easy to give in to. She wants to learn how he does it. To the same question Larry only answers he doesn't know why he wants to stay married. Or if.

"Doesn't this little conversation tell you both something?" I ask.

They smile shyly at each other and nod their heads like schoolchildren. What it tells them, exactly, remains unsaid.

The Carletons have a different answer to the question each time I ask. The Carletons have lots of answers. I let the Carletons amuse me now as they amuse themselves. Sometimes, when they're particularly silly, when they plagiarize entire speeches from *Phil Donahue* shows about "sharing their feelings," I'm the cabdriver who picked me up in front of the L.A. Hilton: I just let the meter run. When they run out of steam I ask them, "Are we finished fucking around now? It's your money, you can bullshit from now until doomsday if you want."

96

Mrs. Carleton blushes, says she's afraid she doesn't know the words that express her feelings for her husband.

"I could whisper a few to you," Mr. Carleton says.

"Try," I say.

"I like the quiver in his voice when his feelings are hurt. It's the only time I feel safe touching him."

I look over at a contrite Mr. Carleton who's looking at his wife with genuine affection. With all my heart I'd like to take that moment from him, but I don't. I'm hovering ten feet above my body, telling myself how to behave, what to do. If I'm angry at Mrs. Carleton's tenderness, at her revelation about her husband, I understand why I feel that way, how little it has to do with them. I have real, legitimate moments of lucidity. At the same time, as soon as I leave my office, blocks of hours seem to disappear, as if the sweep of the minute hand were an eraser, as if I could go on vacation from myself.

Of course I survive these weeks. But only by removing myself from vulnerable places such as my apartment. I go out to eat. I survive on meanness. If there are no tables for one at a restaurant (as there usually aren't), I say I'm waiting for someone else, for my wife. Or if they give me a hard time, I say "for my mistress." If I'm within earshot of anyone else, I get a table. I get particular pleasure out of paying my single check to the maître d'. "Stood up," I tell him and smile. I never go back to the same restaurant twice, unless the service is bad. If they make me wait a long time I come back and read the *Sporting News* on line. I leave a very large tip. If they make me wait longer the next time I leave an even bigger tip. Or I request a table for six. The rest of them, I say, are out parking the car.

Revenge fantasies. I keep the phone number Evelyn gave me Scotch-taped to the television screen as a reminder not to watch. Now the television would be like a tornado, sucking me into it. There are moments, though, usually when I let myself drink, when I pick up the phone and dial the number, prepared to disguise my voice. I want to tell Evelyn her husband has been in an accident. Or I want to tell her I've just shot my uncle. He was coming off the set of *Barnaby Jones* and I shot him because I held him responsible for the breakup of my marriage. Or I want to tell Evelyn not to come back to the apartment, that there's another woman living with me and I wouldn't take her back under any circumstances. I'm afraid of what I'm thinking. Or what I might do. I have picked up the phone twice. Dialed the number and let it ring. Once I thought I heard her voice. "Hello." And then I hung up.

One morning I cancel my appointments and take the subway downtown. I have every intention of talking to her as she goes to work, of telling her she'd better come back. But then, sitting in the luncheonette just opposite her office building, looking into a muddy cup of coffee, I decide I just want to see her face. I want to see if there's grief there, if there's a twinge of regret. What sense would my command make? There's nothing persuasive about my voice.

But what if she's with someone else? It's cold out; men and women with briefcases, some carrying takeout cups of coffee, pass by me in the window. At ten to nine I stare at the steps leading to her office building. Workers are scurrying up the steps in rows of five and six, buried in their hats and overcoats. No one is talking. I look for her walk, for clothing I recognize. If she's huddled in the crowd I don't see her; if she's walking among them I don't know how I could expect to see any expression on her face. And what if she saw me, if she saw the desperate look on my face or my newly acquired and barely controlled rage? Would that make her want to come back? Would she tear up the papers she made me sign in triplicate?

At nine-thirty, finding no trace of my wife, I take a cab up to the Metropolitan Museum and wait for it to open. I wander through the halls watching tourists from Tokyo and Syracuse gaze at the paintings. The canvases don't interest me, the carved figures of dead Egyptians interest me less. I have no hobby, so I do the devil's work.

☆

Rick Chandler, my neighbor, has somehow heard the news, or has guessed at it. He rings my doorbell, probably having tried the telephone, which rests now beneath a couple of pillows. He smiles. "Trick or treat?" I say.

"Would you like to come over to play some cards?" he asks. It is the question of a ten-year-old boy. I won't make it easier on him.

"I don't play cards."

"Maybe some other night," he says and shrugs. He looks over my shoulder into the living room. "You should come over for a drink."

"I'm having guests over. Thanks for asking, Rick," I say, closing the door. I turn on the radio — loud — and I talk over it, just in case he's listening at the door. I want to see no one, I want no one's kindness, especially Rick Chandler's.

I take care of myself the best I can. I understand the banality of self-pity, which is why I indulge in it: it makes me feel less alone. I gather all the objects I associate with Evelyn in boxes and put them in the front closet. I picture hundreds of separated or newly divorced clients doing the same. Silverware her parents gave us, a set of plates she bought for an anniversary ("I feel so bourgeois," she'd said joyfully). Books: the collected early works of Marx and Engels, economics texts from college, unopened cookbooks, any volume that had her name, maiden or married, on the inside cover. The clothes she didn't take. Clothes she picked out for me. A Waring blender. I take everything I want out of the closet and close it up. From now on the closet's out of bounds.

And then, of course, there's the bed, where we spent so much time together. I no longer sleep on it. I pull out the convertible couch and sleep in the living room. I go into the bedroom only to pick out what I'm going to wear the next day. Otherwise I live exclusively in the living room and kitchen. After a while, though, in those two rooms I become extravagant. I buy posters, reproductions of paintings with bright gaudy colors; I put them on the walls with thumb tacks. If, after a few days, I tire of them or decide they're ugly, I take them down, put them in the closet, and buy new posters. Or I throw the old ones in the incinerator. For a few minutes a day, sitting on my couch/bed with my legs crossed, listening to classical music on the radio, catching up on my case load or staring at the walls, I feel safe. I feel like that client of mine who'd rather drive his car than fly in a plane because he thinks he's in control of his own fate. That's what we think, and it would be inconvenient for either of us to behave otherwise.

I indulge myself. I buy two new suits, one charcoal pinstripe (uncharacteristic) and the other khaki cotton (more characteristic). I buy a maroon and white polka-dot tie at Bloomingdale's, flirt with the saleslady, and wonder for a moment if she finds me attractive. I cut off the conversation before I have a chance to find out. Mornings, before I go to work, I exercise. Nothing fanatical, just push-ups, sit-ups, running in place. I think of growing a beard and then reject it. I've seen too many midlife crises, in my office and out, to duplicate them exactly. Every night before I go to bed I repeat this litany: I'm involved in my work, I'm not unattractive, I've helped people get better, I'm not a failure.

After three weeks like this, my nerve endings raw from sleeplessness, my energy gives way. I feel my thighs ache, my shoulders and neck stiffen. My head feels warm. I lie on the couch with a virus, a low-grade fever, sipping hot tea. I want someone to take care of me, to bring me juice and aspirin, to put her lips to my forehead and check the fever. But there's no one here and I finally have to face the fact: I'm a family counselor without a family.

17

THE IRONY DOES NOT ESCAPE ME. What saves my life in the weeks that follow Evelyn's leaving is my job — listening to troubled couples, filling my time and thoughts with their problems instead of my own. It's the same job, the same way of seeing that caused us so many problems and may have ultimately cost me my marriage. The irony does not escape me, but I'm grateful now for my sense of duty, instilled in me by my mother, who to this day pays a price for it.

Although Evelyn and I visited her parents regularly, we managed to see my mother no more than three or four times a year. We had a standing argument, Evelyn taking the idealistic stance, how we owed my mother the pleasure of our company, whereas I took the pragmatic view, that we never left her apartment without getting into a serious disagreement. The truth is not contained in our argument. The truth is that it pains me to see my mother locked away in her monastery of a two-room Port Chester apartment, to see how she's never recovered from my father's leaving. In the twenty years since he left, she's never, to my knowledge, let a man take her to dinner, no less take her to bed. And though I know my mother has always counted on Evelyn's and my marriage to serve as proof positive that "love survives," I see no way of avoiding being the bearer of bad news. If love does survive, it will have to do so without our assistance.

My mother's squat brick apartment house is an anomaly in Westchester. Situated in front of the New Haven railroad tracks, it stands mere blocks from the sprawling estates and country clubs that infuriated Evelyn every time we got near them. "The escape hatch of the rich," she used to say. And even I had to admit the area seemed safe enough to walk around late at night — a claim I couldn't make for my own neighborhood, which seems light years from here.

When my mother greets me she takes the Jewish mother's prerogative, hugging me for an uncomfortable amount of time, then holding me at arm's length. "Let me look at you," she says.

"What choice do I have?"

"You look tired. Are you taking care of yourself?"

"The best I can," I say; then I return the favor, looking over this short and stout woman everyone used to say resembled Joan Crawford in the 1940s. And it's true, looking at the old photographs, with her dark hair in a pageboy and an earnest gaze that seemed simultaneously to reveal and conceal everything, that she fit my vision of the movie stars of her age. Now her hair, pushing out of the front of her babushka, is a yellowing gray; her face is puffy, her hands stiff and arthritic. She looks all of her fifty-eight years.

The apartment itself is dark and cavernous, takes no account of the seasons. The curtains are drawn, plastic covers the furniture, cartons of possessions — dishes, records, clothing — are stacked neatly in every corner of the living room. On the walls hang the remaining mementos, the museum of our family history: my mother's ballet shoes over the couch, pictures of my high-school graduation, photographs with my old college girl friends (with a photograph of Evelyn imposed over the girls — revisionist history, Evelyn used to say), my diplomas, and photos of Evelyn's and my wedding.

"You'll have to excuse the condition of the apartment," she says. "It's a horrible mess."

"It looks fine. All those cartons so neatly stacked."

"Very funny. You know I'm trying to get out of this place. They just raised the rent another ten percent. There's a criminal element moving in."

"Ma, you've been trying to move out of here for the last five years. Why don't you just resign yourself to unpacking some of your things?"

"I want to be ready at a moment's notice," she says. "Have you tried looking around for an apartment lately? You know what three-fifty a month gets you around here? Bubkes, that's what." I decide not to take the first piece of bait. I keep quiet. "So sit down. Have you eaten?"

"I'm not hungry."

"Where's Evelyn?"

"That's why I'm here, Ma."

"God," she exclaims, placing her palms on her cheeks, "she's been hurt. She's injured. I knew it: I had a dream about it. Is it serious?"

"Take it easy. She's not hurt. She's fine."

"Let me sit down," she says. She walks, almost limps over to the couch. "Never mind the furniture. Sit, sit, tell me about it."

Pulling a dining-room chair close to my mother, I take a deep breath and sit down. For the first time I utter the words, making it real. "Evelyn and I have separated."

"I knew it was serious. I knew something terrible had happened. It's written all over your face. Your eyes are puffy ..."

"Stop. There's no need for melodrama. I see troubled marriages every day in my office. It happens to almost everyone."

"I'm supposed to find that consoling? My son isn't everyone, you know. When did it happen?"

"About two weeks ago."

"And you're only telling me now? What have you been doing since then? Why didn't you call me?"

"I honestly don't know what I've been doing. Working, I guess. I knew how upset you'd be and I wanted to wait till I had things under control."

103

"Is there another woman, Michael? You can tell me if there is."

"I don't think anyone else is involved. Just us."

"Then you'll both come to your senses."

"I doubt it. Evelyn seemed very determined."

"She walked out on you?"

"It's more complicated than that."

"She packed her suitcase and you're still living in the apartment, right? How complicated could it be?"

"We've been having trouble for some time now."

"Trouble is one thing. Michael, you just said you saw troubled couples all the time. What about those years of schooling? All those books. Don't they mean anything?"

"You're being a great help, Ma. What do you want me to say?"

She puts her hands on her knees, sits up straight. An act of will. "I'll make some tea. Would you like some?" I nod. She walks to her tiny kitchenette, puts the kettle up to boil, and with her back to me, says, "I could come down and clean. Or make some casseroles you could freeze."

"Thanks, but I need some time to myself right now."

"I understand. I understand." The kettle whistles, my mother pours the boiling water into a pot and brings it, along with two cups, on a tray into the living room. "It has to steep for a while. You're not completely alone, you know. You have a family."

"I know."

"I'm behind you a hundred percent. But let's talk about something pleasant for a while."

"I don't want to talk about anything pleasant, Ma. Listen, have you seen Uncle Burt on television lately?" I ask, trying to ease into an explanation of what happened. "He's back from England, you know."

"I don't watch television. It rots your mind. I read books. Good books that'll improve myself. Your uncle Burt's a fag."

"I know that. You're still mad at him?"

"Why should I be mad?" she says. "What's happened happened. What are you smiling at?"

"I guess at how well you hold a grudge. You could do me a big favor, Ma. I've been thinking about this for a long time and now it's important. Can you tell me what went wrong?"

"With your father and me? Sure, I'd be glad to. It's no news. Your father had a glandular problem."

"Hey, I'm serious."

"No one could be more serious than I am. It was genetic: he was a skirt chaser; he had to be loved by everyone."

"In my profession that's what we might call a symptom."

"In your profession, in your profession. Are you trying to imply that your father didn't love me? We had seventeen wonderful years together. Then he threw me over for a young woman. Glamour, that's what he was after."

"You felt you had no warning."

"Michael" — she leans over to me, pours out the tea, almost whispers — "your father was everything to me. I know things are different today, but I cooked for him, washed for him, entertained, gave up dancing . . ."

"And look what happened."

"And you married an independent woman. Where's the insurance? I was glad to do it. I never had a single regret." Cupping her tea in both hands, my mother grows quiet, withdraws into herself. "I did throw him out once. We'd been married three years. He came home at four in the morning with lipstick on his underwear."

"On his underwear?"

"Filth. That's what turned your father on. I locked him out of the house and he begged me, on his knees, to let him come back. I loved him," she sighs, "so I took him back."

I look at my mother, whom I've brought to the edge of tears. Recreating the scene of the crime, the useless replay, once more. She puts down her cup and relaxes her body, sits back on the couch, her limbs limp, defeated. And what frightens me most, despite the vitality of her anger, is that after all these years she still doesn't have the slightest idea why he left. And I think if my poor, good-hearted and naive mother ever did get out of her apartment, if she ever met someone else, the same thing could happen to her again.

"I know what you're thinking, son. Don't take pity on me. I don't appreciate it. I'm a survivor: I'm doing all right. Just try your best not to end up like me. It's no fun living alone like this."

"I know. You did fine. You raised me, after all."

"You were always such a smart aleck." She shakes her head. "By the way, the tea tastes like poison. This is what you get for the A&P special."

"Are you managing all right financially?"

"Don't ask."

"I just did."

"I'm making ends meet. There's Social Security, disability. I babysit. There's other things in the fire."

"What 'other things'?"

"You haven't forgotten the alimony and child support your father owes."

"That's a dream, Mother. If you haven't nabbed him in twenty years, what hope could you possibly have?"

"I know his every move. If he takes one step into New York State I'll have him in jail before you can say legalized prostitution."

"And just how do you know his every move?"

"I know. I have a detective working on the case. You remember Uncle Harry? He gets a third when he catches him."

"Uncle Harry must be a terrific detective. You're wasting your time . . ."

"It won't be such a waste of time if we get the money. I could move out of this dump in a minute."

"I'd rather you let me help."

"We've been through this before. You have to understand," she says, "I still have a little dignity left. I don't want to talk about it anymore."

Argument started and completed in the usual time. History repeats itself. I stand up to go.

"So," she says, "is there anybody new on the horizon?"

"I told you: it's only been a couple of weeks."

"Don't let your life go to waste, Michael. You're an attractive man. You could rot waiting for her to come back."

"Actually," I say, lying, "there is someone. I just met her a little while ago. Her name's Laurie."

"Really," my mother says, getting up from the couch to open the drapes. "Let's put a little light on the situation." We both squint from the sudden, intrusive glare. "So what's she like?"

"She's beautiful. A Madonna. A horticulturist. She knows everything about plants and pots to put them in. Men are falling at her feet."

"You'll sweep *her* off her feet. You were always great with the girls: you got it from your father."

"Thanks. That was when I was fifteen and your memory's bad."

"You're smart as a whip, gentle, good looking, decent: she'll be lucky to get a hand on you."

"You should be my manager."

"Stay away from show business: it's a filthy racket."

"I was thinking of boxing."

"Another filthy racket. But I'll do it."

"Take care of yourself, Ma," I say, putting my arms around her as much as I can. It's not the same body that held me as a child, but for once I leave my mother in decent spirits. Her care and belief in me might keep me, for a while, afloat. And for the time being I'll keep my fantasies about my parents, our differences or duplications, to myself. And as my mother says as I walk out the door, "Get on with it."

18

I'VE COME TO CLAIM my cactus," I say to the woman checking over figures at the cash register. It's a few minutes past closing time, I've just spent my thirty-fifth birthday at the office with other grievers: I'm determined, especially after my visit to my mother, not to be permanently among their number. "I hope you're a woman of your word."

"Excuse me?" Laurie says, looking up from her calculator — then she smiles in recognition. "Oh, it's you. Sorry, that was a limited-time offer."

"We had a verbal agreement, Ms. Reid. In front of witnesses. I'd hate to have to take you to court. My wife's got connections with the law profession."

"Not that guy in the office. The Man Without Qualities?"

"The very same."

"Sorry I busted in that day. I should have called first, but I had no idea you were in the middle of a divorce. You doing all right?"

"A little better now, though I'm still a bit shaky."

"Well, then, I've got just the thing for you," she says, walking over to the display window and returning with a beautiful red-flowering cactus.

"It's stunning," I say, taking it out of her hands. "I know just where to put it. Now, how about having dinner with me?"

"Uh-oh."

"That's a gratifying response. I mean, we've already had a first date."

"That was different. Nothing personal, but I'm not too hot on divorcés."

"It was better when I was married?"

"If you want to know the truth, yes. The cliché holds true: you know where you stand with a married man. But you," she says, wiggling her right forefinger in front of her, "you're a shrink. You should know better. Fluctuations of mood, you extend yourself, you pull back out of fear, and so on, and so on."

"Well, this is very disappointing, I must say." I shake my head. "I told my mother we were already dating."

"You didn't." She laughs, searching out my expression.

"She was heartbroken by the separation. I had to tell her something."

"This is a very effective seduction strategy. Your mother, for Christ's sake. Put the plant down. You'll drop it."

"I told you I was out of practice. Look, Laurie, don't look so worried, I'm holding it with both hands. You're making me feel very sleazy. Is this a really crude thing for me to do? Am I out of line?"

"It's not at all crude. It's mostly pretty noble."

"Noble?"

"Because you didn't come back after our lunch at the Greenery. I was sure you would."

"Don't think the thought didn't occur to me. Several times. At the most inopportune times."

"That's why I think you're noble. You must have acquired your wife's sense of moral justice at some point."

"Let's just have dinner tonight and see how it goes."

"No dinners. I want to stay away from your interior life. Besides, I'm afraid I'm seeing a friend tonight."

"Is this your way of softening? I told you, I'm out of practice. You can be the man: you lead."

"All right," she says, tapping her forefinger on her chin. "For the day only. You need to get out of the city. How about cross-country skiing in Vermont? My friend will lend me his car, I'm sure of it."

"Oh, Laurie, I'm sorry, I hate outdoor sports. And skiing is the worst: white turtlenecks, hot toddies, goose steps . . ."

"What's your shoe size? I'll rent the skis. My treat. In case you don't like it I won't feel guilty."

"Good. I won't feel guilty either," I say, leaving Tendrils, Etc., with my cactus in a plastic bag, heart beating fast against my rib cage: I have all the nervous excitement of a teen-ager on his first date.

☆

Sunday morning is unbelievably cloudless, crisp, and bright, beams of sunlight glaring incisively against the store windows. I lean against the door of Laurie's store in Rick Chandler's down jacket, twenty minutes before she's supposed to arrive. She pulls up to the curb in a white Triumph wearing silver-reflecting sunglasses and a yellow ski parka. She honks the horn, motions for me to get in. It's been so long since I've been in a car it seems equivalent, especially with the Triumph's futuristic dashboard and instrument panel, to entering a space capsule. I hold on to the armrest with one hand and the emergency brake with the other, but as we drive up FDR Drive, onto the Cross Bronx Expressway, up the Major Deegan, as we leave the familiar city, I feel less and less anxious, my pulse seems to slow, I relax into my seat. Laurie and I talk nonstop all the way to Vermont, though she stops me when I get too nosy or too confessional. I fill her in on the life of the family counselor, before and after separation from his wife, and she tells me a little about her friend, a horticulturist who teaches at Columbia, and apparently makes a salary sufficient to fund his sports car. "He's not very professorial," she says.

"That's a relief."

"To both of us."

We park at the edge of a row of birch trees, the only trees, thanks to their white bark, I know by sight. It's at least ten degrees colder (wherever we are) and there's a brisk wind, but there really is snow on the ground, virgin white and crystalline in the sunlight — a different breed from what we get in Manhattan. "We must get mutant snow south of Riverdale," I say.

"Enough talk, Jarriman. Put on your skis."

Laurie opens the trunk of the Triumph; with her assistance, leaning on the car door, I snap on the narrow cross-country skis. And before I take my first step, I slide and fall. "I'm very athletic."

"You'd better get used to it. Everybody falls. We're going to follow this trail through the birches over to the left. We'll go over a log bridge about a mile up, then turn right. About three miles down, the trail leads to a beautiful lake. How are your legs?"

"I'm glad you asked."

"This is more exhausting than it looks. I'll lead, you follow," she says, then instructs me on how to walk, how to push off the poles, how to slow down going downhill, how to fall.

"That's all there is to it?"

"That's all the book-learning part," she says, and then she pushes off, gracefully and powerfully, gliding over the snow the way a sailboat moves across a lake with a good tailwind. I take my first few steps, slide backward, fall, get up, fall again. I haven't traveled thirty yards before I'm sweating all over Rick Chandler's down jacket. Laurie looks back at me, turns around with one pole, then backtracks. "Come on, fellow," she says. "Let's get to the lake before dark."

"I think I need more instruction."

"That's exactly what you don't need. Just put one foot in front of the other. Establish a rhythm. Don't think about it."

"Valuable advice," I say.

"I think you'd try to talk your way past the Pearly Gates," she says, shaking her head. "Now come on, follow me. I'll slow up a little."

Gradually I catch on a little bit, though even when she slows down I can't catch up to her, but I am skiing more than I'm falling, one foot clumsily following the other, knees slightly bent, my body arching forward so I feel the pure ache of muscular exhaustion. I take small chances going downhill, tucking under my poles to gather speed: I crouch, I glide, I slip and get up again. And I arrive at the lake, slightly out of breath, not too long after Laurie has unpacked her knapsack and arranged some Middle Eastern tacos on a tablecloth spread over a fallen log. "Not bad," she says. "Isn't this exhilarating?"

"I'll let you know when my pulse returns to normal," I say. But looking over the frozen lake, at the solitary figure ice-fishing in dead center, at the forests of birch and pine forming an eggshell around the border of the lake, I have to admit I take in and am taken aback by the silence — a calm I think I've never felt before — which I let wash over me. This is it, I think: the banal, reverential silence, the realization or the hope that whatever problems I've invented for myself, they'll somehow pass, and I'll survive or I won't. But in the presence of this beautiful woman I hardly know I feel as good as I can remember feeling. "You ought to be a travel agent," I tell her. "Actually, maybe we should team up: I shrink the clients, then send them out here with you. It's very gestalt."

"Let's not mix pleasure with business." She smiles and hands me a taco. We eat without speaking, then pass the canteen of red wine she brought in her knapsack. Then we watch the man fishing until he comes up with a tiny wriggling fish, and we both applaud.

"Thank you very much," I say. "This means a lot to me." Then I lean across the log and kiss her on the cheek.

"Thank you," she says. "That was nice."

She holds my gloved hand, I stand up and take her in my arms, I can feel her body heat and frame through the parka — it's simultaneously strange and comforting — and I give her a real kiss, I hold her tight and she returns my embrace. "How did that feel?" she asks.

"Very good. A little confusing, but good. It's exciting."

"It's supposed to be. Beginnings are always exciting. It's middles that are hard."

19

WHATEVER ELSE CAN BE SAID about the Carletons, whatever stress they endure week after week, they always appear neat and trim. Today Mrs. Carleton wears a tailored lime green suit — a little early for spring — a silk blouse, and bright yellow Vera scarf, while Mr. Carleton's gray suit — I recognize it as one of many — seems molded to his trim body. For a man of thirty-eight he seems in remarkable shape. "Racquetball," he tells me as he and Mrs. Carleton sit in different places. "My pulse is under sixty. But let's get down to business. I've been angry all week."

"Good," I say. "That's a good sign."

"Easy for you to say," Mrs. C. says. "You don't have to live with him."

"Well, what's been making you . . ."

"George wants to move out," Mr. Carleton interjects.

"And how old is George again?"

"Fifteen going on six," Mrs. Carleton says.

"She just can't stand to see him grow up. She's too dependent on him."

"I know how I should feel," Mrs. C. says plaintively. "I'm working on it."

"The least you two could do after all this time," I say, "is talk to each other directly." They face one another and Mr. C. grimaces. "Since we've talked about George before," I add,

113

looking down at their file, "I think it would be a good idea to bring the children into therapy with us for a while. And stop worrying about *should* so much, Mrs. Carleton. Your son *is* only fifteen."

Mrs. Carleton stretches her legs and leans back in her chair. "We've been through Network Therapy and structural therapy," she sighs. "Once we had *his* goddamn parents flown in from Indianapolis. Everybody says the same thing: the problem's between us and we've been using the children to mediate our arguments."

"George wants nothing to do with it anymore," Mr. C. says. "He just wants to move out."

"You think he might be trying to tell you folks something?" I ask.

Mrs. C. considers the remark for a moment, then asks, "You think we're not giving him enough freedom to be himself?"

"I think we ought to let him move out if he wants. Give him a taste of the real world. That would show him," says Mr. C.

"Does George have his own room?" I ask.

"He shares a room with Elaine," Mrs. C. says.

"And his sister's thirteen?"

"We have no hang-ups about bodies, thankfully, Mr. Jarriman. We got over that years ago," Mrs. C. says proudly. "George has a very healthy sex life right now. He doesn't have to sneak around."

"Let's save the talk of George's sex life for another session. I'm more interested in the layout of your apartment: whose room is where and how big?"

"The layout?" Mr. C. shrugs his shoulders. "Let's see. First there's an entrance with a foyer and a large closet. Then the living room, about yea big." He motions with his hand as though approximating a large fish. "Then a hall . . ."

"You forgot about the dining room," Mrs. C. says.

"I didn't forget about it. I was just getting to it," Mr. C. insists. But soon they're arguing about which room goes where, how many rooms there are, who has the southern exposure. I ask them to draw separate maps, just to see where and how

114

large the children's room is, but when I compare their sketches they look nothing like each other: Mr. Carleton apparently has the bathroom coming off the balcony.

"You people have lived there how long?"

"We're interior people, aren't we, dear? You can come and look for yourself if you think it's so important."

"Of course it's important," I say, and though Mr. C.'s suggestion is probably contentious, I decide to take him up on the offer. I know therapists who see clients in their homes — I don't usually like to give up the control of the office, but the Carletons *are* desperate, and need something, I'm not sure what, that will help them take their counseling seriously. "Will George be there?"

"I hadn't thought of that," Mrs. C. says. "I suppose we could call and ask him to go out for a while."

"I'd like to meet him."

Mr. Carleton narrows his eyes and crosses his arms. "I suppose you know we were referred to you because of your reputation with childless couples. George isn't the problem: we've already spent several thousand dollars finding that out."

"I never said he was the problem. And I didn't take you on because you were a childless couple."

"I think it's a wonderful idea," Mrs. C. interjects. "You've never seen our place, and I think the change might do us all some good."

We put on our coats and hats and walk out into the brisk March air. Mr. and Mrs. C. walk arm in arm, like the elderly couple they'll probably become, and I suddenly feel like an intruder in their lives. On the other hand, as I watch them jabber away at each other in psycho-lingo while we wait for a cab, I think they're the intruders, and I'm embarrassed to be seen in their company outside the office.

The Carletons live, it turns out, in posh surroundings, on East Eighty-sixth Street. It hadn't really struck me, I suppose because the Carletons look so hopelessly Midwestern, just how wealthy they are. Their doorman nods and opens the door for them (I suddenly become self-conscious about my herringbone overcoat left over from college — no match for Mr. C.'s elegant camel coat); the lobby features gold-flecked wallpaper and a fountain with a cherub spitting water. In the elevator Mrs. C., while getting out her keys, mumbles that she hopes "Lizzy's been to work. The living room needs a desperate cleaning."

She opens the door slowly, peeks around the corner, then turns around. "It's all right. She's been here." We follow her in. Mr. C's perception about the foyer's all wrong, but at least the living room is where it's supposed to be. And furnished in a mishmash of styles: a Colonial loveseat, a Swedish modern deck chair, and an expensive brown leather couch. The effect is not so much aesthetic mismanagement as ordinary neglect. To the right of the living room is a hall that leads to an archway and two closed doors. Mrs. C. leads the tour and points to each door as we pass.

"Our bedroom, George and Elaine's room, and then the bathroom."

"Your bedroom doesn't have a real door on it," I say, pointing to the bamboo curtain in the doorway.

"I think the people before us used it as a dining room," Mr. C. says, scratching his head.

I look in. A water bed, a hookah beside it, a collection of self-help books mixed freely with what look like Quality Paperback Book Club selections of classics in every field.

"I know what you're thinking, Mr. Jarriman," Mrs. C. says, shaking a finger at me. "We usually make love after the children leave for school."

"On a schedule? And what's happened since you've both been working?"

"This is George and Elaine's room," Mrs. Carleton says. "I think Elaine's at her dancing lesson. She's a darling. George should be studying here right now," she says, turning the doorknob.

Sure enough, there's fifteen-year-old George in boxer shorts and dark glasses, studying his geometry text while listening to the stereo with earphones. He's leaning back in his chair, bobbing his long, dark, and stringy hair from side to side, oblivious to our presence. "George." His mother shakes him. "We have a guest. Take those things off."

"Jesus Christ," George says, leaping out of his chair as if he'd just been stung by an insect. His earphone cord stretches, nearly knocking the stereo off his desk. "You just scared the shit out of me. Get out, all of you," he shouts, pushing his mother out the door. "Can't you see I'm not dressed?"

"Is that marijuana I smell?" Mr. Carleton asks, sniffing the air as George guides him out of the room. George is still attached to his earphones, though, and can't hear a word his father says.

"I don't smell anything," I say.

"We've been having a small problem with drugs." Mr. C. shakes his head. "It's not just us, it's the school system. The teachers are selling it."

"I'd rather have him smoke at home than sneak around with his friends," Mrs. C. intrudes. "It doesn't seem to have affected his grades."

"I'd rather he didn't smoke at all," Mr. C. says.

"You just walked into his room without knocking," I say. "He had every right to throw you out."

"Our door is always open," Mr. C. defends his wife. "We're a family here."

"Listen: you're worried about George's taking drugs, he can't even escape to his room to get out from under you. You're excluding him now from a very important family activity."

"We're not excluding him from anything," Mr. C. insists.

"You two have elected George as the safety valve, someone to attack to make sure nothing around here really changes. Is that it?"

"Our son is very independent," Mrs. C. says. "We want to treat him like a person, like a grownup. We just can't make him go because we say so."

"You're his parents. If you make reasonable rules, if he

understands why you make them and he cares for you, there's no reason why he wouldn't follow them. Let's sit in the living room and wait for him to come out."

"Would you like a drink?" Mrs. C. asks as I sit down on the Swedish deck chair.

"I don't think either of you understand the seriousness of the dynamic of what just went on here."

"George was very rude," Mrs. C. says, sitting down next to her husband and holding his hand. "We will have to talk to him about it."

"God damn it, Jarriman," Mr. C. says, "I told you George had nothing to do with any of this. We have our problems like anyone. But you know what the problem is: you've read our files."

"I don't know what you're talking about, Mr. Carleton. This isn't some kind of guessing game we're playing: your future happiness is supposed to be at stake. I don't have to tell you that, do I?"

"You certainly don't," Mrs. C. says. "We're deeply committed to our relationship."

"Let me put it this way: I'm running out of patience. The next time I see you two I want George and Elaine with us. Otherwise I don't see how we can proceed."

"Don't threaten us," Mr. C. says, standing up. "We don't need you to come and judge our house. We'll make it all right. Don't you worry."

"If that's how you feel," I say, putting my hands on my knees, rising, "that's fine. We won't have to waste one another's time. If you change your minds, you know how to reach me."

Mrs. Carleton stands up, runs to George's room, and violently knocks on the door. "George Carleton, you come out here. This minute." No answer. "George, for God's sake, there's a nice man who wants to meet you."

"Why don't you tell him your marriage depends on it?"

Mrs. Carleton looks at me, purses her lips. "But don't you see? He won't come out. We're trying."

"Don't beg him, dear," Mr. Carleton says. "We have other

118

alternatives. We'll try, Mr. Jarriman, that's all I can tell you."

"You really think we have other alternatives?" she asks him.

"Of course," he says. "Of course."

I leave the Carletons to their own resources, which are many. It's good to be out in the chilled air: I hail a cab and it strikes me that this is the direction Evelyn and her lawyer friend headed. Perhaps this is the very neighborhood where she's staying. The irony does not escape me that the Carletons, the foolish Carletons, are still together, pop psychology or no, while Evelyn and I are not. And it's just possible the Carletons will make it, with or without the approval of their counselor or their son.

20

A WEEK PASSES without the Carletons. Half my plants are thriving and the rest are drooping, though I give them equal love and misting and more than their share of vitamins. It must be some kind of sign, but I'll need Laurie to interpret it for me. Annette Eller, sadly, is floundering. She says she feels as if she's hit bottom. Having given Larry permission to avenge her many affairs, having given up other men, she can't stand it that Larry's taken up with a fellow doll maker on the assembly line, a woman "without a brain in her 'Weeping Wilma' head." Weeping Wilma is Ideal's latest and most successful doll, a best seller at Christmas — if you push in her stomach or slap her behind or face, she cries "real tears" until you rock her to sleep. "A brilliant idea," Annette says, "isn't it?"

Annette regrets interesting Larry in other women, regrets having catalogued her affairs for him, regrets having gone into therapy in the first place. "Look where it's gotten me." She sighs. "Now I have nothing." What can I say to her? I repeat Laurie's advice, and for better or worse, add my own. "Middles are hard, but don't give up now. You've come so far. I understand how you feel, but if you still want your relationship to succeed, I don't think you'll find an easy way out of it. It's difficult and painful."

Annette seems far from satisfied when she leaves my office, but resolves to bring Larry back into counseling with her. Now that he's seeing "Weeping Wilma," he's back to telling her she's the one with the problems; he's perfectly well adjusted. She says she wants him back — but she's so shaky when she walks out the door I'm not sure whether she'll have the strength to ask him. "Call me," I tell her, but I'm sure during the whole hour she hasn't heard a word I said.

Days like this I used to look forward to coming home and complaining to Evelyn, or listening to her complain about bureaucratic foul-ups and difficult clients. We'd conspire together to invent insidious punishments for those who caused us grief. Childish things, like ordering half a dozen pizzas to be delivered to them, or imitating a gangster on the phone and warning them to get out of town. Sadly, we never acted on the fantasies. Now, with a great deal of caution, I'll seek out Laurie, who's gradually become more of a confidante and given me entrance to her life. Occasionally I'll call her and she'll simply say, "I'm sorry, I'm having a friend over," or "Thanks, but I have work to do," or "I hope you'll understand but I'd rather be alone tonight." Laurie seems to say what she thinks, guiltlessly, without commitments, naturally, and with little room for inquiry. If those strategies sometimes set me on edge, given my current confusions, they also sometimes put me at ease.

Tonight, dressed only in her powder blue terry-cloth bathrobe and a paisley scarf ("I just got out of the bath," she says), she greets me happily with a peck on the cheek in exchange for the bottle of wine I have brought. I chose a Bordeaux, the exact label and vintage recommended in today's *Times,* so as not to take any chances. Laurie's shelves overflow with oversized pots, the shiniest green plants I've ever seen, and a collection of ceramic dishes hanging above the mantel. The walls are decorated with posters for sculpture and pottery shows, and perhaps because she's put up wooden blinds instead of curtains, her apartment looks much like one of those small uptown art galleries near the Carleton's apartment. That is, except for the potter's wheel, which sits in the middle of the room, and which — since I often sit in the rocking chair and she sits on the couch — I have to talk around. Tonight, though, Laurie pats one of the cushions of the couch and I sit next to her, only inches away from her bare, curled under, and slender legs.

"I'm really glad to see you tonight," she says.

"And vice versa," I say. "You do look a little down. What's the matter?"

"Just general malaise. I'm probably spending too much time by myself."

"You mean you never get used to living alone?"

"Do you ever get used to being married?"

"I'm afraid you do."

"Well, then," she says, "that's the difference. You get used to it in some ways, I suppose, and then there are days you wish there were more."

"And some days you wish there were less."

"Then you don't miss Evelyn?"

"That's not what I meant. I miss her very much." I watch Laurie tear the foil top off the wine. "You have to let it breathe, you know."

"Thanks," she says, uncorking the bottle with a jerk. "Damn, I almost spilled some."

"Well, this is a first. The first time you've felt worse than I have."

"I don't think that's true, Michael. You talk about being sad, but I'm afraid you're the type who lives in shock for a while. I don't think it's really hit you yet."

"I hope that's not true. Say, have you ever wanted to get married?"

"Not since I was sixteen. I have wished that relationships would last longer than they do, but . . ." She shrugs.

"But what?"

"But they don't. Or they haven't."

"I know," I say, and as I pour our first glass of wine we both grow quiet, as if sadness were tangible enough to sit between us, to separate us. I think about my life alone, not for the next few weeks or months, but for the life my mother has, or doesn't have. And for the first time since Evelyn's left I'm crying, I'm not thinking, the grief flows effortlessly. When I look over at Laurie she too is crying, until I catch her eye by putting my fingers to her cheek. Then she looks at me and breaks out into a tiny laugh. "Look at the two of us," she says. "We look like Lassie just died."

"And she was such a good dog."

"Faithful, loyal. She'd lick your hand, get the newspaper . . ."

She leans over to kiss me, and as she does her bathrobe opens slightly and I can see the top of her breast, the small, dark brown aureole lifting to the nipple. I put my arms around her, bring her body close to mine. Her tongue is in my mouth, enters slowly and tenderly and withdraws. My whole body seems to give rise as she leans back and soon I'm on top of her. I open her robe, her flesh is warm and pliant, I kiss her neck, then her breasts and stomach. We're both still crying, but she pulls me close to her, unzips my pants, tugs them off, and pulls me into her. I'm only conscious that this is the first time I've made love to anyone in months, and my nerve endings feel as if they've rubbed against a stucco wall: I'm raw as a bruise, dizzy, uncentered.

Afterward Laurie is smiling; she goes into her bedroom and dresses while I'm paralyzed on the couch. "That was nice," she says, buttoning her blouse as she reenters the room.

"It surely was. Nice isn't the word for it. I wonder what it means."

"It means you're truly hopeless," she says, tugging at my arm to get me up. "You're not with one of your clients now: it doesn't have to *mean* anything. Let's go for a walk: I want to show you around some of the galleries."

I take Laurie's hand and walk the streets I used to feel were too dangerous to walk at night. We walk in and out of galleries, but I hardly notice a single painting or piece of pottery: I look carefully into her face, her expression, which looks as lovely and straightforward as ever. It betrays no change. Then why is it, walking down Houston Street, I feel the city growing darker, I can't read the street signs, I hardly know where I am or whom I'm with?

21

Evelyn's wish for children is granted, although not with me. After three months of resisting the temptation to call her, to ask her to come back, I give in to the desire to hear her voice, using the excuse that I'd like her to pick up the rest of her things. What I'm not prepared for is a man's voice at the other end of the phone: when he says, "MacLean residence," I'm stunned into recognition — my wife's taken up with the mortician and his son. How I neglect the obvious! My best bet is to hang up, but my hand is paralyzed on the receiver.

"Michael, is that you?" he asks. "Evelyn's been trying to reach you for weeks."

"How did you know it was me? The heavy breathing?"

"I just knew; most people say 'Hello.' Hold on. Evelyn, it's Michael."

Evelyn comes to the phone out of breath, in her most lilting and disarming voice. I can almost see her face flush with excitement. "Michael, how have you *been*? I've been worried to death about you. I even called your mother."

"Great. I'm doing all right. Not bad," I say, trying to disguise the wavering timbre of my voice. "I leave the phone off the hook. How are you doing?"

"Fine, fine. I'm doing fine." And after a moment of silence she offers the grim details — how she's moved in with Ross and Benny, Ross's twelve-year-old son, and how they're taking wonderful care of her. When I ask her if she wants to pick up the rest of her clothes she says that it's too crowded there as it is. Why don't I just come to dinner so we can talk? And because I can think of no reason to say no, because I'm desperate to see her again, I accept.

When the time comes, though, when I knock on the door of Ross's fashionable Upper East Side apartment, I'm unprepared for her. She's adorned in a new hairdo — her long brown hair has been clipped into a mass of woolly tangles and curls — a perm. "What have you done to yourself?" I ask.

"I'm changing my life. I hope you like it. I was afraid you wouldn't recognize me."

"I recognize you all right."

"Let me take your coat," she says, lifting it off my shoulders. "Is it cold out?"

"It should be. March comes in like a lion, doesn't it?"

"It's April, Michael. It's almost Easter."

She puts my coat into the foyer closet, steps aside, and motions me into a thoroughly modern living room, equipped with chrome and canvas furniture, a tweed couch, yellow parson's tables, and ceiling-to-floor brushed chrome lamps. Evelyn's contribution, she says, is the array of plants: ferns, jades, ivies, exotic cacti. "I got the idea from you." She smiles. The clash of metal and greenery, of austerity and humidity, takes some getting used to, but nothing compared to seeing Evelyn with another man. Ross is reading on the couch in his informal attire: a red, short-sleeve Izod shirt, khaki slacks, and brown loafers. He looks something like an unimaginative college senior, though the short-sleeve shirt reveals a muscular build, and when he stands up to shake my hand, firmly, I realize he's two or three inches taller than I am, and with his angular features, squarish jaw, and wavy hair, objectively better looking. A weight-lifting lawyer. Just my luck.

The three of us stand in the middle of the room, exchanging, for a moment, whatever pleasantries we can make up: we all agree how good it is to see one another again, how good we all look, how comfortable we feel, considering. In the background I hear the familiar murmurs of television from a bedroom. "Benny," Ross says, "come out here and introduce yourself to Michael." Benny sticks his head out the door and frowns. "But, Pa," he says, "*Space 1999* is almost over." With the exception of his hair, which is dark and straight, Benny is the exact replica of his father, right down to the khaki pants.

Evelyn walks into the kitchen, which is divided from the living room by a butcher-block table and a huge sideboard. Ross, as uncomfortable in my presence as I am in his, excuses himself to help Evelyn with the salad. "Why don't you show Michael to your room, Benny? Maybe he'd like to watch the tube with you."

Benny's a dutiful son, understandably a little reticent around strangers, but attentive nonetheless. He tells me he likes history and social studies, he does well in school but can't stand his science teacher, who's a dork. His room contains numerous posters on the walls (Tom Seaver, Wonder Woman, the Bee Gees, Kiss) and hundreds of outer-space toys (robots, polyethylene monsters, electronic gadgets). As he shows me around, he keeps one eye on the television set. "I don't want you to miss anything," I tell him.

"That's all right. I've seen this episode before: it's a black hole rip-off. What do you do for a living?"

"I'm a family counselor."

"You mean you have to listen to everybody's problems?"

"It's not as bad as it sounds," I say, but he doesn't look convinced. As we walk out to the living room we catch a glimpse of Ross and Evelyn holding hands in the kitchen. When Ross leans over to kiss Evelyn on the neck, Benny and I both cringe a little. We look at each other, break into nervous laughter, then cup our hands over our mouths and retreat into his room. "Do they do this often?" I ask.

"All the time," he says. Then, after pausing a moment, he asks, "Didn't you and Evelyn?"

"In the beginning, yes. I assume just like your mother and father."

Benny does not answer. He leans back on the bed, his hands

folded behind his neck. I think I can detect the discomforting sting of memory in his abstracted expression: the melancholy moments of family conflicts, similar, perhaps, to how I must have felt after one of my parents' arguments, or after one of my battles with Evelyn. I have the urge to reach out to him, but fear I may have already gone too far. "You want to talk?" I ask.

"About what?" He rises to turn the volume up on the television. "This is the good part. When everyone on the ship is jarred by an asteroid and almost throws up."

Ross and Evelyn come in together. "Looks like Benny's found a captive audience," Ross says. "Drinks are served in the living room, Michael. I think the wine has sufficiently breathed."

I excuse myself to Benny, walk behind the happy couple into the living room, and sit in a canvas director's chair opposite Ross on the couch. Evelyn takes another trip to the kitchen to pick up the wine and glasses. On the parson's table to my left I notice a bronze version of the blindfolded statue of justice, with an enormous oil well tipping one of the scales.

"You like it?" Ross asks. "An apartment-warming gift from my ex-wife. Clever, isn't it?"

"Extremely. And considerate too."

As Evelyn places the tray on the cocktail table, a glass drops onto the rug but doesn't break. "Jesus," she hisses. "Ross," she adds, "could you ask Benny to turn the damned television set down?"

"It's not that loud," he says.

"It's giving me a splitting headache. We'll all go deaf."

"Say," he says, patting a cushion of the couch, "have a seat." She walks over to him and sits. He slips his arm around her waist and says, "Now, what are you so upset about?"

"I just want the volume turned down. That's all."

"No, really," he insists. "Think about it for a second."

She's quiet for a moment, takes a deep breath, then breaks down. "I guess I had a difficult day at work." Then, in her elevator voice, she adds, "And I suppose I'm a little tense about Michael's being here."

"That's better." He smiles. "Benny, could you turn the volume down a little. It's hard to hold a conversation in here."

"Sounds like you've been in therapy, Ross," I say, fearful I might have just witnessed the kind of tactics couples use on each other after leaving my office. I resolve to change strategies, effective immediately.

"Yes, I have," he says. "It's done wonders for my ability to relate to people. In fact, I really admire your profession. Had I been smart enough to go years ago, I might still be married today."

"That is unfortunate."

"Michael." Evelyn frowns, pouring wine into the glasses, then changes the subject. "Ross and I have been involved," she says, then blushes, "in organizing AFDC mothers. They've been getting, with all the recent cuts, a royal screwing."

"I know how they feel."

"I hope you're not going to make things more difficult than they already are," Ross says. "It wasn't easy for Evelyn to invite you here tonight."

"It wasn't easy for me to accept. What I want to know, Evelyn," I say, "is why you didn't tell me you were involved with someone else. It's a terrible shock to me."

"Ross and I weren't involved," she says, "*that* way. I went to him for help when things went haywire for us. He was very gracious and understanding."

"I'm sure he was."

"We didn't sleep together, Michael, until after I left you."

"Oh, spare me."

"Excuse me for interrupting," Ross says, "but what happened between you and Evelyn had very little to do with me. I don't think you'll get anywhere until you shift the terms of the disagreement."

"I certainly will not excuse you. What went wrong with Evelyn's and my relationship is very complicated. What really happened will only unfold over time. There are no easy answers. But we'll figure it out, don't you worry about it."

" 'Figure it out' sounds so removed, so mechanical. Aren't you pained by it? It must hurt to see us together."

"Of course it hurts. You want an affidavit?"

"We have no right to pry into Michael's life now, Ross," Evelyn says, as though I weren't there. "Though Ross *has* been through this before, Michael, and I know he only wants to help."

"Let's leave the lay therapist out of this, Evelyn," I say, standing up to leave. "He wasn't an eyewitness. Or at least I don't think he was."

"Let's be friends," she says, walking over to hug me. For a moment I forget, kissing Evelyn on the forehead, that I've been sitting in Ross's director's chair, that Ross is in the room, that it's his room, that Evelyn is no longer my wife. When I look at his smiling face, at his uplifted wine glass proposing a toast to the future, I don't know what I'm doing here, why I don't just walk out. But when Evelyn leads me by the hand to the butcher-block table and says, "I made lasagna, your favorite," I sit down without speaking, I lift my fork to my mouth. I eat.

22

A T FIRST GLANCE it looks as if the window of Laurie's store has just been cleaned. The Boston fern seems to leap out of its clay pot, the irises are a vibrant yellow. The plants look so appealing I decide to call Laurie when she gets to work and tell her how good for business a clean window can be. But as I approach the store on my way to the office I cannot see my reflection. An African violet has been tipped over the edge of the window frame. The window itself has been removed with a razor blade, by-passing the security system. Inside, the cash register lies on its side, its drawer splintered open as if exploded by a small grenade. The opened refrigerator door has misted up; dirt and footprints are all over the hardwood floor.

I run up to my office and call her. "Laurie, this is Michael. Be calm," I say. "Your store was robbed last night."

"Oh, God Jesus," she says. "Shit."

"I'll call the police and run back down to make sure there's no looting. Unless you want me to come get you."

"I can't believe it," she says.

"Do you want me to come get you?"

"If you could go down to the store, that would be really helpful: I'll be there as soon as I can hail a cab. I'll be all right."

But Laurie, who arrives at the store shortly after I've liberated a policeman from a nearby coffee shop, is far from all right. "They pulled the goddamn split-leaf tricanium out from the roots. It'll never recover from the trauma." She runs to it, cups dirt from the floor, and repots the six-foot plant. "Get me the watering can," she says, as if she were performing a delicate operation. Before I can reach it the policeman is leaning over the plant with her, pouring water out of the can.

"It'll be all right, lady," he says. "We have a pointer at home. When he wags his tail he always knocks over the coleus."

"This isn't a coleus," she says.

"Apparently the coleus is a very hardy plant," I tell the policeman.

He nods.

"Do you want to do something about these footprints?" I ask him as Laurie starts removing more dirt from the floor.

"Nah," he says. "In robberies like this you almost never get the guy. Unless there's an eyewitness."

Laurie stands up and surveys the store. "Why didn't he just take the money?"

"How much did you leave in the drawer?" the policeman asks.

"Ten dollars."

"Well, that's why he knocked over your plants. You pissed him off. He probably took some he liked. Ten bucks isn't even cab fare to Westchester. You ought to leave more in the drawer. And leave it open."

"And you guys, you fucking guys," she says, "ought to patrol the streets instead of trying to tell me how much to leave for him. As though it were a Christmas present for the doorman."

"Take it easy, Laurie," I say, watching with one eye the policeman closing up his notebook and starting to walk out the door. "She's understandably upset."

"I didn't rob the goddamn store," the cop says. "I thought this was *your* store. Then who is he?" he says to Laurie.

"He . . . he's my friend. Look at this," she gasps. "The refrigerator. The door's open. I don't know how many of these violets will survive."

"Are you insured?" I ask.

"I don't know. I suppose so. But these plants are going to die. What a fucking mess. Why me? Why didn't he just rob a bank?"

"Take it easy," I say, taking her hand. "There's nothing you can do now. I'll stick around and help clean up. I'll stay with you, I'll stay with you."

She pulls me close to her and hugs me. "You can't imagine how this feels, Michael. It's like a violation, a rape. Especially the way things have been turned over. It doesn't make sense."

"It's irrational, Laurie. Terror's supposed to be."

"Please, no psychoanalysis now," she says, letting me go. Then, turning to the cop, she adds, "Aren't you going to do something?"

"There's nothing much we can do," he says, shaking his head. "Just take a careful look around and see if the pattern is repeated. Ask people in the neighborhood if anybody saw him."

"It's not fair," she says. "You can't stay here, Michael. You've got clients."

"I wrote a note on my door saying that appointments would be postponed," I say, lying; though I'm worried someone might leave the office despondent, I have no intention of leaving Laurie now. "I want to help."

"I'll be all right," she says, watching the policeman walk back to the street. "He probably has to return to his doughnut surveillance. I'll be all right. When I get out of this city. It wasn't so bad when my apartment was broken into. All they got was my camera."

"Do you have a broom?"

She silently points to the back room.

"We'll clean this place up in no time. I can look up a glass repair place in the Yellow Pages and you can call your insurance company."

Laurie sits down on the counter next to the cash register, and with her hands on her hips, looks out the windowless window and sighs. "I suppose it could have been worse."

"You could have been here."

"I would have killed him. The cop was a lot of help, wasn't he?"

"I thought he was kind of charming about the coleus. Besides, I interrupted his breakfast. You know how useless a man can be before his breakfast."

"I'd forgotten. It's been a while since I've seen one."

"It must be at least two weeks, right?" I laugh.

"Never with you."

"That's right: it's the one meal we've missed. That's something to look forward to. How about this morning?"

"I can't leave the store."

"I can walk to the Carnegie Deli in ten minutes. I've timed it before."

"That's sweet."

"I'd like you to be able to count on me."

"I am," she says. "I feel a little better already."

When I return, my arms full of bagels, cream cheese, cheesecake, large Styrofoam cups of coffee, a quarter pound of lox, and a side order of pickles, Laurie sets a couple of paper napkins on the counter. "Picnic," she says. "Just like the country."

"You're not really thinking of leaving the city, are you?" I ask.

She shrugs her shoulders. "I've been thinking about it. I don't like this kind of stress."

"I'd miss you," I say. "Who else in the city would put up with me?"

"Now, now, no self-pity. This is my day for it. But I really don't think human beings were meant to live this way. So many occasions for fear." She shakes her head. "And in the springtime I always want to be somewhere else."

"That's like some of my clients. Only they feel that way most of the time." I look at my watch: it's almost eleven-thirty. "After we eat I'd better get back to my office. Will you be okay?"

134

"Sure. I'm fine now. You'd better get back. Otherwise all those crazy people'll be running around loose."

"They're not crazy. They're just people in trouble."

"Michael," she says, as I'm halfway out the door, "thank you for staying. I know how responsible you are. How difficult it was for you to take time off."

"I enjoyed it," I say. "I'll call you later. It was good for me."

23

DURING THE CARLETONS' next scheduled appointment George Carleton appears by himself, wearing his dark glasses, but also wearing a shiny black mohair suit with thin lapels and a thin black knit tie. He wears a taxi-driver hat, and when he takes it off, I find myself staring straight at his shaven head. I gesture for him to sit down. "Where's everyone else? I left the hour open just in case you all decided to show up."

"I don't think they're coming today. They don't know I'm here. You see, I'm cutting school."

"Oh?"

"Yeah. I just came in to thank you," he says, pausing to clasp his hands together and stretch out in his seat, "for having me sent to military school."

"Military school. I'm afraid I don't know anything about it."

"Well, you see, let's see, after that day you came to visit I got sent home from school for smoking dope in the lavatory. There was a big deal, the administrator sent for my parents, and when they got home — I think Dad was humiliated — they told me how you said it was time to get tough with me and give me some discipline. Dad made this great speech, right out of *The Waltons*, and that's when military school came up. We had a long discussion in which they let me say zilch, and therefore we all agreed. So I'm going."

"Your parents misheard what I said. I wanted you to get back into therapy with them. How do you feel about it?"

"How do I feel?" George shrugs and scratches his bald head. "I feel great about it. Ever since Mom went to work the joint has been a madhouse: growl, growl, growl. I figure it's about time to get into some serious push-ups with a bunch of Nazis. Who knows, I might get strong enough to beat up my old man."

"You'd like that."

"Oh, yeah, a statement like that really makes you guys go ape. I've seen that look before: it's the joy of watching a genuine maladjust."

"All right, George, you got me. What would you like?"

"I don't know what I'd like. I came here to, you know, tell you how much I appreciate all you've done for me and warn you my father's getting pretty fed up with you. I think he's considering Rolfing now. Or something quicker."

"And you're worried about your parents?"

"Nah. They'll come out smelling like roses. They thrive on this kind of nervous energy, on wearing you guys out. But then again, they do keep you in business."

"It's a shame, isn't it?"

"Let me tell you something," George says, leaning over my desk and waving his finger in the air, "parents aren't worth it. They're nothing but trouble. Power hungry. I'm never getting married, I'll tell you that."

"Don't give up on them, George. They're confused, but people change. I'd like to see you all together if you want."

"You can look me in the eye and honestly tell me you think they're going to change?" George doesn't wait for an answer. "No, for the time being you're welcome to them. Good-bye," he says, saluting in military fashion. "Just practicing." But before disappearing behind the door, he adds, "You might think about making an honest living someday."

24

A COMPLETELY DISHEVELED Annette Eller walks into my office, fifteen minutes late for her appointment. Her yellow car-rental-agency jacket looks slept in, her shirttail hangs out of her navy blouse, her eyes are puffy, her blond hair generously shows its dark brown roots. "Sorry I'm late, Doc," she says, taking a deep breath and standing before my desk. "I don't suppose it matters much." When I say nothing she adds, "I mean I'm afraid this is our last appointment."

"Oh?"

"You're a family counselor, aren't you?" I nod. "Well, then, you can't counsel me anymore. I'm not a family. It's common fucking sense."

"What happened, Annette?"

"Do I have to spell it out for you? The stupid son of a bitch took off with Weeping Wilma."

"I haven't heard that tone of voice in a while. Why don't you sit down and catch your breath."

"You're not going to make me cry. You can make me sit, but you can't make me cry. It's not worth it. He's not worth it."

"Take it easy: I don't want to make you cry. Did you talk to him before he left?"

"He talked. I listened. It was disgusting. He says she's marvelous, she says he's sexy. Sexy, can you imagine? You saw him in here. Christ, even his mother thinks he's forty years old. And listen to this: they made a pact with each other — to remain absolutely faithful until death do them part. I hope it's soon. We'll see how long that lasts," she laughs. "Larry runs out of tricks in about a week and a half, and his best ideas come out of *Penthouse* letters: 'I get off on a couple of Big Macs spread on an amputeed Vietnam vet.' " Then she slumps in her chair, her limbs limp, her face staring into her lap, as if exhausting her prepared speech she's ready to fall apart.

"I've never seen you so angry."

"You're a master of the obvious, Doc. Six years thrown out the window. You bet I'm angry."

"You're a lot stronger than you think, Annette. You don't have to try to be so tough."

"Ha."

"I know something about how you're feeling. It's devastating to lose someone you love ... someone you share a history with. There's almost nothing worse. You understand, though, no matter how absurd it might seem to you, why that pact of fidelity was important to him."

"Everyone makes promises. And everyone breaks them."

"That's true. But it says something about how wounded he feels."

"My heart bleeds for him. How do you think I feel, for Christ's sake? I made a *commitment,* as you like to say. I gave up everything for him."

"And it wasn't enough. Devotion helps, but you had a lot to overcome."

"Tell me about it."

"I don't have to tell you about it. You're not the only person who's gone through this, though. People can only endure so much before they lose faith. They might not choose to lose it, but it happens. I think Larry wanted to trust you. He just couldn't."

139

"I don't know who was stopping him. I shouldn't have dragged him in here. Or told him about the guys at the agency. I was just being naive."

"Don't worry so much about blame. A couple usually elects one person to have an affair. It's a pretty desperate signal often, but it's a signal. Now you have some deciding to do: whether you'll want to fight to get him back or whether you want to put your emotional energy into starting over."

"Or maybe I'll just want to forget about the whole thing."

"You could do that. But I meant it when I said you were strong. You were brave to bring things out into the open. It did show a real commitment."

"I suppose I don't feel very brave."

"That's all right, Annette. You've got rebuilding to do. But I don't think you've wasted your time here or struggling with Larry. I doubt that you'll make the same choices again."

"Yeah, I'll make different mistakes."

"I'm sure. Why should you be exempt? The point is . . ."

"The point is irrelevant, Doc, no matter how fast you think and talk. The point is my fucking husband took off and I'm back to point zero." Annette gets up from her chair, moves to the window, and stares out at the sky. "This talk is getting me nowhere. I'm going home."

I move toward her, look at her profile carefully, but it's impossible to know what she's thinking. "I wanted it to work, too. A lot. You deserve some happiness. I think, in a while, you'll have the opportunity to get it." I take her limp hand, clasp it hard, and she begins to cry, noiselessly. It takes a lot of will power not to cry with her, not to tell her I know exactly how she feels, but I stop myself: my sympathy is not at stake. "I'm sorry if I made you cry. I'm here if you need me. It might be good to have someone to talk to."

"I don't think so."

"All right, but you don't have to go through this alone. Seek out some friends, someone who cares about you. Do what you have to do, but don't spend all your time on regrets."

"He's asking me not to be human." She shrugs.

"It's true," I admit, watching her open the door and leave. I'm unable to help her, and I experience in her leaving the leaving I was deprived of: Evelyn's. This time I'm watching it happen and I still can't change it. And I can't follow my own advice: I think of all the things I might have done to keep the Ellers together, where I could have been more firm, where more yielding. I don't think I could have done any good. But I want to call Larry and tell him what a mistake he's making, how Annette's no longer the same person who hurt him.

I sit in my chair for an hour, first going over the Eller file, then just sitting and staring. At home, for the first time since Evelyn left, I turn on the television, but I can't keep my attention focused on the screen, and I change channels furiously. The situation comedies are ridiculous caricatures, cynical in their stupidity; the mysteries are not mysterious enough; and the educational channel, which offers a ballet and a show on heart disease, teaches me nothing I want to know. Not even the familiar visage of Uncle Burt would console. The phone rings and I run to pick it up, hoping it will be Annette or even Larry, but it turns out to be Laurie. "Hi, Spinoza," she says. "I've called to check on my plants. Are they wilting, are they underwatered? Do you need personal counsel?"

"Huh? I think they're okay."

"You weren't supposed to answer that question seriously, dummo. I didn't call to make you feel guilty. How'd you like to get out of the boring old house and see a little jazz at Sweet Basil? Ron Carter tonight. He's *très* accessible."

"I don't think so tonight, Laurie. I don't feel up to it. I'd rather be by myself tonight."

"Is this supposed to be a dose of my own medicine? My first rejection? It'll be my treat."

"No, it's nothing like that. I had a very draining day and it's too much to ask me to be human."

"And you think you have to suffer with it yourself, then," she says. "All right. Call me if you need me."

I go out for a walk, pick up a copy of *Time* at a candy store, and go back upstairs to read it, avoiding the faces of neighbors in the elevator. Half the population of Cambodia, I find out in an update, is still starving. The unemployment rate is rising, marriages are on the decline. That's worth a paragraph. Now I understand why I used to spend so much time watching television. If Annette Eller has a set, I hope she's watching it, or better yet, I hope she throws it out the window.

25

EVELYN STILL WANTS to be friends. She invites me to dinner
once a week during the month of May. I force myself to tell
her about Laurie and once in a while she reveals her own
fears about her relationship with Ross. He's a very strong and
forceful figure, she says. She finds it difficult to stand up to
him sometimes. She's taking an assertiveness-training course
at NYU. ("Don't laugh," she says. "It's a women's issue, a
political problem, not just a problem for me and Ross.")

During these dinners I watch Ross and Evelyn call each
other "dear," argue over insurance, bemoan the dwindling
federal funds for the inner cities. They appear so domesticated, so married, it's difficult to remember the time when
Evelyn was my wife. Sometimes, when she tries to treat me
like a younger brother, asking me if my practice is thriving,
if I'm eating well, if I've gotten someone to clean the apartment, I become resentful ("I can vacuum a goddamn apartment by myself"). I retreat to Benny's room, preferring discussion of his sadistic science teacher or the merits of Isaac
Asimov over Ursula LeGuin.

Benny and I get along famously and share the discomfort
(though he would not verbalize it) of feeling like intruders on
this new coupling of his father and my wife. I take Benny to
the park to throw the ball around, to the Cloisters to look at
the tapestries, to the movies to see *The Empire Strikes Back* (his

seventh time, my first). At first Evelyn seems pleased by the attention I give Benny, but on the Saturday afternoon when Ross is working at the office and I ask Evelyn if I can take Benny to a Mets game, she eyes me suspiciously. "Why do you keep taking Benny so many places, Michael? I thought grown-ups and children had nothing in common."

"No fair," I say. "That was a long time ago."

"And why, of all things, a baseball game?"

"You know how much I like baseball."

"No, I certainly don't," she says, but as we're edging toward the door she shrugs and lets us go.

I am determined that Benny will enjoy watching this ball game more than I enjoyed the Giants game when I was his age. In the subway on the way to Shea Stadium we go over the starting line-ups: Tom Seaver, his favorite player, has been traded to the Reds and is pitching today, so Benny's loyalties are divided. I assure him it's all right to feel that way. As a special treat before the game, I decide to take him to Frank's Bar and Grill, the Queens bar run by my former hero. Thomas has owned the bar ever since he retired in the mid-1960s. Eventually the Pirates did trade him, but unfortunately to the expansion-team Mets, who lost as many games their first season as any team in history. Thomas batted nearly .300, and spent the waning days of his career as the best player on the worst team in baseball. I still admire his perseverance. I point him out to Benny as we enter, this now two-hundred-eighty-pound red-faced Irishman who stands behind the counter shaking whiskey sours in front of life-sized blowups of players sliding into third base. I get up the courage to speak to him before ordering. "You were quite a ballplayer," I say. "I remember."

"Uh-huh," he says. "Thanks. Now what'll you and your boy have?"

I order a draft for me and a Coke for Benny. When we take our seats I tell him had Thomas been on the Yankees when he was at his best he'd probably be in the Hall of Fame today. He just never had the publicity of the New York sportswriters.

Benny is singularly unimpressed. "Are you sure it's the same Frank Thomas?" he asks. "He looks awfully fat to have been a ballplayer."

"I'm sure," I say, not particularly anxious to explain the metaphysics of growing older to a twelve-year-old. "I'm sure. How old are you, sonny?"

"I'll be thirteen in a couple of weeks. Want to come to my party?"

I nod.

"You'll have to bring a present."

"That's all right."

"I'm just kidding, Michael. What happened? You leave your sense of humor at home?"

"No, I'm just a little distracted. Nostalgic, actually. I remember when he was in the majors."

"You're not exactly on Social Security yet."

"Thanks a lot. I suppose next you'll tell me what a bright future I have ahead of me. Finish your Coke so we can make batting practice."

In spite of my efforts, my explanations, my decoding scorecards, my lessons in who covers second base on steal attempts, the game doesn't offer Benny much excitement. Seaver gets knocked out of the box in the third inning ("He's lost something off his fast ball," I tell Benny), but the Reds come back, rally for four runs in the fifth inning, and are beating the defenseless Mets, 8–5. Not much of a game. We leave in the top of the eighth to beat the crowds back to Manhattan. Benny's silent on the return trip, and my feeble attempts at conversation ("Does your father take you to many games?" "No." "Do you see your mother often?" "Pretty often." "Do you like Evelyn?" "She's all right.") only make him withdraw even more, so I leave him be.

☆

When we get back to the apartment, Evelyn is at the sink washing dishes. Her eyes are red. Ross is sitting at the butcher-block table, resting his chin on his palm, a morose look

145

smeared on his face. "Uh-oh," Benny says to me. "Argument city. I'm going to my room. You're on your own."

"We're here," I say. "The Mets lost."

"That's nice, dear," Evelyn says, wiping her eyes with her plastic glove.

"No, it's not nice," I say. "We were rooting for the home team."

"Did you just call him 'dear'?" Ross asks. "Did I hear you call him *dear*?"

"I'm sorry," she says, beginning to cry again. "It's an old habit."

"What's the matter?" I say to Evelyn.

"Why don't you mind your own business?" Ross snaps.

"I guess I'd better be going."

"That won't be necessary," Ross says. "I'm going for a walk." He stands, looks past me, takes a zipper jacket out of the front closet and slams the door behind him.

"So what happened?" I ask, sitting down at the butcher-block table.

"Did you two enjoy the game?"

"Evelyn, can't I help?"

"Ross was angry I let you take Benny to the game. He thinks we're seeing too much of you."

"Don't tell me the therapy king is jealous . . ."

"No, I don't think it's that. He doesn't understand why I keep asking you here, why we want to remain friends."

"That's understandable. If you were living with me, I wouldn't want your ex-husband around. Especially before he's recovered from losing you."

"He's questioned my motives. He thinks I haven't let go yet."

"Well?"

"Ross is very smart. He thinks it's destructive for both of us and I'm just being thoughtless and selfish. And it would be better for you if we made a clean break."

"Since when is Ross so interested in my welfare?"

146

"Michael," she says, turning around to face me, "he doesn't want me to see you anymore."

"And?"

"I don't know. We've shared a lot of time together. I don't know if I'm ready to let you disappear from my life."

"This has been a bad time all around. The Carletons are giving me a supreme pain in the ass, they're going to send their son to military school, and" — I pause — "Annette Eller's husband left her. I think she's given up on therapy."

"You're kidding. I know she meant a lot to you."

"She was making real progress. She made a real commitment to him."

"That's awful," she says, taking off her plastic gloves and sitting next to me at the table. Then she clasps her hand over my open palm. "You must be really broken up about it."

"I am," I say, but now, looking at her tear-streaked face, I'm not thinking of my work. "It hurts me to see you unhappy like this."

"I've been happy enough. Generally. He's been good for me in lots of ways."

"Like catching up on your cooking."

"That's not fair. I enjoy it."

"I know it's not fair. Who's trying to be fair? You know, Evelyn, when you left me I really felt I was on the edge of something important. I've been trying to forget about my father. To put him behind me."

"You can't do it, Michael. I've heard you say that a million times. How can you expect me to believe you?"

"I miss you, Evelyn. I want you back." She pulls her hand away and stares behind my face. "When I made love to Laurie I felt like a criminal."

"You made love to her?"

"It's legal. I don't think you've exactly won the chastity award this year." Evelyn frowns and closes her eyes. "Is it too hurtful for you to see me? Am I ruining things?"

No answer. Evelyn, in all her confusions, in her new hairdo

147

and an apron that says WHAT I NEED IS A WIFE, is so touching I can hardly stand to be in the same room with her.

"I don't want to talk about it now," she says, and we sit at her table, ex-husband and ex-wife, in mournful silence.

"What's for dinner?" Benny says, coming in from the bedroom. "I'm starved."

"Oh, my God," Evelyn says, shooting out of her chair as if we'd just been caught in a primal scene. "In all the chaos I forgot to put dinner up. We'll have to call out for pizza."

"I think I'd better be going before Ross comes back from his walk."

"I think you'd better," she says, running into the living room, thumbing through the phone book. "I don't know how it slipped my mind."

"Don't worry about it, Evelyn," Benny says. "Pizza will be fine."

I put my arm around Benny at the front door. "You're a pretty terrific kid."

"I like pizza. Thanks for taking me to the game," he smiles. "It was lousy."

"Next time a double-header," I say. "The percentages will be with us."

So without saying good-bye to Evelyn, who's frantically getting salad material out of the refrigerator, I walk out the door, wanting to apologize for all the confusion I may be causing her. But the truth is, I'm not sorry at all.

26

HAVING LEFT ROSS AND EVELYN'S in a total quandary, having uttered sentences about wanting Evelyn back before I knew what I had said or if that was in fact how I felt, I fall back into a deep depression, full of regrets. I should never have accepted Evelyn's dinner invitations. I lacked — there's no other word for it — suspicion. Why had she invited me in the first place? Had she lost her nerve, wanted to make me jealous, or worse yet, make Ross jealous? Or was she simply worried I might not survive her leaving? She may have been right. When I think of Evelyn now I think of the first dinner at Ross's, her murmuring "Let's be friends" when that's the last thing I want, kissing me into a state of vertigo from which I haven't yet recovered.

In the meantime my clients are familiarly needy, full of demands and confessions. It's what they pay me for. One couple denies each other affection, another wants a written contract for household duties, while Mrs. Parrish, to my surprise and dismay, suddenly confesses that while her husband was in Iwo Jima in the Big War she had had an affair with a flatfooted 4-F shoe salesman in Brockton, Massachusetts. Mr. Parrish, devastated, confesses that in all their years together he has not so much as looked at another woman and announces that he cannot live with such a deception. As far as he's concerned she can move out tomorrow. After altering my schedule to give them another appointment, after convincing Mr. Parrish not to throw away some thirty-odd years of marriage with one sentence, they agree (temporarily) not to separate, though Mr. Parrish will not sleep in the same bed with a "lying wife." And though I offer Mr. Parrish a number of reasons why his wife might not have been able to tell him, how it might have been partially his responsibility, how all of us have parts of ourselves we fear bringing out in the open, the truth is, as sophisticated as I'd like to feel, I understand completely his feelings of devastation. I shared them the moment I walked into Ross and Evelyn's and saw them together.

Then how could I keep it from Laurie that I'd seen my wife again? That I felt as if I'd betrayed Laurie by talking to Evelyn that way? The truth was I hadn't meant to say anything, but looking at Evelyn, red-eyed and defenseless in front of the sink, I felt as if I had no other choice. The romantics, even if their reasoning was wrong, may have been partially right to glorify suffering in love. It wasn't so much that suffering was glorious but inevitable, and shared suffering as well as joy counted for something. With Evelyn it counted a lot. My feelings had been real, my commitment to what I'd already lost. How could I keep that knowledge from Laurie, when I hadn't returned her phone call in more than a week?

"Is it dinnertime already?" she says, answering the telephone cheerfully. "A midnight supper perhaps?"

"I'm sorry. I meant to call days ago. It's been a hellish time."

"That's all right."

"Laurie, I just called to tell you I don't know if you can really count on me."

"What do you mean?"

"I mean I've been seeing my ex-wife. I mean I still have feelings for her."

"You're getting back together?"

"It's nothing like that. She's living with another man. That lawyer."

"Then what's the problem?"

150

"It's not a problem. It's just that after your early warnings about men in my situation I feel awful about it. I thought you'd like to know. You should probably hate me."

"I don't."

"You don't hate me?"

"No. I don't want to hear about it."

27

I LOOK OUT THE WINDOW: the six leaves on the one tree in front of my office are in full bloom. I hope for a balance of rain and sun so they'll prosper. June. The solitude of my apartment is bearable, occasionally a sanctuary, the one place I'm usually spared other people and the ringing telephone. Which is why, at 10:00 P.M., I'm shocked by the phone ring, why I fear some client's in trouble.

"Hello, Mikey," a voice squeals, "you recognize my voice?"

"No. Who is this?"

"It's your uncle Harry. Your mother's brother. I'm calling from Brooklyn. You remember me?"

"Sure, Uncle Harry, I remember you." My memory of my uncle is of the vulgarian who told a lot of jokes no one seemed to find funny. Uncle Harry's had a hard time of it: long ago he dropped out of law school, took up serving summonses while working part-time in a clothing store. Now he's become a detective of sorts, extending his job as summons server to tracking down missing husbands and wives, slapping summonses on them, garnisheeing their salaries, and splitting the money with the wronged spouse. A very speculative profession, Harry's is. "What do you want?"

"I'm sure your mother has kept you abreast of my work in Las Vegas."

"Not really."

"She's mentioned this business with your father, hasn't she?"

"Briefly, yes."

"Well, there's been an important breakthrough in the litigation and I'd like to discuss it with you."

"Shoot."

"Not on the phone. This is an urgent matter. I wouldn't disturb you at this hour if it weren't. I'd like you to come down to my office so we could talk about it now."

"Now?" Uncle Harry assures me the matter won't wait. He gives me the address of his office in downtown Brooklyn, says he'll expect me within the hour. I take the subway to the Broadway stop in Brooklyn and walk the remaining blocks to his office, hoping the threatening clouds won't drop a storm. The streets are deserted at this hour, and Brooklyn looks as though someone were about to or already had dropped a bomb on it. Uncle Harry's office is on the fourth floor of a building that houses a stereo warehouse and wholesale hospital supplies. The elevator is broken, so I take the stairs. The office doors are decorated, to use the term loosely, in the remnants of art deco, and that includes the lettering on Harry's translucent glass. HARRY WEINTRAUB, PRIVATE DETECTIVE. No sooner do I knock on the door than it opens suddenly and I'm pulled into it by the shirt collar and pushed against the wall. Harry slams the door with his foot. "You stupid son of a bitch," he says, his bald skull poised, like a bull, to butt my face, "what the fuck do you think you're doing?"

"Hey, what's going on here?"

Harry tightens his grip on my shirt, pushes me against the wall again, then draws me closer to his scarlet face. "I'll tell you what's going on. As if you didn't know. You didn't happen to take a little trip to the West Coast recently, did you?"

"Sure I did. I had a convention."

"My ass," he says. "And did you arrange a meeting with one Burt Jarriman?"

"How did you know about that?"

Harry removes his hands from my shirt, makes a fist, and

rotates it in my direction. "Are you a shmuck? Is that what your problem is, that you're a shmuck?"

"If you don't take your hands off me, Harry, and tell me what the hell's going on here, I'll have you arrested on assault and battery."

Harry releases his grip, motions for me to sit in the swivel chair in front of his desk. "Wonderful," he mutters. "Now the shmuck wants to have me arrested." He walks over to his file cabinet, pulls out an eleven-by-fourteen manila envelope and a cassette recorder. He sits down, taps his fingers on his desk, leans forward, and looks me in the eye. "You understand, don't you, that you might have ruined everything? I've been working on your mother's case for three long years, and for what? Her lawyers gave up on her years ago: they'd rather see her out on the street."

"What are you talking about, Harry, for Christ's sake?"

"I'll tell you what I'm talking about. I'll tell you. I've been on your father's trail, I've watched his every move for the last ten months. Nobody told me how to find him, it's not like he's listed in the phone book, you know . . ."

"Get to it, Harry."

"And you take one little trip to L.A., talk to your father's brother of all people, and now he knows I'm trailing him. He could've taken a business trip to the city any day now. I have information that he's been here half a dozen times to close deals with William Morris, and he's slipped out without being noticed. But he takes one more trip and I'll have his ass in handcuffs faster than you can say 'judgment to pay child support.' But now" — he shakes a finger at me — "but now . . ." He pulls a packet of photographs from the envelope. "Here. Take a look at these. Recognize these two?"

The first photograph is of two men sitting at a table in a restaurant. The man on the left is Uncle Burt; his arms are crossed and he's leaning over to talk. The other man, in profile, is clutching his drink.

"I took it with my Minolta," Harry says proudly. "That's your alleged father, in case you're wondering."

I pick up the photograph and study it. After all these years trying to convince myself I'd seen my father on television, on the city streets, in parked cars, when confronted with an actual photograph I don't recognize him at all — he's a total stranger. His hair is wavy but slicked down and receding high up on his forehead. His features are not at all pronounced, they have no angularity to them. In profile, a round nose, an oval chin, soft, although not heavy, cheeks. As though his face were pliable, made of clay. He's wearing a dark suit and a white tie. Very dignified, in a flashy sort of way. I search the photograph for every detail, but find no resemblance between us.

"Don't tell me you don't recognize him."

"To be honest, I really don't."

"Well, that's him. You can take my word for it. Here, take a look at these." He hands me the rest of the photographs, all different angles of the same pose. Nothing registers. "Your mother's heart would be broken if she knew you went out to see Burt," Harry says, shaking his head. "What an act of disloyalty. For shame."

"That's none of your business."

"Listen, asshole, your mother and I have spent a lot of time and money on this case, and now your father knows we're looking for him. I don't know how we'll get him back here. I've racked my brains. Fortunately," he adds, leaning back in his chair, "he wants no part of you."

"Bullshit. What do you mean my mother *and* you have spent a lot of money? You haven't taken anything from her, have you?"

"Expenses, I'm working for expenses only. Your mother's family."

"I don't believe this. How can you take money from her when she doesn't know where her next month's rent is coming from?"

"This is an investment, shmuck. Your mother's going to have a nest egg for her old age."

"She's in her old age now. This must be against the law." I stand up. "How many years do they give you for extortion?

155

If you have a license, I'm going to make sure it's revoked."

"Listen to this," he says, "before you open your big mouth." He loosens the collar of his shirt, one of those nylon ones you can see an undershirt through. "Your uncle Burt has this comedian. He's terrible. Crude. A real no-talent. I heard him six nights in a row in this dump of a hole, The Steamboat. I didn't crack a single smile. Burt wants your father to handle this fool, to get him into one of the small lounges of Caesar's Palace. Your father does a lot of business there. He's an agent now. He handles chorus girls. That's perfect for him, isn't it?"

"I don't see what this has to do with me."

"Sit down and I'll tell you what it has to do with you. Your uncle spilled his guts about your little meeting at the studio. He told your father he could arrange a meeting if he'll just give this comedian a shot. Listen." He pushes the playback button on the tape recorder and lifts his eyebrows. The voice is undeniably Burt's, the cultured jewel thief, the criminologist. "Allie," he says, "the boy just needs a break. Three days. If he doesn't go they can cancel. An opening act to somebody."

"I can't push anyone at the Palace, Burt."

"That's your father," Harry says, and yes, the voice comes back to me now, the man with the explanation at the luncheonette, who yells from his car in the traffic jam. The voice that turns me into a child again, hanging on his every word.

"Your son came to see me in Hollywood a little while ago. He wanted to know about you, about how you're doing." My father says nothing. "He's married now. He's a shrink. Listen," Burt says, "I'm not asking you to stick your neck out for me. He's good. I've got to get in on your end of the business. How long do you think I can keep getting these stupid bit parts?"

"I know what you're thinking, Burt. But I don't want to see him."

"Allie, you're looking at him. Listen to him, he's got the audience. He's got them."

"Yeah, all three of them," my father says. "I wasn't talking about him."

"Allie, for God's sake, Michael is your son. Maybe he's fed up with his mother. Maybe he wants to put the past behind him."

"And maybe he doesn't. Maybe he wants to put me in jail. Maybe his mother still wants blood out of a stone."

"He would have told me, Allie. Jail never came up. He misses you."

"I'm not taking your boy on, Burt. You might as well take him around to the smaller clubs in Reno."

"He's got a long-term at The Steamboat. He's ready, Allie. They're both ready."

"Forget it. I've got twenty years built up here. I have a life."

Harry stops the recorder. "You don't want to hear the rest, Mikey. Your father's no fool. He knows something's cooking. He knows we're close."

"What do you want from me, Harry?"

"I've thought it over, Mikey," Harry says, shuffling his papers, putting the photos back in the envelope. "I just want you to rectify your mistake."

"I haven't made any mistake."

"Your mother could use that money. He owes her eighty-five thousand in back child support. That's almost fifty thousand she could put into a house and get out of that hellhole."

"Fifty thousand for her? Did I hear you right? And the rest?"

"She had nothing before. I told you, handcuffs as soon as he steps off the plane."

"You take another penny from my mother and you'll be in handcuffs."

"I don't want to argue with you, Mikey. All I want you to do is lure him back into the city. Tell him you want him to meet your wife. Tell him how you've missed him all these years."

"You heard him. He doesn't even want to see me."

"That was partly to get Burt off his back. But if you were there, face to face, how could he resist? His own son, successful, grown up. A mensh. You're a bright boy: you could convince him. Use psychology on him," Harry says, pointing to his temple. "Use your head for once."

"They ought to lock you up."

"Think about it, Mikey. Don't be selfish. Think about your mother locked away with all those cartons."

"You think about it, Harry. Why haven't you thought about it?" I walk out, my legs rubbery, but I'm not thinking about my mother's apartment. My father's voice, his stern refusal, keeps ringing in my ears. His fear, unbelievable, that I'd want him in jail. I won't believe any of it — the photographs, the chemical resolutions, the thin spool of magnetic tape — it doesn't add up to a father. To my father.

28

I RUN FROM HARRY'S OFFICE to the el, the sound of my father's tape-recorded voice still ringing in my ears. The cloud cover has dissolved and the late evening chill is oddly penetrating: I should have worn more than a short-sleeve shirt. I put my hands in my pants pocket and wait half an hour for the train. Fortunately, Harry's neighborhood is so broken down not even a mugger would bother prowling the deserted platform twenty feet above the street. There's only one person sleeping in the subway car, an old woman lying down next to a glassy-eyed cop holding a German shepherd on a leash. A hell of a way to travel.

A moment of sanity: I get off the subway at Laurie's stop. There's no way I'm going back to my apartment. I walk the three blocks north and west to her place, my teeth chattering from the cold. I look up from the street to her window but I don't see any lights on. It's nearly one and I'm suddenly afraid of waking her up, so I keep walking, looking for a phone to call from. When I finally do find a booth in front of a closed drugstore, the receiver's been severed from its cord. Given two equally unattractive choices, I decide on the uncharacteristic one, asking Laurie for help; I run back to her place and knock, tentatively, on the door. After a minute I hear a throaty voice almost whisper, "Josh? Is that you?"

"Laurie?"

"Michael?" she asks, opening the door slightly, then closing it to remove the chain. "What are you doing here at this hour?"

"I didn't wake you up, I hope."

She shakes her head no. "Well, that's good. I tried to call but there isn't a working telephone booth within a mile of this place."

She puts her hands on her hips — she's fully dressed in jeans and a navy silk blouse — and stares at me, shaking her head.

"I could come back later if this is inconvenient."

"Sure," she says, looking down at her watch. "Why don't you try me about four in the morning. I shouldn't be doing anything then."

"I'm sorry. I wanted to call first."

"What's the matter? Your eyes are all red." She reaches out for my hand. "You're freezing. Are you ill?"

I shake my head.

"Get in here, for Christ's sake." She takes me into the living room and sits me down on the couch. "Let me get you a drink. All I have is Scotch: is that all right?"

"I don't want anything, thanks. I just didn't want to wake you up."

"What is it?" she says, sitting down next to me on the couch. "It has something to do with Evelyn. Is she all right?"

"It's my father."

"He's dead. Oh, Michael, how did you find out?"

"No, he's not dead."

"You don't have to talk now if you don't feel like it. Just relax for a few minutes. Here, I'll massage your neck." She guides my head down and with her forefinger and thumb kneads the muscles in the back of my neck. "God, are you tight. Does this feel any better?"

"I think so. Listen, Laurie, I really am sorry for barging in on you like this. I don't have any right."

"Will you stop it?"

"My father doesn't want to see me."

"How do you know? I didn't even know you were looking for him."

160

"I'm not. But I heard him say it in his own voice." Lying down with my head in her lap, I tell Laurie the story — piece by piece, from Harry's phone call to the moment I leave his office. She listens silently, attentively, punctuating my remarks every so often with comments like "Are you sure it was him?" and "Your uncle Harry sounds like a real creep."

"You're really shaken," she says when I finish. "You should hear your voice quavering."

"It's the first time I've heard his voice in twenty years. And to hear him say that."

"But why is it so important *now*?"

"I suppose because now I know how he feels. I always thought he had a reason."

"I'm sure he does."

"Well, it's not good enough. I am his goddamn son."

"You're also a grown man now," Laurie says.

"Thanks for reminding me."

"Hey, hey," she says. "Take it easy. *I'm* not the one who left. I'm here. Can't you feel my hand on your forehead?"

"Yes, I can. I'm sorry. I'm just angry. At him, at myself for letting it eat at me, and at my goddamn uncle for ripping off my mother."

"Why do you think he still has so much power over you?"

"My father? Because. Because" — I pause, trying to clear my head — "for so many years I was afraid to admit how hurt I was."

"You're refusing Harry's proposal out of hand? Maybe you should try to see him."

"After what he said? No, I've thought about it. Way before Uncle Harry. The father I want to talk to doesn't exist."

"That seems like a pretty intellectualized response."

"I don't think I'm comfortable in this position."

"I can move. Should I get you a pillow?"

"That's not what I meant," I say, sitting up, pressing my palms against my temples. "I mean I had to go to school for years before I could say things like that."

"Well, see, that's your problem."

"Please. I'm already feeling inadequate about my work."

"It's true, then. You really don't like being in this position."

"I don't like to impose, that's all."

"Bullshit."

"No, I'm not used to being so self-absorbed. Say, speaking of which," I say, looking for the first time since I came in at the dining table, "what's this?"

"What's what?"

The table is set with dinner plates, a vase of flowers, a linen tablecloth, crystal, two poured glasses of wine next to a salad bowl, and candles with burnt wicks that look as if they'd been lit, then quickly put out. "You're expecting someone."

"No, not really."

"Wait a minute. Wait just a minute. Who was Josh, anyway?"

"Was? He *is* my friend."

"The horticulturist?"

She nods.

"And you were expecting him."

She shakes her head.

"Then he's already been here."

She nods again.

"But he didn't drink his wine. Or stay for dinner."

"Very observant."

"You don't want to talk about it. You had an argument. I'm sorry. And here I am unloading on you as though you had nothing else to worry about."

"That's all right. I'm glad you're here. I wouldn't have been able to sleep for a while anyway."

"Was it about me?"

"Don't be so vain."

"Listen, you never set up such a fancy meal for me, you know."

"Well, you're sounding in slightly better spirits," she says, moving from the couch to the table to nibble on a piece of lettuce. "That's not true," she says, speaking with her mouth full, "is it?"

"I think so. A tablecloth. Crystal. A view. It looks like a regular Top of the Sixes."

"Not quite. Does that restaurant still exist? I haven't heard about it in years."

"I've never been there. We should try it sometime."

"We'd never get through the door." She sits on the couch again, gestures for me to move closer to her, then holds a forked tomato close to my mouth. "Now come on and eat. It's good for you."

I shake my head in refusal.

"It's a shame: it'll just go to waste."

"It will? Are you okay? Do you want to talk about it?"

"No, I don't. I'm not like you that way, Michael. I like to keep separate relationships separate. They're private matters."

"I was thinking as a friend," I say. "Someone who cares about you, who wants you to be happy."

"Why don't you stick to thinking like yourself?"

"All right, I will. What the fuck does this guy think he's doing coming over here at this time of night? Watering the violets?"

"He was coming over to apologize for being so pig-headed."

"Will you accept substitutions?"

"At this hour," Laurie yawns, "I'll accept almost anything."

"Then you don't want me to go back to my place tonight?"

She shakes her head.

"Should I clear the table?"

"As payment? Why don't you just help me make the bed: I did a laundry today, so I have to put on new sheets."

"You know," I say, following her into the bedroom, "I've never spent the night with you before."

"My judgment must be slipping."

She throws me two pillowcases. "Here, you can start with these," she says. Her bedroom is stark and functional, with a mattress on the floor, a brown, braided rug beside it, an old wrought-iron lamp, the standard student's bookcase of bricks and pine boards supporting her art books and horticulture manuals. I put the pillowcases on the pillows, toss the pillows

163

on the bed, and help her tuck in the (flowered, naturally) top sheet. "Say, watch what you're doing down there. Military corners, Buster. Or else the covers will all be on the floor by morning."

"Military corners? Laurie, I never would have expected this from you."

"What's the matter, you don't know how to make them?"

"Of course I do. It's how Evelyn and I . . ." The blood suddenly rushes to my head. "Are you sure I should stay? Listen, there's something I have to tell you."

"I know, this is your first time. I'll be gentle. Can't it wait, Michael? I'm really wiped," she says, casually beginning to unbutton her blouse. I can't help but stare: her naked pose is so domesticated and yet exciting that I don't know what to say. Or do. "If we're lucky we can get a couple of hours sleep."

I undress, slip under the clean sheets next to her, and press against her. "Thanks much," I say, leaning over to kiss the back of her neck. "You've done more than your duty tonight."

"That's okay," she says, turning around to face me and pulling my buttocks close to her body. "If you want to, you can do yours now."

Afterward, staring at Laurie's ceiling, my head filled with tangled images of my father and uncles, of Laurie and Evelyn, I move toward Laurie and whisper, "Are you asleep yet?"

"I'm trying."

"I'm not sure I should be doing this."

"Too late. You've already done it."

"I feel like I'm sending out some very mixed signals. And this thing with my father only complicates matters further. What do you think?"

"Right now I'm thinking I have to open the store in less than four hours. Can't we save the rest of the talk for later?"

"Sure," I say, and though I don't sleep, I do lie still with my hands behind my neck. I turn every so often to look at Laurie's sleeping face, and for the first time in more than a decade, I spend the entire night with a woman who's not my wife.

29

Whatever Ross and Evelyn's desires in the matter, Benny decides to invite me for dinner on the occasion of his first real date and his thirteenth birthday. "It'll be a feast," he says on the phone. "Evelyn's cooking up crêpes Florentine, and chocolate mousse for dessert. I want to repay you for taking me to the game."

"Did Evelyn put you up to this?"

"Unh-unh," Benny says emphatically.

"And it's all right with your father?"

"We talked about it and he said whatever I wanted to do I had final say."

"In other words, a fight."

"This place has been like *Star Wars* the last couple of weeks anyway, so it's not likely to make any difference."

"If you're sure I'm not going to cause trouble."

"Listen, man, after all the trouble I went to you'd better show up. The eats will be great."

Reluctantly I agree to come, though when I get off the phone I feel as if I just had been in an argument with a fifty-year-old. And though I'm prepared for a not very pleasant evening, I'd do almost anything not to ruin Benny's first date.

☆

When Evelyn opens the door she puts her finger perpendicular to her mouth. "Come on in," she whispers. "There's been a change of plans: Benny's decided he has to get to the dance an hour early."

"Well, where is the birthday boy?" In my hands I'm clutching the latest edition of the Doubleday baseball encyclopedia. "I've got a lot of advice to give him."

"Michael, be quiet. He's in the bedroom dressing. If you say one word I swear I'll break your arm."

"Take it easy. I was only kidding." I put the book down on the parson's table and sit at one end of the couch.

"Not there," Evelyn says. "That's Ross's seat. By the light. He's very fussy about it."

"All right. I'll stand up. Can I take Benny and his date to the gym?"

"They don't hold dances in gymnasiums anymore," Ross says, tugging on his cloth belt as he comes out of Benny's room. "Besides, they won't need an escort: they're going to walk to the dance, and Marion lives right here in the building."

"Marion," I say. "That sounds so grown up."

"Grown up." Ross laughs. "That sounds like something a thirteen-year-old might say."

"My, aren't we the mature ones? Don't tell me you're not at all excited. Or did you pass by adolescence completely, moving from the oral stage to adulthood in one fell swoop?"

"Michael used to be a real terror with the girls on Long Island," Evelyn says, trying to ease the tension. "His mother says they wouldn't leave him alone. Or vice versa."

"See how much things change," I say.

"Or how they remain the same," Ross says.

Benny walks into the living room, hands in his pockets. His hair is slicked down (though it curls over his ears); he's wearing a yellow oxford shirt and a crew-neck sweater tied around his neck so he looks as though he just stepped out of a Sunday *Times* ad. "What's everybody looking at?" he asks.

"Michael's telling us about his childhood sweethearts," Ross says. "A case of arrested development," he adds, under his breath. Evelyn glares at Ross, but he ignores her.

"Childhood sweethearts. Whoaaa," Benny says, walking over to the television, turning it on. A monster movie's on Channel 9, one of those films in which a toothpick Tokyo is devoured by a caterpillar. It's usually the kind of movie Benny can't tear himself away from, but tonight he switches to the weekend news. Evelyn and I look at each other and shrug. He turns to face us for a moment and says, "I've seen it before: it's not very good," then goes back to the news.

"Don't you want to see what Michael brought you?" Evelyn asks him.

"Shhh. I will in a minute. I want to see this story."

"I'm afraid you're not going to get much of his attention tonight," Evelyn says to me. "He's been like this all day."

"It's understandable," I whisper, almost mouthing the words. "He's just nervous, but he thinks he's not supposed to be."

Ross walks over to Benny, sits beside him on the floor, puts his arm around his son, and watches television with him. Evelyn motions for me to follow her into the kitchen, where she puts on her apron and begins to beat the batter for the crêpes. "Ross has also been a little touchy today," she says.

"I suppose he's nervous, too."

"It might be a little easier if he'd just admit he's jealous . . ."

"You're not pitting the two of us against each other, are you, Evelyn? Well, are you?"

She stops beating the batter. "I don't know how you can even suggest it. First of all, that kind of manipulation requires a strength I really don't have right now."

"That sounds bad."

"Confused, definitely. Bad, very possibly." She returns to her batter. "I don't really want to talk about it. I'm not up to it."

"No one ever asked you to be Superman, hon."

"Superperson, please," she mutters. She wants to make

peace. "But let's do change the subject. I'd rather hear how you've been doing."

"Not all that well. It's often lonely. Though I don't dwell on it. I may lose the Parrishes now."

"What do you mean 'lose' them?"

"I mean it came out that Mrs. Parrish had an affair. A long time ago. I suppose it's an accumulation of things. It's crazy."

"You can't blame yourself for that."

"That's what the textbooks say, but I'm brokenhearted about it. Truth is, you can and you can't. You want to take credit for those who do change, so it's not exactly fair to deny some responsibility for the ones who don't."

"This doesn't sound like you, Michael. Since when are you equating separations with failures?"

"Since when? You want to know since when?"

"I thought that subject was off limits," Evelyn says.

"You know you could get arrested for batter abuse, you've been knocking that stuff so long."

"I'm sorry. I wasn't thinking. Well, there's no law that says you have to be the foreman. You make the crêpes," she says, handing me the pan, "and I'll work on the sauce and the filling."

The crêpe pan heats on the stove, I place it in the batter, it hisses, and I return the pan to the stove. "Too fat."

"You don't have to eat that many," she says.

"No, I meant the crêpe. Why, do I look too fat?"

"No, you look marvelous. I was just distracted."

"I know, or you wouldn't have said that."

I actually make her blush. "Michael, you're incorrigible."

"That's what I've been trying to tell you," Ross says, walking up behind Evelyn and kissing her on the neck. "The news is just about over. What's he incorrigible about?"

"Everything," she says. "Dinner will be ready in a few minutes."

"Good," Ross says. "Benny's been getting itchy and I'm starved. He turned the monster movie back on."

Ross and I sit at the table while Evelyn sprinkles parsley over the crêpes. "Okay, Ace, dinner's ready." He motions to Benny. "Why don't you turn the set off and have a seat?"

"Dad," Benny says, without turning from the set, "I'm really not hungry. I'd rather not have anything to eat."

"You've invited Michael to dinner, Benny. You're being very rude."

"Michael will understand. He's had his share of childhood sweethearts."

Ross looks at me and I put up my hands to indicate I understand. Evelyn carries in the salad bowl and sets it between Ross and me. "All right, Benjamin," she almost sings. "The monsters can wait. If you don't eat now you won't be ready on time."

"I'm not eating tonight, Evelyn."

"After I spent all this time cooking?" Ross motions for her to be quiet. "But I made crêpes, his favorite." Her voice trails off into the air.

"All right. Let's start with the salad, then," Ross says, loudly. "You don't know what you're missing, partner."

In a few minutes there's a knock on the door. "Already?" Benny says, turning off the set and running to the hall to answer it. Marion has arrived. She's a pretty little blonde with a forest green sweater, a tartan skirt, and a green ribbon in her hair. We get up from the table, but Benny motions us away behind his back and blocks her entrance. "He's ashamed of us," Evelyn whispers to Ross, while Ross pulls me from the foyer by the back of my belt.

"I'm ready," Benny says to Marion. "Did you hear what just happened in Namibia?"

"No, what?"

"I'll tell you about it," Benny says, walking out the door, waving to us without looking behind him. His absence, as soon as the door is shut, is almost like a hole in the wall. Though Evelyn has returned to the kitchen to fetch the crêpes, the ritual of dinner has been rendered meaningless.

Ross sits on the couch, his hands behind his forehead, his legs stretched out. I try to make myself invisible, picking up a copy of the *Harvard Law Review* off the cocktail table; I leaf through the pages, but Ross's discomfort is pervasive. This is the first time he's brought out my sympathy. I'm touched by his feelings for his son, and I try to draw him out. "It's hard to believe he's grown up so fast, isn't it?"

Ross turns to face me, seems genuinely startled by my presence. He puts his hand to his chin as if he had a beard. A technique he might use at the witness stand. "Tell me, Jarriman, why do you keep coming here?"

"Because I keep getting invited."

"No, that's not what I meant. I mean, what's the attraction of it? Evelyn seems to think you get something out of it."

"Is that what Evelyn thinks? I think it's something of an accomplishment that we can still be friends. But I certainly don't want to cause conflict between the two of you . . ."

"Is that what you think?" he laughs, and at that moment I could knock the alligator right off his Izod shirt. "No, I don't think *that's* the problem. That's not it at all. Forget it. Just forget I brought up the subject."

"Oh, no, Ross. You just don't drop a bomb like that and then say 'forget it.' I want to know what you're getting at."

Evelyn enters the room, her hands encased in two red oven mitts that say HIS and HERS. "Dinner's ready," she says, her timing perfect.

"Michael," Ross says, "I couldn't care less about your 'friendship' with Evelyn. I don't think you do, either. It's Benny who brings you here: why don't you admit it?"

"What's to admit? You have a wonderful son. You ought to be proud of him."

"That's just the goddamn point. He's *my* son."

"Who ever said he wasn't?"

"Don't get your back up. Don't be so defensive. It's just that you're not Benny's father and he doesn't need your protection. Nobody's abandoning him."

"Ross, damn it," Evelyn says, "why don't you lay off? Benny wanted Michael here tonight. It was his idea, not Michael's."

"All I'm saying" — Ross lowers his voice, talking slowly, choosing his words with deliberation — "is that if Michael wants to start a family he should go somewhere else. He's got no future here."

"I'll put the crêpes back in the oven," Evelyn says.

"Don't bother on my account," I say. "I think I'll be going."

Evelyn follows me into the foyer, her hands still in the oven mitts, begging me to stay. "We'll all calm down," she insists.

Even Ross seems remorseful. "I didn't mean to hurt your feelings, Michael."

"All you had to do was tell Benny you didn't want me here. I didn't come here for a therapy session: you should stick to the law. You'd make a lousy therapist."

"And you'd make a hell of a father."

"Why are you being such a bastard, Ross?" Evelyn pleads, and apologizes again.

"If you want to see me again, Evelyn, you know how. It will have to be somewhere else."

I try to read Evelyn's inscrutable expression when she doesn't answer me, but no response is forthcoming. Or, rather, I see so many confusions in her eyes, in the way she purses her lips, I can't filter any single signal out. At least I don't find the signal I want to read. So I leave.

I take the elevator, pull up the collar of my sport coat, and walk into the late spring air. It's a crisp and clear June evening. When I look up beyond the tall apartment houses of the Upper East Side I can actually see the dull shine of a few stars. Walking to the subway, I look back only once, knowing well I may have seen my wife, excuse me, my ex-wife, for the last time. For once Ross, in all his cruel directness, his uncontrolled control, is probably right. Benny's not my son, he doesn't need my protection. It's not likely I could shelter him from the world of adolescence, or worse, the world of men and women. All you can do is prepare yourself to make mistakes and learn to live with them. If you can do that much. Marion will kiss him on the cheek tonight, maybe on the lips, maybe more. Maybe not. In any case, it's not my problem, just as Evelyn's confusion is no longer my problem or pleasure. I feel the blood rushing through my body, my pulse quickening, my hands curling into a fist. I can't make Evelyn come back to me, and I can't know, once their door is closed, what comfort Ross provides her in my place.

30

THE LETTER READS:

> Dear Doc,
>   I've recommended my boss come to see you. He's a
> genuine certifiable, and should provide you with hours of
> fun. He refuses to believe I've turned a new leaf over,
> and he won't keep his paws off me. He says he's heart-
> broken about losing me, but I think his problem lies
> somewhere else, if you know what I mean.
>   Don't ask him about me and how I'm doing. He won't
> know.
>
> > Yours,
> > Annette

The man who hands me the letter is middle-aged, forlorn
enough to be heartbroken, but just as I tell him he should be
seeing someone who works with individuals, the phone rings.
"Michael, this is Evelyn. I'm sorry to interrupt you at work
but this is urgent. Can you meet me at the garage of Ross's
apartment house in half an hour?"

"Half an hour? In the garage? I'm in the middle of an
appointment now. Can't it wait?"

"I'm taking off from work right now. Believe me, I wouldn't
have called you at work if it wasn't important."

"What's the matter? You sound absolutely frenzied."

"Michael, there's no time to waste. Get your ass over there."

"All right, I'll be there." I tell Annette's boss that there's an emergency and I have to leave.

"Someone's really gone bonkers, eh, Mr. Jarriman?"

"I certainly hope not. But it sounded very important."

"Will I get a refund for this?"

"You haven't paid me anything, Mr. Gordon. There won't be any charge for this consultation, I assure you. You should be seeing someone else."

Once I've reassured Annette's boss, I put a note on my door canceling the rest of my morning appointments, and with the man still putting on his coat and hat, I run out the door and hail a cab to Ross's. Because of the morning traffic, though, Evelyn's already sitting in the driver's seat of Ross's station wagon, honking the horn so I'll be sure to see her. My mind races a mile a minute, cataloguing all the possible tragedies that could have precipitated her phone call, not daring to say aloud the one I'm hoping for. I get into the car, one of those Ford wagons with phony-wood side paneling. "What's happened, Evelyn, is everyone all right?"

She puts the gearshift into drive and pushes hard on the accelerator, her eyes intent on the road ahead. "I want you to take it easy, Michael. We're going to take a little ride to Westchester."

"My mother. It never occurred to me. She had a heart attack."

"No," she says, putting her hand on my leg and patting it, "she's physically all right. Your uncle Harry called. I've never even met the man, but he sounds like a complete idiot . . . he called me because he didn't know we were separated."

"He's the detective on my mother's case and he didn't even know we were separated? I could strangle him . . ."

"Anyway, he said he wanted me to tell you because he was afraid, after he saw you last, that you wouldn't be able to keep your composure."

"He's got some nerve."

"Your mother's been evicted, Michael. They're putting her out on the street right now. This very minute."

"Evicted?" I slam my fist on the dashboard. "She never even said a word. She never asked for a penny."

"You know your mother. Paying her bills, I'm sure she thought, was all she had left."

"A marvelous existence. I could kill the bastard. He's been sucking her blood for I don't know how long."

"You'll get your chance. He's up there with the movers. He tried to get an injunction, but he screwed it up . . . he just doesn't know what he's doing."

The thought of my mother on the streets, the ultimate disgrace for her, for any of us, is unbearable; it presses down on my body, reduces me to silence.

"The important thing," Evelyn says, "is that we're there to help. That's why I brought the station wagon."

She weaves her way through the traffic on FDR Drive, honking her horn, driving recklessly over potholes and old mufflers, up the Hutchinson River Parkway. I hold on to the dashboard for fear of my life.

"Ross will help," she says. "He's an excellent lawyer."

"I don't want his help."

"It's not the time to refuse anybody's help."

"Thanks for the advice."

"Or do you want to end up like your mother?"

We arrive at my mother's apartment complex in less than fifty minutes, but the movers have now been there for a couple of hours, and thanks to my mother's having carefully packed all her cartons, they seem almost done. There's the couch covered by plastic, there's the refrigerator with all the messages on it, there's the dining table. A few neighbors are watching. Uncle Harry's gesturing wildly at a lawyerly-looking man with an attaché case tucked under his arm as if he feared Harry was about to remove it from his body. And there's my mother, sitting on the curb, staring off into space in the same housecoat and babushka she was wearing when I last saw her.

Evelyn parks the wagon right in front of her, but it takes her a moment to recognize us when we get out of the car. "Mother . . ."

"Darlings," she says, clasping her hands in the prayer position. "Thank God you're here. And together again. It's the only thing that matters."

"Don't be stupid, Ma. You've been thrown out on the street."

She stands up to hug me while she reaches with one hand for Evelyn's arm. "It was a dump. Not worth a *hundred* a month. Thank God I'm getting out of here: they don't deserve a red penny of my money. Harry's going to help me."

I run over to Uncle Harry and before I know it I deck him on the sidewalk with a single punch. He sits there for a moment, putting his fingers to his lips. "He hit me. His own uncle, and he hit me. This is going to cost you, Michael Jarriman. Look," he says, showing me his fingers, "I'm bleeding. I've got witnesses. You saw the battery," he says to the man with the attaché case.

"Go fuck yourself," the man says, walking away from him. "You've made your bed," he says, pointing to the bed on the sidewalk, "now lie in it."

Evelyn approaches the man, full of questions. She introduces herself as an interested party. "You gave proper notice? Was a hardship claim filed? I assume you got the necessary papers."

"It's a pleasure to talk to someone who knows what she's doing. Here are all the papers," he says, taking an envelope out of his attaché case. "We've gone out of our way to be fair. You'll see photocopies of all the notices."

"Why wasn't I notified?" I ask the man. "I'm Michael Jarriman, her son."

"Because they specifically requested it," he says.

"Michael, it doesn't pay to argue," Evelyn says, after looking through the papers. "I've seen hundreds of these. They've got the law on their side."

"That's what I was afraid of. Ma," I say, shaking her, "what suitcases do you need? Where'd you put your clothes?"

"It doesn't matter," she says. "I've got nothing. I need nothing. The important thing is that you and Evelyn are with me. You don't want that Laurie."

"Which suitcases, Ma?"

"Any of them. See how a tragedy can bring a family closer together? It's important."

"Michael," Evelyn says, "just grab whatever suitcases you see and throw them in the back of the car. I'll call a storage company. You can't just leave your mother's furniture in the street."

I begin to pack the back of the wagon while Evelyn goes off looking for a phone booth. My mother is busy leaning over the cartons, all of which are carefully labeled: dishes, linens, books. She rips one open and brings a brown cigar box to me. "Here, look," she says, grabbing my arm. "I saved these for you. I knew you'd want them." She removes an envelope of photographs and puts them in my hands, photographs taken years ago, of Evelyn's and my wedding. Two bright-faced people obviously in love. Then a photo of the two of us when I open my practice, one of Evelyn in front of City Hall looking serious with her briefcase, then a newspaper clipping of Evelyn taken from the early 1970s, when she organized a work slowdown until the city agreed to pay certain benefits, and the single article I've written for a professional journal. An odd chronicling of our history.

"Put those away, Mother. We're not together. You're only making things worse."

"My eyes are deceiving me. Is that woman an Evelyn look-alike? And I suppose you're not my son. Is that what you're trying to tell me?"

Evelyn returns, pushes Harry aside when he tries to describe what went wrong. My mother turns to her with the photographs and Evelyn, though she winces momentarily, looks at them patiently, guides my mother to the front seat of the car, and sits with her. "That's wonderful, Ma." "You'll catch cold: it's better to wait in the car." "We'll take care of you. That's right: the family's together now. Don't worry about a thing." Once she's soothed my mother, she comes back outside to talk to me. "I took care of the storage people. The third company said they could come today: they were a little more expensive, but I might be able to have Welfare take care of part of the bill. I called them and we've got an appointment tomorrow afternoon. We'll get food stamps."

"Let's take her back to my apartment. There's plenty of room for her now. It's too big for someone alone."

"I don't think she should leave the county or rely on you yet. We can't give them any excuses for denying benefits. You should let your mother make the final decision about where she'll live. I don't think she'll move in with you, though. It'd destroy her. She's a little delirious now, but that's natural."

"Evelyn, you're being totally marvelous. I don't know how to thank you."

"She's my mother too, you know. You think I could live with myself if they threw her into a home? Thank God I've got some experience in these matters — at last my work's come in handy."

"What do you mean *at last*?"

"I might as well tell you — I've been thinking of quitting. Ross wants us to have a child. We talked about it a lot after you left last time."

"You'd be crazy to quit. You really believe in what you're doing."

"I know. Look, it's crazy to have this discussion now. Let's take your mother to a motel, then we can come back and wait for the storage people."

"Maybe we've both invested too much in our work," I say. "That doesn't mean you have to give yourself up."

"Later, Michael. The car's full. Let's get out of here."

We get into the car; my mother is weeping, the full impact of her eviction having finally hit her. Harry knocks on my window; I roll it down. "You should have gone to Vegas, Michael. Here, it's not too late," he says, handing me a piece of paper with two addresses on it, "office" and "home." "This is how to reach him. Your mother needs the money. Now especially."

"You're going to need it too when I sue you for fraud. If I don't kill you first."

"Michael," Evelyn sighs, then pushes her foot down on the accelerator before Harry says another word. My mother says, "Don't leave me. Alone. I want my children with me." Evelyn stops the car in front of a Best Western motel; I get out of the car and register my mother. When I get back, Evelyn's holding out a can of Coke and a pill for my mother. "Here, take this, Ma. It will relax you."

"I hate pills," my mother says, but she takes it.

"What's that?" I ask, taking a couple of suitcases out of the back seat. "What are you giving her?"

"A sleeping pill."

"Where did you get those?"

"My shrink prescribed them."

"Your shrink? You? Come on."

"Don't laugh. It's an honorable profession."

"Since when?"

The three of us open the door to my mother's new temporary residence. It could be Anywhere, U.S.A. My mother walks into the bathroom, flushes the toilet to see if it's working, looks behind the shower curtain to see if the tub's clean. "No glasses," she says. "There's toothpaste on the mirror."

"We'll take care of it, Ma," Evelyn says. "Here, you lie on the bed. Turn on the television. It'll take your mind off things."

"I hate the television," she says.

"We all hate the television," I say. "Just listen to somebody for once. Watch it."

"Good advice," Evelyn says, tucking my mother in as I turn on a soap opera.

"Good reception," I say.

"Michael, I think we should go back. Everything's still on the sidewalk."

"When the case is settled," my mother says, "I'll pay you back. Every penny of it. But don't leave me now. Don't leave me alone."

"We'll be back in an hour, Mother, I promise," I say. "Now you just relax."

Evelyn and I run back to the car. I watch her face while she's driving: she's intense, efficient, compassionate. She's totally wrapped up in my mother's situation. "I think we can build a good case for emergency housing," she says. "I know a couple of people in the department up here and we can break some of the red tape."

"And you want to quit."

When we return, Harry and the man with the briefcase have gone, a few small children are playing around the cartons and another is sitting on the couch, reading. The storage company arrives, they load up my mother's collection of possessions in no time, and I write out a check for them: two months in advance. Evelyn double-checks the items in the truck against a list she's made up, while I run up to the apartment to see if anything's been left behind. On our way back to the motel she stops at a liquor store, instructs me to wait, and comes back with a bottle of bourbon. "This is your brand, if I remember correctly."

"I think we've earned a drink. Several of them, in fact," I say, opening the bottle in the car and taking a swig. "Pretty degenerate, huh? See what's become of me?"

"Pretty degenerate. We've been running around like a couple of lunatics, but I think things are under control now."

"You do?"

"No." She smiles. "But one mustn't lose hope."

When we get back to my mother's room the shades are drawn, just as in her own apartment, the lights are out, and the TV's on, but my mother's eyes are closed. She's asleep in the fetal position. Evelyn covers her and kisses her on the forehead. "Our poor baby," she says, then joins me sitting on the other bed. We look at each other and take a deep breath. She takes my hand and presses it to her cheek. "I feel flushed."

"I'm totally exhausted," I say, removing my sport coat and loosening my tie. "I sweated through everything."

Evelyn takes the sport coat and hangs it up, then comes up

behind me and massages the back of my neck. "How's that feel?"

"Wonderful," I say. "Now what?"

"Let's just rest for a moment. I don't think any of this has registered yet. Like your threatening to sue Uncle Harry. I can't believe it."

"Can you believe," I say, pointing to my mother, "that in the middle of all this she took out our wedding pictures?"

"She really loved us, you know."

"In the past tense? She was right about one thing, though: a crisis brings a family closer together. Don't stop," I say, holding her hand to my shoulder. "It does feel good."

She stops and sits beside me on the bed. She takes my hand, raises it to her lips, and kisses it. I can't keep my hand from shaking. "There, there," she says. "Let's lie down for a minute." We lie down, side by side, for the first time in months, clutching each other so tightly I can feel the pulse in her fingers. I undo the buttons of her blouse; she closes her eyes but doesn't pull away. I take off her bra and caress her breast. "Evelyn, I still love you."

"After all this?"

"I know it's stupid. I can't help myself." She unbuckles my belt, then kisses my ear and whispers, "We shouldn't be doing this."

"We shouldn't? We're still legally married."

"Forget legally," she says. "Your mother's in the room."

"She'd be ecstatic if she were awake."

"She'd be hysterical if she were awake."

We take off the rest of our clothes. I look at her carefully, at her body, this woman's body that is simultaneously so strange and familiar, and I enter it, I enter her, my wife.

"I don't know what this means," she says.

"I don't care. Just think of it as gratitude if you have to." Then Evelyn relaxes her body, tenses up just before she comes, and lets out a tiny welp, a whine, a vibration of her voice I'm not likely to forget. Then we both lie back, my arm under her neck, side by side.

"I think I'm going to Las Vegas, Evelyn. I think he should pay for this."

"I think it's the right thing to do. Now."

"If he has anything resembling a heart he's got to give her something."

"And she'd much rather take his money than ours. I mean yours."

"Then you're behind me?"

"A hundred percent," she says. "One hundred percent. Michael," she says, turning to face me, "I'm going to have to tell Ross about this. All of it."

"And what do you think will happen?"

"I just don't know," she says. "I just don't know."

III

31

SPURRED ON BY EVELYN'S CONFUSION, I take the first available flight to Las Vegas, a Friday "night flight" on which I am joined by potential gamblers. They pass their time playing cards, talking about odds or the once-in-a-lifetime chance to see Sammy Davis, Jr., in person. It's a noisy group. I make notes furiously on my napkin, listing a number of reasons why my father should support my mother, beginning with the humane and ending with idle threats of lawsuits to garnishee his salary. The questions I wanted to ask him about our past together, about his leaving, seem much less important to me now that my mother's been evicted. For once I can put myself aside.

Circling over the city before we land, I'm taken aback by the colored lights on the famous "strip," this long, singular road growing out of the desert, this wet dream of a utility-company executive. No wonder they say it's always daytime here. No photographs, no slick Hollywood movies, could have properly prepared me for the gaudy glamour.

Except for the slot machines upstairs, the airport resembles a normal one, so I find my way to the car-rental agency rather easily. A patient young woman maps out in red the way to my father's house when I show her Harry's card with the address. I drive through the city, the streetlights making it easy to read my map; I look at the couples parading from one casino to the next, at the marquees filled with recognizable names from *The Tonight Show,* and singers from the age when my father was at home: Tony Bennett, Peggy Lee, and Vic Damone. As I drive away from the center of town I pass the all-night justice of the peaces, the instant weddings and divorces offered at "reasonable" fees, then the pawnshops, the less expensive and less accessible motels, and at last the McDonald's, the Kentucky Fried Chickens, and Bonanzas, which let you know you're still in America. Then a few more turns to the suburbs, the houses becoming more elegant the further I get from center city, the darkness heightened by the shadows of the mountain ranges, which seem simultaneously to threaten and to protect the city from the rest of the world.

Though my father's name is not on his mailbox, I double-check Harry's card against the number on the house and know I have arrived. I park across the street, turn out my lights, and stare at the building for a moment. What a contrast to my mother's squat apartment house. My father lives in a large and sprawling stucco ranch, New Mexican style, cream white. There are two cars in the circular driveway: a silver gray Cadillac and a maroon Datsun sports car. His nearest neighbors are city blocks away. There's no grass where the lawn ordinarily would be: instead a lone palm tree sprouts out of the moss-and-gravel pavement in front of the house. Near the palm stands a small fountain where I imagine birds are supposed to splash, but there's no water in it.

I get out of the car. The air is chilly: a desert night. A single light is on in the kitchen, and I see a figure pass by the window. A middle-aged woman wearing an evening dress and a pearl necklace. Is it Lisa, the same woman I met at my father's office so many years ago? I move closer to the house, peer into the kitchen, for the first time unsure whether incompetent Harry even knew my father's correct address. But as I look beyond the cactus plant in the kitchen window, I see the man Harry showed me in those photographs. He's sitting at the kitchen table, sipping a glass of milk; the woman has brought him something else from the refrigerator. She stands behind him while he eats, rubbing his shoulders. He looks up and smiles, pats her hand with his, and puts down his fork. The shock of this domestic scene, so harmless yet so intimate — it's almost as if I'm watching it on television. My father stands up and moves away from the table: next to his wife he's shorter and stockier than I remember him. So he doesn't look like me, I think. But perhaps seeing yourself in your father is like listening to your voice on the tape recorder: everyone recognizes you except you. Though there are still traces of black in his hair, his sideburns are shockingly white, and as he bends I see the same bald spot, the family trait, I saw in Burt's hair.

When my father takes his plate to the sink I have a clear view of the living room, beyond the kitchen. The room is all white, from the white plush rug to the white couch and matching set of armchairs. A fireplace houses two unlit cardboard logs, and a baby grand piano (the same one we used to own?) stands to the side.

He moves toward the window and the sight of his face so close to mine is frightening enough to make me retreat to the car: this isn't the meeting I first envisioned, with me as the intruder violating his privacy. In a few minutes he opens the garage from the inside, wearing a black silk suit; he steps outside and sniffs the air. Behind him is his wife, adorned in a small wraparound fur. By Eastern standards it's late, but it must be time for the second shows out here. They get into the Cadillac and I have no choice, after he's a block or two ahead of me, but to start up my rented Chevette and follow them back into the city.

The Steamboat is a small, three-story brick hotel with a false-front water wheel to the side of the entrance. Every hotel seems to have a theme, somebody's television daydream or overaged fraternity party. The Steamboat simulates the nineteenth century: the doorman wears a straw hat, a white shirt with a black-and-red garter on his arm, and red suspenders. Hollywood's riverboat gambler.

I park a few blocks away from the hotel and wait in the car for a few minutes, actually contemplating buying a ten-gallon hat for a disguise — at that moment I understand the long-term effects of television on my life. Then I walk to the hotel. The Captain's Table, the small lounge of The Steamboat, lined with slot machines, is about the size of my father's living room. And there he is, seated with his wife and four other people his age, about three feet from the stage. The only other patrons of the lounge are sitting at a table, staring at their empty glasses: they look as if they've been there since morning. I take a seat in the back of the room, as far from my father as I can get. Within thirty seconds a waitress, dressed in a red silk short skirt and black net stockings, asks me what I'd like to drink.

"Nothing right now, thanks."

"You might as well," she says in a Southern drawl. "There's a five-dollar minimum for the stage show."

"I'll take a bourbon with water on the side, then." And within another thirty seconds she returns with my drink and a hand for the money. "That was fast."

"Let's just say you caught us on an off night," she says, putting the money in an empty glass on her tray and returning to her seat at the bar.

The stage consists of a small platform raised about a foot off the floor, and the platform is shaped like a lifeboat. A lifesaver inscribed with THE STEAMBOAT hangs from the ceiling, and each of the tables is lit by a small yellow lamp in the shape of a paddle wheel. No vulgarity is overlooked.

Seemingly from out of nowhere a man in his early twenties, tall and thin, his face made up almost ghostly white, his eyes dilated, appears on the stage. "Hello, you all," he says. "I'm Rickie Marx, no relation to Karl or Groucho." He looks around the room, his head like a turret, at the silent audience. "A shame, isn't it? You're a good audience, though. Last night's audience was something else: a mortician's convention. I swear to God," he says, crossing his heart with his fingers, "I couldn't tell the salesmen from the customers." I look to my father, who's wincing, squirming in his chair. He whispers something to his wife while the others at the table stare blankly at the stage. "So you don't like dead jokes, is that it? A tasteful bunch. Well, let's talk about our favorite subject. S-E-X," he whispers into the microphone. "If I say it any louder I get too excited. I tell you, the world confuses me today. Women's lib., Save the Whales, gay rights. I went into a San Francisco bar the other night, over at Castro Street — you know the kind — and I ordered a Scotch. The bartender asked me how I wanted it and when I said 'straight up,' he threw me out on my butt." A moan comes from my father's table. "You don't believe me? I swear it's true . . ."

My father puts his palm to his face, shakes his head. A man at the table, seeing my father's expression, lets out a short, hollow laugh. Marx, startled by the sudden noise, breaks the imaginary veil of the audience. "That was funny?" he asks, staring right at my father. My father looks around the room to make sure Marx is talking to him, pauses when he sees me, then turns around in his seat and starts talking to his friends. I close my eyes, let the bourbon slide down my throat, and gesture to the waitress that I'd like another one. If it's going to be a long night, I want it to be as painless as possible.

Although no one laughs at his jokes, although there are only eight people in the room, Rickie Marx goes on with his routine; some of his jokes I can almost remember from *The Ed Sullivan Show*, others are too crude for the sleaziest of burlesque houses. My second drink arrives and is finished in about the time it takes him to tell a joke about, though I can't believe it, a farmer's daughter. Then Marx motions to the off-stage piano player, and bellows out a slightly off-key rendition of "Bewitched, Bothered and Bewildered." My father rises from his chair in the middle of the song, puts his wife's fur around her shoulders, and motions for her to get up.

When he approaches my table on the way out, I can't help but turn my face, stare off into the paddle-wheel lamp. Then, as his body is literally close enough to touch, I look directly into his face. The face of a sixty-year-old stranger. But he does return the look, I'm sure, his expression first bewildered before a sneer appears on his lips. This can't be a look of recognition, I decide, because he keeps walking. He's probably simply puzzled as to why anyone would come to see Rickie Marx of his own accord.

So it seems I've missed my first chance to claim him, to tug on his arm and ask, "Don't you recognize me? I'm your son." And since he's now seen my face, I decide not to follow him for a while; perhaps I'll have another drink and find a hotel room, then look for him in the morning. After Marx's routine The Steamboat seems peaceful again, save for some pre–rock-and-roll standards played by the piano player: "Gigi," "Begin the Beguine," "Smile," and so on.

When I get up to go to the bathroom, my legs are not quite sturdy and my gaze is dulled. I feel a pleasant buzz, though I cannot quite walk a straight line. Once inside, though, I see exactly what's behind the false front of The Steamboat: two greasy mirrors, sinks full of iron deposits and dirty enough for any Exxon station, and a toilet without a door or toilet paper. Ammonia permeates the air. It takes me a long time to pee — I can feel my heart race as I do, and zipping up my pants I come to the conclusion I'm not just a little loose, I'm certifiably drunk. Washing up, I stare into the mirror: the eyes are puffy, the mouth down-turned in a permanent frown. Could anyone tell that I'm my father's child? To be drunk is to be filled with self-pity. Nevertheless, I want to go for the show-biz gesture, to smash the mirror.

I don't know how long I've been staring at the mirror when someone else walks into the bathroom. I drop my eyes to my hands: I'm still soaping them up, rubbing off the top layer of skin with the abrasive chemical soap. When the stranger turns away from the urinal and moves to the sink to wash his hands, I feel as if I must be going crazy: it's the face of my father, unless the man in the club wasn't my father at all. But he already left.

I smile briefly in the mirror and the man returns the smile in his mirror. I shake my hands dry, and since there are no towels, I wipe them on my pants and move toward the door. This is no time to introduce myself. No sooner do I place my hand on the door handle, though, than I'm pushed into the door with enormous force, my face smashed into the wood. I can hardly breathe. My legs collapse and I begin to sink to the floor. I look back and I'm beginning to black out when I see this man, elbows to his chest like a football guard, exerting a force on my back I can't believe comes from a sixty-year-old man. "I can't breathe," I say.

"How'd you like to make that a permanent state of affairs?"

"Stop it, will you, for Christ's sake? You're hurting me."

"All right, you son of a bitch," he hisses. "Who sent you? Who told you to follow me?"

"What are you talking about?"

"I spotted your car in front of my house, punk. A green Chevette. Don't think I wouldn't call the cops." He leans into my body, increasing the pressure. I feel his breath on my neck. With one hand he grabs my hair and pulls it back so my cheek is against his. "Now: where are you coming from? Come on, tell me, or I'll smash your face in." But before I can catch my breath he says, "All right," and slams my forehead into the door. Again and again. A cracking noise. My own blood in my eye. I'm stunned back into childhood: my parents arguing at dinner. He tells me not to play with my food. I put my fist down on my plate and he pulls his belt from his pants. Stings my arm. I feel the sting now in the identical place. With all my strength I push my body away from the door and bang him against the opposite wall. I turn around and with the back of my hand I slap his face hard. Then I slap it again. "You stupid fucking asshole," I shout, "I'm your son. I'm your god-damn son."

32

H<small>E DROPS HIS HANDS</small> from his chest and stares at me. He says nothing. He touches his fingertips to his lip, which is bleeding slightly. There is no expression on his face. Then he takes his hand and smoothes down his hair. "I was afraid it might be you," he says. "I was afraid it might be you but I couldn't believe it. I mean, why didn't you just come up to me?"

"After all these years?"

"Of course after all these years."

I put my hand to my forehead, which is also bleeding. Enough so it coats my palm. "You hurt me. Didn't you know you were hurting me?"

My father steps forward to examine the wound. He takes off his silk tie and dabs my forehead with it, then wraps it around my head like a bandage. "I'm sorry," he says. Then he wraps his arm in mine and leads me out through the Steamboat lobby. A few tourists take their eyes off the slot machines for a moment to watch, but only a few. My father opens the rear door of his Cadillac and I slide in. He says something to his wife I can't quite hear. I fold my hands in my lap: sitting in the back of his car with my head bloodied and bandaged makes me feel like a criminal. I've been discovered, I've confessed. His wife turns around, extending her hand to me. "I'm Lisa. We met a long time ago but I don't suppose you'd remember."

Once in the house, he takes me to one of the bathrooms, which is decorated with full-length mirrors, a sunken bathtub, and Egyptian tile, all circa 1958. He sits me down on the toilet seat, takes a bottle of peroxide and some Q-Tips out of the medicine chest, removes his tie from my head, and tends the cut. It sizzles and bubbles up. "Don't worry, it won't hurt. It's peroxide," he says. "That's a nasty cut, though."

"I'm afraid I ruined your tie."

"Oh, Allie," Lisa says, standing on tiptoe to get a look at me over my father's shoulder. "I hope you haven't hurt him. Badly."

He glares back at her. "Listen, hon, this isn't exactly how I pictured my reunion with my son."

"Me either. I'll be all right," I say, moving to rise, but he pushes down on my shoulder with his hand.

"Let me wrap it in gauze," he says, "to prevent infection. So you're a shrink now, I understand."

"Actually a family counselor. Burt must have told you."

"Oh, I have my methods."

"So I saw."

"This is still a rough town, Michael. You never can be sure whether or not you've stepped on someone's toes."

"You don't think it's funny that I'm a family counselor?"

"Just because I divorced your mother? Don't be silly."

"That looks good," Lisa says. "I mean the bandage. Michael, I can't tell you how happy you've made us. We've been waiting for this day for twenty years. You must believe that."

"Not now, Lisa," my father says. "It's been a very long night."

"Well, it's true, Allie. Your own son should know that."

He bends down to look closely at my forehead. "Not bad. I'm not exactly Doctor Kildare, but I think it'll hold together. Lisa, could you make up the guest room for Michael? I think we all could use some sleep."

Fifteen minutes later I'm undressing in a room decorated

with hardwood beams, dressers, and bed. In the next room I can hear murmurs, my father and his wife talking, but I can't hear the words. I can't help thinking that if Evelyn were here with me she would have observed how Lisa waits on my father hand and foot. And I'd have to worry that she might tell my father so. But that was an old Evelyn, not the same woman who wanted Ross's child. I turn out the lights, get under the covers, close my eyes. In a few minutes the door opens slightly. I see the figure of my father in his pajamas. He walks in, sits on the edge of the bed, and straightens the blanket up to my neck. "I just want you to know," he says, "that whatever's happened, whatever the reason for your being here, it's good to see you."

"I'd like to say it's good to see you too."

"Then why don't you?"

"I don't know. We have some difficult business to discuss."

"I know that," he says, kissing me on the top of my head. "We'll talk in the morning."

☆

But I don't wait for morning to wake. My head throbs. It takes a minute to focus my eyes, but then I notice light leaking from the bottom of the door and I follow it. There's the silhouette of my father — he's looking out the living-room window at the mountain peaks, which are illuminated by the house floodlights.

"Staring out of windows is a family trait, you know," I say.

"Having trouble sleeping too?" my father asks. "Jesus, it's after four. I guess I'm a little excited by your being here. I'm not sure what you expect."

"Neither am I. Should I turn on the lights?"

"No. You might wake Lisa up. Actually I'm out here," he says, walking toward me, then collapsing on the couch, "because we had an argument. Lisa thinks I ought to give your mother something. As a gesture."

"You're a little ahead of me. But I'm afraid she needs much

194

more than a gesture: she's been thrown out of her apartment. And she deserves the support."

"You didn't let me finish. Not because she deserves it, but as a gesture to let you know . . ."

"To let me know what?" I ask, sitting beside him on the couch.

"It doesn't matter," he says, throwing up his hands. "I can't do it. I won't do it. I don't know if I can make you understand." My father stands up again, begins to pace with his hands behind his back. The way an expectant father might pace in a 1940s-movie maternity ward. "Let me put it this way. I can only be direct with you. I wasted some seventeen years of my life with your mother. Living with her, those last years especially, was like having an enormous weight around my neck. I felt like I was choking to death. And once I left, well you know what she did."

"What do you mean?"

He sits beside me again, this time leaning back in the corner of the couch. As far away as he can be on the same piece of furniture. "Let me tell you a story. When I first moved back to the city with Lisa I used to call to speak with you. Your mother wouldn't let me. She said an adulterer was a bad influence. She said she'd get a court order and have me arrested if I appeared anywhere near the house. This was the fifties, remember: she might have been able to pull it off. An adulterer, for Christ's sake."

"Can't you understand how hurt she felt? Here she was, married all these years, probably no other man ever touched her, and she didn't have a clue she might be left with nothing."

"If she didn't have a clue it was her own fault. The clues were everywhere. Let's go out for a walk," he says. "I'm afraid I'll raise my voice and wake up Lisa. She shouldn't be involved in this. Her only urge is to protect me."

My father opens the sliding glass doors, and the two of us, dressed in pairs of his pajamas, put on shoes and walk toward the mountains with the floodlights behind us. Our bodies make elongated shadows on the desert floor and when my father gestures with his hand it's as if a cloud has passed overhead. There's a thin layer of frost on the shrubs and the lawns of the other suburban houses. Within a matter of minutes my hands and feet are almost numb. Several hundred yards from the house, my father says, "I used to be very restless when I was your age. Your presence reminds me of it. I can feel the tension."

"Mother still talks about it."

"I always had one foot out the door. Not just in the marriage. But I like people here," he says. "My life is peaceful. At sixty you feel like you deserve at least that."

"I can understand that. I have to tell you, though, I think the way you went about it was wrong."

"Wrong? Leaving your mother was wrong? She really poisoned your mind. There are divorces every day. You're a family counselor, you should know that."

"That's not what I meant. Packing up and running away like that," I say, stumbling over the words; they don't sound right, even to me. "I mean, didn't you care what happened to us?"

"Your mother made it impossible," he says. "If you don't understand that, you don't understand anything. Case closed."

"Then you have no regrets."

"Absolutely none."

"That makes us very different," I say, and as soon as I've said that the weight of moral judgment, the clarity and harshness of it, seems to lift from me. "Then tell me what it was like to leave a son behind. What is it like to start over, from the beginning?"

"You really want to know?" He turns to face me. "You won't like it: it felt great. It was like" — he pauses — "it was like waking up one day and realizing you're not dead. It saved my life."

"That's quite a testimony," I say. I look at this man who's so concerned with his own survival, a man who has hurt me and others I love, and I'm unable to hate him. For him to admit making a mistake would mean tearing down everything he's spent the last twenty years trying to build up. His whole life in the desert. In a dispassionate moment I can see it's necessary for him to hate my mother. Having told my clients so many times blame is not the issue, how can I ask him to confess? With your own father, though, it's not quite the same. He has a side to his story — in his terms it might make sense. But my mother has nothing, and I've been injured in ways I'm just beginning to understand. "You know, I used to tell my friends in college when families came up that your leaving didn't matter very much. I don't remember much about you when I was growing up. If I'd admitted that it hurt me, I think I felt I'd go under. I think I invented the idea that I could take anything. It worked for a while. But I paid a price for it."

"Is this your idea of a moral lesson, Michael?" he says, thoughtfully. "A lot of time has gone by. We can waste it by dwelling on this garbage or we can try to enjoy ourselves."

"Those are our only two choices?"

"As far as I can tell. Look," he says, pointing in front of us, "the sun's beginning to rise over the mountains. I didn't know that's where it came up."

"And you've lived here how long?"

"Long enough to know better. I'll tell you the truth: I never notice things like that. I come from the city, and I think I could live anywhere. I'd rather be indoors."

"Let's go back, then. I'm freezing my ass off. Also my feet. Also I think I'm getting hungry."

"That's a good sign " he says, and we turn away from the rising light he found so beautiful a moment before. Awkwardly he puts his arm around my shoulder. As if he'd never embraced a man before. And in a moment he lets his arm drop to his side.

"I'm glad you're happy with Lisa," I say.

"I'm happy as a lark," he says, but I can hear in his voice his distraction, his mind moving somewhere else. "I've never been happier in my life."

"You know," I say, trying to bring him back, "I really do

understand about your leaving. My wife and I have recently separated."

"Burt didn't mention that."

"Burt didn't know. It hadn't happened then. I suppose that figures in somewhere about my being here."

"For a divorce? I know a lot of people. If you want my advice, put her out of your mind completely. Move somewhere else if you have to, start seeing other women, unless you already have one." He speaks with the clarity of someone who's given this advice before. Or taken it. "You have to live your life."

"Now you don't understand. I've tried that. It's not what I want. Though I wish Mother had heard some of that advice." At the mention of my mother's name, though I won't betray her by saying so, I'm overtaken by a wave of guilt, a fluttering in the stomach. I think of her so many miles away, my last image of her being tucked in by Evelyn at the motel. If she could see the two of us together now, I honestly think it could kill her. I walk in front of my father as we approach his house. Opening the sliding door, I smell fried onions. Lisa's in a flannel nightgown, standing at the stove frying eggs.

"Hello, boys," she says in a cheerful voice. I'm sure she'd like nothing better than for us to get along, for our lives to be mutually repaired, the way it happens in TV movies. "Did you have a nice walk?" she asks.

"Yes, we did," I say. "A little chilly, but nice."

33

My father has appointments he can't break. We eat quickly, discussing nothing in particular in Lisa's presence; I replace the gauze bandage with a Band-Aid, and by eight o'clock we're out of the house. In the car on the way to Caesar's Palace he explains, in an animated voice, the nature of his job. "You see," he says, twisting his lower lip slightly, as if offering confidential information, "I'm an agent for 'alleged talent.' If you were paying attention to that comic last night, Rickie Marx, you'll have an idea of what I mean. Not that I'd take on anyone that bad, mind you . . . but close. It's also the price you pay to live out here, and every once in a while you come across somebody really good and you can forget about the Rickie Marxes of the world."

"It's the same thing with people I work with."

"Yeah?" he says. "Anyway, this thing at Caesar's Palace today, I want to prepare you for it but I don't exactly know what I'm in for. I owe this guy Eddie Shansky a favor. He took on one of my dance acts at Caesar's without even an audition." My father shakes his head, I want to tell him to pay attention to his driving, but the road's surrounded by so much harmless desert even going off the road wouldn't cause any problems. "You pay favors back in this town. That's one thing. I mean, in the bathroom, for example, you could have been from Eddie. You might have misunderstood something."

"Misunderstood what?"

"I'm not complaining, mind you. There are plenty of rewards to my job. Not the least of which I'm driving now. And in spite of what anybody says, show business is a people business. I happen to like working with people."

I say nothing. It's silly to interrupt him, to get my two cents in. Instead I look out the Cadillac window at the now almost familiar road approaching downtown, as we pull up in front of the columns at Caesar's Palace. A man dressed in a toga takes my father's car keys, and after receiving a dollar bill, drives the car away.

I've seen enough gambling movies not to be shocked by the luxurious decor of the Palace: the golden chandeliers, the plush, deep-red rugs, the infinite rows of slot machines and infinite suppliers of quarters. It's the mezzanine that surprises me, the closed doors of the Chariot Room, the Spartacus Lounge, the Appian Way: a scene that so approximates the conference rooms of the Los Angeles Hilton it takes an act of supreme will not to immediately run to a room on the twentieth floor.

My father opens the doors to the Colosseum, an enormous room the size of a college gymnasium. With his back to us, a short, skinny man in black tights snaps his fingers for some fifty young, attractive women in various states of dress, from leotards to short skirts and halter tops. The women stand still in rows of five, hands behind their backs in military at-ease position.

A man in a navy pinstripe suit with close-cropped blond hair and one of those ageless faces approaches my father with an extended hand. "Allie, so good to see you." The way he hangs on the word *see*, it's almost as if he'd expected my father to disappear from the face of the earth. "Listen, I really, really appreciate this." He chooses his words carefully. He could be a Wall Street lawyer, a member of the mob, a young psychologist out of a Midwestern university.

"That's all right. Eddie, this is my son, Michael."

"I didn't know you had a boy, Allie." He looks me over,

cuffing me lightly on the side of my head. "He must be your younger brother, eh, fella?"

"Now, what was it you needed me for?" my father asks.

"Sure, we'll get right to it. You must want to spend some time with your boy. You see, we're opening a new routine for Shecky, and I need your advice on the dancers. Fruity Elvin over here," he says, pointing to the man in tights, "got them down to something over forty, but now's where I need your advice."

"I can give you an hour," my father says.

"That's fine. Wonderful. And I'll see what we can do for Burt. We can always find a place for someone with his skills." At the mention of Burt's name my father turns his face from Eddie and me and walks toward the man in tights. Eddie calls after him. "By the way, Allie," he says, lowering his voice when he gets my father's attention, "it's topless."

"Jesus, Eddie." My father shakes his head. "What is this, the squeeze?" Eddie smiles at him and shrugs. "Every time I do one of these freebies," my father says, turning back to me, "I think of your mother. In New York I wouldn't have to touch this." Then he paces in front of the dancers with his hands behind his back. He's not interested in my response. And as the music starts up, the theme from *The Pink Panther,* my father smiles slightly, keeping time with his foot.

"Three-four time," Elvin says. "One, two, three, and kick." The women step forward, step to the side, step back, raising their arms in the air as they kick to every fourth beat. Human gyroscopes. My father walks up and down the rows, studying each dancer's legs, her composure, facial expressions. After a little while he says, "To the left side of the room, please," "Sorry, no thanks," "Not this time," "That's close, but not exactly what we need today," "Very good, to the left please," and "Too theatrical." The rejected women drop their heads or walk to the corner of the room, expressionless, pick up their purses and changes of clothing. The chosen lean against the wall, chattering to one another or catching their breath. In twenty minutes, about the time it takes to play one side of a record, my father has thinned out the number of dancers to fifteen. "We'll take a short break here," he says.

"Amazing, Allie. Good work," Eddie says. Eddie's now chewing gum, has his arms crossed in front of his chest, as if he's seen one too many Lee Marvin movies.

"You wanted half a dozen with two standbys, right?" Eddie nods to my father, and then my father walks over to me. "I'm afraid this isn't very interesting. You want to wait in the coffee shop until I'm done?"

"No, that's all right. I don't want to lose track of you."

"It's not all like this," he says. "I've handled people like . . . never mind. I'll tell you about it later. We'll be out of here soon." The self-consciousness already seems uncharacteristic. "You're in for a treat, then."

The same music starts up again; the women now line up single file as they dance. Most of them are heavily made up: their faces painted with color, their expressions vacant or absent. My father walks up and down the row with Eddie. "Okay, girls," he says. "Same routine. Tops off, please."

A few of the women casually begin removing their tops, as though they were undressing before the mirror or in a women's locker room. One jokes in mock shyness. "But, Mr. Jarriman," she says, unbuttoning her halter, "no one ever told me show business was like this." Another woman does shyly turn her back as she rolls the top of her leotard to her waist. She's the one with the smallest breasts, and couldn't be older than seventeen. Surprisingly, the sight of these half-dressed women is not the least bit sexual; the atmosphere is colder than what could safely be called clinical. My father looks at the women and nods; I begin to wish I'd followed his advice and gone downstairs.

He paces the room again, this time absent-mindedly. Then, as if he's suddenly snapped out of a trance, he passes by them, one by one, with his final judgment. "Very nice," he says. "Definitely." "Posture," he tells the next one, shaking his head. "Too old." Then, as though he were reaching out to shake a stranger's hand, he holds his palm beneath one woman's breast and holds it there, supporting it. "A little too much sag." Finally, as he approaches the shy young woman who turned her back to undress, he says, "Come back in a couple of years. You'll be good."

"What am I supposed to do in the meantime," she says in a nasal twang, "caddy?"

"Develop," he says, making a muscle. "I've seen it done. Don't be discouraged."

The music stops, the dancers fall out of line. The runners-up take their rejection professionally, that is, without emotion. I'm feeling a little sick to my stomach.

"That should do it, Eddie," my father says, brushing his palms together with a clapping noise. "My hands are clean. Let's get out of here," he says to me. "I wish you didn't have to see this."

"That's all right." But the truth is, I can't look at him for a while. "I would have stayed downstairs, but I don't have much more time."

"You don't approve," he says as we walk to the door. "It won't *hurt* you to see this. That son of a bitch, Eddie. I could kill him."

"Approval doesn't really enter into it," I say. And it's true, I'm more embarrassed for him than ashamed that he should be humiliated in my presence. But I also know that the man I've wanted to talk to all these years doesn't exist. I invented him for the same reasons people like the Carletons invent counselors to solve their insoluble problems. "But I really should get back."

"Really?"

"I have a lot of commitments. Clients who need me, and," I say, smiling, "a couple of women to care for." Laurie and my mother quickly come to mind, but I know it's really Evelyn I'm thinking of, selfishly, the recent insane and exhausted moments we spent in the Best Western motel in view of my mother.

"I suppose I understand." My father sighs. "But really, you let me off so easy with your mother. I expected you to come down a lot harder on me."

"What for? There wasn't anything I could have said to have changed your mind, was there? I told you she'd been evicted. It was no surprise to you."

"I suppose not," he says. "No, definitely not." We're both quiet for a while, waiting under the hotel columns for the man in the toga to return my father's car. It's a sunny morning, very hot: I'm sweating through my shirt. I look at my father, who seems to be staring off into the mountains again. Or maybe he's not thinking of anything at all. The man in the toga arrives, pulls the car up to the curb. "Good morning, Mr. Jarriman," he says, and the recognition seems to cheer my father up.

"At least let me drive you to the airport," he says. "I'll have Lisa take care of the rented car." I nod in approval, and we're off. He turns on the air conditioner and the radio. His look is serious — it's the same contemplative and distracted look I saw just before he decided which women's breasts were large enough for the show. We get on the interstate, he turns on the cruise control and leans back in his seat. Just before the exit sign for the airport he says, "I'm sorry I didn't live up to your expectations. I'm just an ordinary man."

"Join the club. I'm sorry I didn't live up to your expectations either. I suppose it was wrong to have expectations."

"Lisa will be disappointed, but I'll explain." He pulls up to the curb of the terminal. "All the airlines are in the same building. Remember what I said about starting over."

"You didn't hear what I said about wanting my wife back, did you?"

He shrugs and leans toward me as I get out of the car. "Don't say I didn't warn you. Will you keep in touch?"

"I think I will." And I lean toward him to receive his awkward hug. "I'm sorry if I disturbed your peace of mind for a while."

"Don't be silly. You have my address now, right?"

"Right. I don't suppose you'll be in New York any time soon."

"I don't suppose."

I withdraw from his arms and walk to the terminal without turning around, not because I'm afraid I might see my father crying, but because I'm afraid I'll see him gone. I don't feel grief. I leave Las Vegas no less confused, but comforted by my confusion. The hurt little boy who wants to strike out at his father is still there, but now he's accompanied by a man who wants to forgive, to leave the past where it is.

34

I RETURN TO NEW YORK with no sweeping generalizations
about my history, my family, or my marriage. My father's
tirade against my mother, my mother's unflagging bitterness
about my father, suggest only the constancy of human frailty.
Not so much that pain hurts, but that it lasts. And each of us,
in our most childish of hearts, believes he's been singularly
injured. In my own way I'd expected Evelyn not only to tol-
erate my endless reveries and ambiguities but to find them
noble. It shouldn't have shocked me so when she didn't. But
remembering her response to my meeting with Burt, I resist
the temptation, proud as I am of the illumination, to call her.

All that being said, when I pass Laurie's store on my way
home from work on Monday, I can't help but go in.

"Hello, stranger," she says as I walk in the door. "What
happened to you? Your plants die?"

"No. At least I don't think so. Truth is I haven't paid them
much attention lately."

"My, aren't we the forgetful ones."

"Are you being nasty? I've never seen you nasty before, so
I can't tell for sure."

"I was only teasing," she says, shutting off the fluorescent
lights and taking plants out of the window. "Closing time."

"Because I wanted to call you. I've been away."

"Good for you."

"See, you are angry at me."

"I just got mad." She bends down to spray a plant with her misting can, then leans back, placing her hands on her hips; a long curl of hair falls over her right eye and she gracefully sweeps it away with the back of her hand. "Now, if only this Boston fern'd respond to treatment, I'd hardly have a mark on my record."

"Too bad I'm not Cary Grant."

"It sure is." She looks up at me. "Why?"

"Then I could tell you how pretty you looked when you were angry."

"I don't think you could say it even then. Hey, what's that Band-Aid doing on your forehead?"

"Oh, this," I say, touching it with my fingertips. "I'd forgotten all about it. Just a little something I got in a fight with my father."

"Now there's a family story I could stand to listen to. At least it's got some action."

"I told you I was away. Friends?" I say, extending my hand.

"We'll see."

"How about if I took you up on that offer to listen to some jazz?"

"Too late. Ron Carter left ages ago. Although," she says, "there's a pretty good old-fashioned torch singer at Sweet Basil."

"It would have to be named for a plant."

"No accident, honey," she says, gesturing to a plantless shelf on the wall. "Here, help me close the metal grate so I can get out of this place."

"The grate's a good idea. It must have set you back plenty. This time I pay: I don't care if it is a freebie."

"A Band-Aid on his forehead and he wants to pay for the girl. What's happened to you, Michael? You've become a regular macho man."

She hands me one end of the grate and gestures for me to pull. We walk toward Fifth Avenue to catch the downtown bus, while I tell Laurie of the visit with my father and watch her expression as I shift from episode to episode — her smile when I mention Eddie Shansky and the topless scene, her anger when my father refuses to help my mother. She kisses my hand, I forget what I'm saying in the crowded bus, I look out the window, shaken by my attraction to her. It hasn't diminished. Enough.

Sweet Basil stands in the middle of the original bohemian haven, a neighborhood that has gone through more renovations than the Carletons' psyches. Not far from where Ginsberg and Corso used to drink in the 1950s. While I was growing up it turned into a mecca for middle-class Long Island and New Jersey teen-agers on the move. Two blocks east, in the 1960s, it became the East Coast Haight-Ashbury, with more than its share of runaways and hard drugs and knifings in broad daylight. Somehow the neighborhood's made a comeback: it's one of the safest areas of the city now, a refuge for many of the city's gays. The houses have been restored, the streets don't seem extraordinarily filthy, couples — mostly male and male, female and female — walk the streets with little fear in their faces. A good sign.

The club is something of an anomaly: knotty-pine walls and larger than I remember clubs in the 1960s, it caters to a high percentage of straights. "Heteros' last hope," Laurie jokingly says. Most of all, Sweet Basil seems too clean, too Midwestern, with its wood furnishings and hanging plants, to be the real thing.

Laurie obviously feels at home. She nods at the bartender as we pass, she's given a good table close to the stage. Others wave at her when she sits down. Definitely her turf. I wonder how many men sitting at the bar are or have been her "friends," or if they wonder what she's doing with an uptight guy in a brown, 1960s vintage, herringbone sport coat. In moments of anxiety it's remarkable how quickly those old bourgeois impulses for approval come back. How strong. I reach across the table for Laurie's hand. She smiles and leans in my direction so she can make herself heard.

"So," she says, "after all this, how do you feel about your father now?"

"A thousand different ways. He was such a stranger to me. What amazed me most was how little his leaving had to do with me. In his own way, he's a very charming man. I think he loves the woman he's with; he seems happy in his work."

"Interesting, but that doesn't say how you feel about him."

"I'm angry at him, I'm sad for him, I'm happy for him. How's that for being evasive?"

Laurie shrugs.

"Actually, there are just a few ways I don't want to be like him."

"Like?"

"Like I wouldn't want to be blessed with his amnesia for people he's supposed to care for."

"Well, if that's what you're worried about, forget it. You don't have any choice in the matter, Michael: you're a born rescuer. Your shrinking, your going out to Las Vegas for your mother. Why, the first day you came into the store you were like Prince Valiant trying to recover my virginity. It just so happens" — she tilts her head, and tightens her lips — "I don't need your protection. Which might be why you lost interest."

"Not fair. It's not so horrible for people to need each other, Laurie."

"I know. I don't mean to blame you for it. It so happens it's not always my idea of a good time."

"You know, I do care about you very much."

"And I also know you're still in love with your wife. Remember that day you described her for me? So strong, principled, et cetera, et cetera, how different you were?"

"Yeah."

"Well, it always struck me that you were really talking about yourself: you and Evelyn are probably the last living do-gooders in the city of New York."

"Well, that makes me a little sad."

209

"It shouldn't. You don't have to love everyone and everyone doesn't have to love you. It's not in the contract."

"That's not what made me sad, I guess. Are you still seeing the horticulturist?"

"On the side." She laughs. "Come on, we're not enjoying the music."

I turn to the stage, a stage the size of the Captain's Lounge in The Steamboat; a single blue light shines from ceiling to floor. In the time we've been talking, this is what I've missed: we've been served drinks, my bourbon is half-finished; a short black man with a mustache, gray-peppered hair, and a three-piece navy pinstripe suit has come on to the stage to sing, accompanied by a bass player, pianist, and drummer; the room has filled so much that rows of customers have lined up against the walls to listen. Our dinners, two big caesar salads, have been set before us.

"You look worried," Laurie says. "What's the matter?"

"I just forgot where we were."

"See where all this talk gets you," she says, putting her forefinger to her lips. "Let's listen to Johnny Hartman."

Once I listen, Johnny Hartman's voice seems haltingly deep and modulating, as though his diaphragm and mine were connected by a thread. He stands completely still, allowing his face to express any necessary emotion. He holds the microphone tight and close to his mouth, and his voice glides effortlessly from low octave to high. "He has an oceanic vibrato," Laurie says. "He used to sing with Coltrane."

He sings songs like "We Kiss in a Shadow," "Dedicated to You," and one of my parents' favorites, "My One and Only Love." *The blush of your cheeks tells me you are my own,* he croons, *I give myself in sweet surrender, my one and only love. The very thought of you* ... I am in the Village and Harlem nightclubs I imagine as part of my parents' courtship. My father, in his double-breasted suit, adjusting his collar in the mirror in a photograph my mother took — even then the ladies' man. Dancing cheek to cheek with my mother. They're in their early twenties, he whispers his hopes for the future in her ear: a son, a house in the country where they can take long walks under the trees. In a time before shopping malls and fast-food palaces are hammered into the landscape. My parents are hopelessly distracted into love. What happened? What happened doesn't matter now; nostalgia, too, is an act of will. I look at Laurie, sitting across from me, her palms supporting her chin; she's moodily listening to the music too. She's as attractive as ever. Only now she seems miles and miles away from me.

This is corny, isn't it?" she says, wrinkling her nose.

"I like it."

"I like it too."

"But I think it's a little too much for me. Can we get out of here?"

"Sure," she says, and she lets me pay the check. We gravitate toward Laurie's apartment, which is not far from the club. We walk without talking, her arm wrapped in mine. The Village streets are still filled with couples looking in the closed store windows, walking in and out of the late-night bookstores and restaurants. When we get to Laurie's door she examines my face closely, giving me one of her doctor-to-patient looks. "You want to come in? Could be your last chance."

"What do you mean?"

"I mean I think I'm going to Colorado. New York's no place for a girl like me. The most interesting landscape I see is my store window."

"When did you decide for sure?"

"Relax. I was being theatrical to get your attention. I decided long before I met you and it'll probably take me six months to a year to get things straightened out on this end. I went to college out there, you know."

"No, I didn't know."

"The offer still holds, though."

"I don't think I should. Not tonight."

"Poor Michael," she says, then kisses me on the forehead. "He can't take anything casually. You probably shouldn't have come to see me tonight. You weren't ready yet."

"I know. I'm ..."

"If you say you're sorry I'll brain you." She puts her arms around me and kisses me, lip to lip, tongue to tongue. When she disappears into her apartment I turn away to head uptown, unwilling and unable to think about my feelings for her. I walk the couple of miles to my apartment, and when I get inside the lobby I find a piece of paper taped to the outside of my mailbox. It reads,

> Dear Michael,
>   I've been phoning all night. No answer. Came to ask
> you *not* to call or come by for a while. At least until
> things calm down a little or straighten out. All hell's bro-
> ken loose on the Western front.
>
>   E.

A message personally delivered asking me *not* to see her? Whatever her motives, I decide, putting the note in my jacket pocket, this is one rescue mission I'm refusing to take on.

35

Even from the parking space assigned to my mother at the Best Western, I can hear the music from *The Red Shoes*. Which means my mother is using the portable phonograph I brought her. "There's nothing on the television but trash," she'd complained, as if it were the motel's fault.

"Perhaps there are some X-rated movies on the cable," I said.

"Very funny. You must have gotten the dirty mind from your father," she'd said, and within a week I bought her the phonograph.

Today she seems in good spirits, is wearing a navy blue skirt and cream-colored blouse instead of the usual housecoat. "Come into my castle," she says, inviting me in with the sweep of her hand. And she has seemed to accomplish small miracles with the room, replacing the kitsch art with Degas dancer reproductions and family photos I don't know how she got. In the bathroom is a hotplate and a little refrigerator.

"You're not supposed to have cooking implements in your room," she says proudly. "Go ahead, you can read it on the back of the door. It says so right here."

"So how did you accomplish this coup?"

"One of the chambermaids is a doll. She's going to school part-time. She wants to be a nurse."

"And you're her first patient."

"Let's just say she likes my company."

"Very mysterious."

"Mysterious my bottom," she says. "Have a seat on my couch. Some people actually *enjoy* my company, for your information."

I sit down on the gray-plaid Herculon couch while my mother sits on the edge of the bed. "Of course people do. Was the couch here last time?"

"Evelyn's been here to see me several times. I don't think I bore her."

"I never said you bored anyone. I'm here, aren't I? There's no gun at my back."

"Take it easy. You want some tea? I can make iced: there are buckets of it in the laundry room and Evelyn got some of my kitchen utensils out of storage."

"You've been seeing a lot of my ex-wife."

"She's been marvelous. Let me pull open the blinds. There's a wonderful view of the shopping mall. It's so plastique here, Michael, it makes my apartment look like the Modern Art Museum." She gets up from the bed, lets in the light and the view of an A&P, a Bonwit Teller, a Sears, and a huge parking lot. She strides back to the bed without her usual limp.

"But you're comfortable here."

"At least I can entertain." She walks into the bathroom, puts up a kettle of water for tea. "They said I can stay here until they find me a satisfactory place to live. A real place, not a dump."

"Evelyn again?"

She nods. "I had to sign a lot of papers. Verify that . . . you know. It was humiliating. Don't worry too much: I think she's coming to her senses."

"Ma," I say. "I don't think I want any tea, thanks. Let me take you out to dinner. I hope," I say, hoping against hope, "you haven't been talking to her about us. Believe me, it's not in our best interests."

"Out to dinner, that's a lovely idea. I have one dress in my closet I haven't worn in years. Since there's nothing much to do here, I decided to let it out at the seams to fit the new me. You have to wear something, after all."

"I thought you'd be a little harder to convince."

"Disappointed?"

"Of course not," I say, watching her reach for the dress in her closet, hold it on its hanger against her frame. "It's just that it used to be a fight to get you to walk around the block."

"If we ever did go for a walk you'd have understood. In my neighborhood we might not have made it back alive. Don't laugh. So what do you think: do I look ridiculous?"

I look over the navy blue silk dress with large white polka dots and padded shoulders. Because I know my mother, because I know the dress is at least thirty years old, it does indeed look ridiculous. On the other hand it doesn't look so different from dresses I've seen in those fashionable boutiques, or those worn by punk rockers. "I'd have to see it on you," I say, "but I think it'll look snazzy."

"You really think so?" She looks me over carefully to make sure I'm telling the truth. "I know it's crazy, Michael," she says, "but I feel like I'm on vacation here. Living in the motel reminds me of vacations we used to take in the Poconos or Lake Placid. Only more pleasant." She walks into the bathroom, closes the door to change, and says, "The tea's about to boil. I almost forgot. I'll let it steep for a few minutes. You can change the record if you want to."

"No, I like 'The Red Shoes.' It brings back memories. I really don't want any tea, Ma."

"It's just that they take care of you around here. They'd make the bed and vacuum if I let them."

"If you let them?"

"This is my home," she says.

"Don't get too used to it," I say.

"I know. I suppose when I get a place of my own it'll take some getting used to. It might be a real letdown."

"Don't think of it that way."

"There," she says, swinging open the door. "Have you ever seen me dress so quickly?"

"No, I haven't."

"You see, there's not all that much time left."

Since I can't figure out whether that statement reflects the old Mother or the new, waiting for death or defying it, I decide to let it pass. "So, where should we go?"

"Every day when I shop at the A&P I pass by this nice Italian restaurant, but there's no menu in the window so I can't tell if it's overpriced or not."

"Well, we'll soon find out," I say, and my mother folds her arm in mine, double-checks the lock on the motel-room door, and we walk to the mall, which is only a few hundred yards from her new residence. Looking at her as we walk, I'm amazed she could get the fabric to stretch so much and yet fit her body without making her look like a packed salami. But she was always a master seamstress, and while my father was spending all our money (she liked to tell me) on other women, she repaired all her dresses, mended my father's socks and my shirts until they were composites of woven threads. She took an odd, chilling satisfaction in that necessary deprivation. Now, as we walk into the restaurant, typical of mall restaurants (with the antiseptic smell of boiling, starchy water; the rouge of the elderly; woodlike paneling; and fluorescent lighting), she tells the headwaiter she doesn't want to sit close to the door. She points to a booth in the rear of the restaurant where it's "quiet enough to talk without looking at the shoppers."

We sit down, the waiter perfunctorily hands us menus, then returns to a table where the other waiters are reading newspapers. "They must do a decent lunch trade," my mother says. "It's almost empty now and it's past five. Anyway, I'm not even that hungry. It's just good to get out. Just as I feared," she adds, "it's way overpriced."

"Don't worry about it. You're not paying tonight. Let's start with a carafe of red wine."

"All right. That sounds delightful: I haven't had a drink in a restaurant since" — and her eyes intensify as if she were focusing on a sign at the other end of the room — "let's just say for a very long time."

We order the house wine and sit silently for a while. My mother strains for a number of things to say, beginning words, sentences, but then sighs and takes a sip of her wine. We listen to the waiters' conversation, their complaints about their wives, the size of their tips, the trade the Yankees just made. "They think money can buy them another World Series," one of them says. Another responds, "If they got it, they might as well spend it."

When it's our turn to order, my mother says, "I'll just have a cup of minestrone and the tossed salad. The luncheon special."

"Ma, I'm taking you out to *dinner*. I'll have the lasagna, a side order of clams in garlic sauce, and some antipasto. Are you sure you don't want anything more? You know I can afford it."

"I told you I wasn't that hungry," she says, handing the menu back to the waiter and gesturing for him to go away. "You shouldn't say that in front of him: it's none of his business how much you make."

"Don't spoil the meal, Mother. Please."

"You know how much I could make the lasagna for?"

"Mother." In the presence of absolutely no one I'm totally embarrassed by my mother's dedication to poverty, to her scrimping and scraping after my father left, to her survivor's mentality. Is this what annoyed my father, he so obviously dedicated to the pursuit of pleasure? Not really. What was there to argue about if one person spent and the other saved? No, the resentment came later.

"On my little stove in the bathroom I could have cooked you a really decent meal. We could have watched television afterward."

"I don't watch television anymore, Ma."

"That's good," she says. "Evelyn says you were away for a while."

"Yes, I was. What's Evelyn doing talking about me?"

"She still thinks about you, that's why. You don't want to tell me where you've been? That's all right. You've been with that Laurie, haven't you?"

"No, I don't want to tell you where I've been. I'm not accountable to you anymore."

"You've never been. But you're so touchy with me. It's like I don't even know what I'm saying that offends you so much, it's like I touch you somewhere where you hurt yourself but you don't tell me where, so how am I supposed to know where to stay away from? I don't think it's fair."

"No," I say, as the waiter puts down my antipasto and my mother's salad. And I'm thinking that if this had been three months ago and she'd pushed me about the trip I might have told her where I'd been. How capable of cruelty I was, and how capable I am now of restraint. "No, it probably isn't."

"All I was saying was that Evelyn's been showing me around looking for apartments in the area. We haven't found anything yet but she's hopeful. And I can see she's not happy with the lawyer. Lawyers are crooks. She told me as much herself."

"Eat your salad before it gets cold."

"We don't have to talk about it. But you should talk to someone. Have your little secrets. I won't tell you how I got the couch."

"Okay, Ma," I say, "tell me how you got the couch. Let's have a nice dinner."

But the remainder of the meal is as strained as its beginning. The tension comes, in part, from having expected so much from my mother, because she's been trying so hard (for herself and for me) to change, but she's fifty-eight years old and just as stubborn as I am. I pick up the check on the condition that she can leave the tip. When we get back to the motel room she takes a whiff of the air and says, "Oh, we left the tea steeping. It was Earl Grey." Then she moves over to hug me, her grip tight on the back of my head, pulling me close to her. "I'm sorry," she whispers. "It was so good of you to take me to dinner."

"It's all right, Ma. Any change takes some getting used to. And you can always reheat the tea, right?"

"What the hell," she says, smiling, taking the pot and draining it down the bathroom sink. "We can boil another pot and throw the old one out. You only live once, you know what I mean?"

36

I HAVE MY WORK, and I'm slowly learning other pleasures. Walking around the city, for one. Listening to music. Going out to eat. Movies, novels, even fixing up the apartment.

My office continues to be a revolving door: old families I've been working with walk out, satisfied or not, together or apart; new families, full of trouble, are anxious to begin. Having been a student of Benny's, I begin to take on more couples with children. The family seated before me now, frenzied and frightened, wait for me to take the lead. The father's around my age, dressed in a short-sleeve shirt and dungarees. The mother's a plain-looking woman in a brown polyester pants suit who sits formally, with her hands crossed over the purse on her lap. The children are nine and seven, lively, but distracted: the older girl's wriggling in her chair, the younger coloring a book on the rug. It's the older girl who "has the problem": she's been diagnosed as hyperactive but the prescribed drugs have had no effect. She's restless, "bitchy," the mother says, can't concentrate on her schoolwork. The guidance counselor at school suggested family counseling, which is why they're here. At this point they know something's wrong, but not exactly what.

"I got so depressed when the drugs didn't work. That it might have been something we did . . ."

"We're doing the best we can," the father interrupts. "She doesn't want to listen."

Soon enough questions will be asked, doors will open, their confusions will multiply. I'm tempted to ask if they're sure they want to go through all this, but at this point my job is to listen, to watch them interact, to look for patterns or danger signs. We go around the room: each member of the family tells his or her side of the story. "If only she'd sit still for a moment," the father says.

"If only you'd stop bugging me," the child says, standing up in a burst of anger. She holds her arms tight to her sides. "If you'd stop bugging me," she repeats, but can't complete the sentence. "No more doctors. I don't have to talk to any more doctors, do you hear?" And she begins to cry. Her mother cradles her in her arms while the father stands up and, hands in his pockets, turns away to look out the window. First blood. As they continue talking, interrupting one another, revising each other's stories, they become recognizable, resembling other couples I know: the Carletons, the Ellers, Evelyn and me. I can guide them a little. In their openness and lack of direction, they push and they retreat, they exhaust themselves by the end of the hour.

"Do you think you can help us?" the mother asks. "As you can see, we're a mess."

"We're making a little progress already," I suggest. "I'd like to help with some of the questions."

"I don't want to see any more doctors," the nine-year-old says, but this time with less conviction.

"We're a pain, I know. But what if we could get your parents to bug you less?"

"And she us?" the father asks, smiling, and his daughter responds.

"I'm not promising anything," she says.

"Me either," I say, and the tension's broken some; it's a good time to break. I escort them out the door, the cycle's in an upturn, we've been through something together, and we all fill with a little hope.

37

I SEND WEEKLY CHECKS to my mother now through Uncle Harry, giving him a small cut (to be paid back, he says, when he makes a breakthrough in the case); my mother thinks he's managed to garnishee part of my father's salary, so we've kept her dignity intact. It's a lovely time in the city, a Sunday morning in mid-July. The gray winter's passed, the overbearing summer heat and humidity have not quite set in. My apartment's old enough so I can open the barred windows, air out the apartment, admit the mild breeze.

I walk to the park, which is bright green, blossoming, unthreatening. There are children flying kites, joggers of all ages, bicyclists, softball leagues, even a few couples rowing in the muddy pond. A few of those seated on benches, mostly the elderly, nod at me as I pass, and for a moment I can believe the city's not so uncivilized after all, a person could actually live here and not be in constant fear for his life. When Evelyn and I were together we didn't exactly go out of our way to avoid the park, but we did spend most of our time on the indoor sports of thinking or being socially useful. We equated long walks with aimlessness, leisure with decadence.

I wait on line at Ferraro's, one of many to make a ritual out of the Sunday *Times*. I check to make sure all the sections I want are there: Sports, Arts & Leisure, even the News of the Week in Review. I plan a feast for brunch: cream cheese and bialies, Bermuda onion and scrambled eggs. When I get back home I turn on PBS on the radio. The announcer is introducing the first act of the weekly opera: today it's Verdi's *Don Carlos*. Poor Carlos, it seems, has fallen in love with King Philip's wife. He's torn between politics and love, he can't choose between his loyalty to Rodrigo and his own desires. A perfect candidate for counseling.

Midway through the third act the doorbell rings. Unheard of: no one ever visits me at home, and for a moment I can't decide whether to answer it. When I open the door I find Ross and Evelyn, dressed in their summer regalia: Ross in a powder-blue golfing shirt and yellow pants, Evelyn in an almost translucent cream-colored dress and sandals. "We were out taking a walk," she says, "and we thought we'd stop by to see how you were doing." On tiptoe she peers over my head into the living room. "Is that all right?"

"Sure. Check-out time is eleven A.M."

Evelyn frowns.

"No, it's all right. Come on in. I was listening to the opera."

"I've been trying to call you," she says. "But you're never home."

"I'm home."

Ross sits on the couch, inspects the room. "Nice place."

"It hasn't changed much since . . ." Evelyn says. "I mean there are some new plants and some nice posters on the wall."

"I'm getting used to it."

Evelyn sits in the wicker rocker opposite Ross and begins to rock. "So what's happened since you went to see your father? I've been worried."

"There's nothing to worry about. I handled it all right."

"You don't want to talk about it," Ross says.

"There's nothing much to talk about. It was kind of anticlimactic."

"Oh," Ross says, scratching his head. "Say, you wouldn't like to come to a ball game with us, would you?"

"Excuse me?"

"I got some tickets to a Mets game."

I look over at Evelyn. "I hope you two aren't on some sort of sympathy mission."

"No, it's nothing like that," Ross insists. "I just got some tickets at the office and . . ."

"Don't lie, Ross," Evelyn interrupts. "We decided" — she pauses, looking for his approval — "that no matter what happens we'd like us to all be friends."

"That's a pleasant thought," I say. "Do I have any choice in the matter?"

"Of course you do," Ross says, rising from the couch. "If you'd like us to leave."

"I'm not sure. What brought on this sudden change of heart?"

"Lots of things," Evelyn says. "Benny . . ."

"I can speak for myself, thank you," Ross says. "If you want to know the truth, you got my son excited about baseball. I'd like to learn more about the game so I can spend more time with him. Where I grew up we played mostly soccer and rugby."

"Where'd you grow up, on the Thames?"

"And Benny thought you were being immature about Michael, Ross," Evelyn says. "Why don't you admit it? We've been going through some rough times since we last saw you, Michael. Constructive, but rough."

"I don't think I want to hear about it."

"Anyway," Ross says, "you wouldn't have to pay. I'd appreciate some pointers."

"Who's playing?" I ask.

Ross takes the tickets out of his pants pocket. "The Mets against the Braves."

"Sounds like a lousy game. It says here" — I point to the newspaper — "they're both in last place."

"Please, Michael," Evelyn says. "I'd really like you to go with us."

"All right," I agree, "but I was really enjoying myself before you two arrived."

Driving to the stadium, I sit in the back seat, lean back, and listen. Ross says he's already memorized the rosters. Evelyn tells me about new pressures on the job, how the recent cuts in personnel have demoralized her.

"How's Benny?" I ask.

"He's fine," Ross says. "He always asks about you."

"I'm sorry. I miss him."

"That's all right," Ross says, looking over to Evelyn. It's an issue they've obviously discussed. "We're grateful to you."

We arrive at the stadium twenty minutes before the game, but the stands are mostly empty. There's nearly half a season to go and both teams are long out of the pennant race. New York fans are not stupid: the Mets are no longer the new kids in town, they're far from the miracle Mets of '69, so the fans stay home. Or they jog, take walks, visit relatives in the suburbs.

Ross buys a program and Evelyn grabs it from him as we walk to our seats to join the loyal five thousand. "Who should we root for?" she asks.

"You root for the home team," Ross snaps, turning to me. "Evelyn has no sense of loyalty."

"What's that supposed to mean?"

"You know exactly what it means: it's a totally foreign concept to you."

"Ross," I say, "you have to tip the attendant who wipes your seat."

"I didn't ask him to wipe it. It was perfectly clean."

"You're not talking about *loyalty* loyalty," Evelyn says. "You're talking about loyalty to you. I'm not your Irish setter, you know."

"Never mind," I say, taking two quarters out of my pocket to give to the attendant. He looks at me as if to say he sees all kinds here, then walks off to the next set of customers. "These are good seats. Let's not argue," I plead. "It's too nice a day for it."

"I was only talking about the concept of loyalty," Ross says.

"And I was only talking about who we should root for, for Christ's sake," Evelyn says. That being settled, I take my seat between the two unpracticed brawlers.

225

Evelyn and I stand for the national anthem. Ross remains seated, his arms crossed, muttering, "All hail to fascism." Evelyn and I smile at each other and sit down. "What Ross is referring to, Michael," Evelyn says, "is that I'm thinking I might want to come back. If you still want me to."

"Can we pay some attention to the goddamn game?" Ross pleads. "Why is Swan throwing the ball to Stearns when there's no batter yet? Isn't that taking unfair advantage?"

"They're just warming up, Ross. The game hasn't started yet."

"Oh," Ross says, writing something on the program.

After the first Braves hitter flies out, the second batter chops a routine ground ball to the Mets' rookie second baseman, who boots the ball and throws it over the first baseman's head. "That was lousy," Ross says. "Why are they so lousy?"

"No talent."

"I don't believe in talent," he says. "It's an elitist concept. It depends upon instruction, right, honey?"

"Tell it to the second baseman," I say. "Why this sudden change of heart, honey?"

"Don't be mean. You have a right to be mad at me. I ran away when you needed me. There are problems in every relationship: I think I understand that better now."

"I brought it on myself. I pushed you until you acted out what I feared most: my abandonment."

The third Braves batter hits a long drive off the right center-field wall, scoring their first run. Already the Mets fans are booing, cursing at the pitcher. "That was exciting," Ross says. "Is he a good hitter or is Swan just a lousy pitcher?"

"A little bit of both. It takes two to make a mistake," I say. Ross and Evelyn nod almost simultaneously.

"I've been unfair to all of us," Evelyn declares. "I've caused nothing but grief."

Ross looks past me to Evelyn and narrows his eyes. "What you two don't understand is that I'm the one who made a mistake." He stands up to face the two of us. "I lost Christine the same way. I did it to myself. I was afraid to give up control.

My therapist said so. I was afraid to let them breathe, I was afraid they'd leave me. I'm afraid of women." He nods, as if agreeing with himself. "That's it. I'm clearly afraid of women. Can you understand that?"

"You certainly had me fooled," I say.

"They're afraid of you, too," Evelyn says.

"Would you please sit down?" the woman behind Ross asks.

"Certainly. I'm sorry," Ross says, sitting down. "I wanted to be strong, Evelyn. I thought you'd respect me for it."

"I do respect you," Evelyn says.

"Just when you're ready to dismiss someone as a complete fool," I mutter to myself. "It's all right, Ross. Authority's a problem for fathers."

Ross shakes his head. "I want my son to respect me."

"He respects you," I say, taking his hand. "It's impossible to be perfect. To be a perfect father."

"I know," he says. "I'll never learn."

The Braves keep hitting and the Mets keep muffing chances in the field. Already behind four to nothing, the Mets replace their starting pitcher before they've had a chance to get up.

"This is an exciting game, I guess," Evelyn says.

"I don't know," Ross says.

"Do you think we ought to go?" I ask.

"No, I'll get a hold of myself," Ross says. "I really want to learn about this."

"You see how infielders are moving in toward the plate?" I say. "They're hoping for a ground ball. To cut off another run."

"What difference does it make, if they can't catch the goddamn thing?"

"I don't know," I say.

"You never answered my question, Michael," Evelyn says. "About my coming back to you."

"I've wanted you back since you left, you know that. It's just that" — I pause — "what's to assure this won't happen again?"

"Nothing," Ross says. "Absolutely nothing. At last" — he

claps his hands — "three outs. Maybe now we can get back into this game."

The Mets go down, one, two, three. Only one batter manages to hit a fair ball, a Baltimore chop to the shortstop. Ross sighs, "I thought the Braves were supposed to be lousy too."

"They are," I say. "Probably just not lousy enough."

"I don't know what you see in this game, Michael," Evelyn says. "It has all the excitement of a Zen monastery."

"It is a meditative sport," I say. "But when you think about it I guess it is pretty boring."

"Pretty boring? We still have seven innings to go."

"Eight," Ross corrects Evelyn. "Benny thinks it represents our culture's last acceptable form of hero worship."

"Bullshit," Evelyn says. "Benny couldn't possibly think that."

"I extrapolated it from what he said. He's very bright. He has an overview of the game."

"That's probably why he'd never say anything like that," I say. "What does he think of this mess, anyhow?"

Ross considers the question for a moment. "I suppose we're all affected in the same way. We're at each other's throats, the tension has us all on edge."

"He cares deeply for all of us," Evelyn says. "I think it hurts him that we're all in pain."

"Maybe we should go to him for counseling. Certainly Michael hasn't gotten us anywhere."

I ignore Ross's remark and try to concentrate on the game, but it isn't easy. The possibility of Evelyn's return scares me to death. Almost as much as the opposite. Besides, the pitching is awful; almost every batter seems to go three and two before he strikes out or hits the ball. The Braves score once more in the fourth on a wild pitch and the Mets manage to eke out only one infield hit. The highlight of the game for us comes when Braves third baseman Joel Horner, a temperamental ballplayer and the Braves' only quality hitter, drives theatrically into the third-base stands for a foul ball and just misses it. We can see his pained expression as he tumbles into the front row of seats just a few yards in front of us. "If we were a couple of rows closer, I could have caught him," I say.

"Now that's exciting," Ross says.

"Can we go home?" Evelyn asks. "You still haven't answered my question, Michael. Do you enjoy humiliating me like this?"

"Of course not. I just want to be cautious. I want it to be right."

"Good idea," Ross says.

"Can you be quiet for a minute, Ross," Evelyn pleads. "This is hard enough. Michael, we've invested a lot in one another. We've grown a lot together."

"And apart. But we can't get back together if you're feeling a wave of nostalgia, Evelyn."

"That's insulting. I still love you, you know. More. Now that you don't come to visit, I miss you all the time."

"You do? Then move out of his apartment. Don't be too impulsive. Take some time by yourself and think about it. Make sure it's what you want."

"Then will you take me back? How could anybody be that sure?"

Evelyn reaches out for my hand; in Ross's presence I'm embarrassed by her touch. Also comforted by it. Also guilty about it. I turn to Ross to ask him how he feels about all this, but he's not in his seat. He's moved to the front row with his scorecard, leaning over the stands and peering into the Mets' dugout. It's touching that he would do all this for his son. "You know, Evelyn, it's not fair to Ross to do it this way. It's cruel."

"It was his idea," she says shyly. "Actually it was my idea, but his therapist agreed, and Ross made the final suggestion."

"I guess we shrinks have to stick together," I say. "But give yourself some time. There's only so much chaos any of us can endure."

"I know," she says. "I think I have to leave. I can't stand this anymore."

"You can't? You take the car: I'll tell Ross. You know how to reach me."

"I hope so," she says, walking toward the concession stands and out of sight.

I go down to the first row to join Ross, who's talking to the Mets' equipment manager, pumping him for information. "The reason the Mets are losing," Ross says, turning to me, "is that they have no power hitters. No one to drive in any runs."

"Are you all right, Ross?"

"Is Evelyn gone?" he asks, looking back to the stands. "Of course I'm not all right. I haven't been all right since the first time you had dinner at my apartment. It's just that there's nothing I can do about it. If I don't let her go," he says, but trails off. "I'm not being a hero, Jarriman. She made up her mind a while ago and I haven't been able to persuade her that it's the wrong thing to do, that we can work things out. I don't like you, you know. I don't like how you neglected her, and I don't appreciate the grief you've caused me."

"I know you don't," I say. "That's all right." I sigh. "Evelyn took the car." I make my way back to my seat, then an inning later to the outer edge of the stadium, where I take the subway back to midtown. There's no way to figure out what just transpired, how we all went our separate ways. I get out at the Fifty-ninth Street stop, but I'm not prepared to go back to my apartment alone. I decide to take advantage of one of the city's offerings, an air-conditioned art-theater matinee of a John Garfield double feature. He's so shy and tough, so lovable and pugnacious, that in the wombish dark of the theater I momentarily inhabit his character, the picture moves me. Within a matter of minutes, though, exhausted, I fall asleep.

38

LUCKILY FOR UNCLE HARRY, I'm in a good mood the morning he greets me at my office door. "You start late," he says, as I put the key in the lock. He strikes a pugnacious pose, leaning against the wall, one foot in front of the other, his arms crossed in front of his chest. "When I was your age I'd be working as soon as the sun rose over the Palisades."

"The sun doesn't rise over the Palisades."

Harry shrugs, straightens his tie as I open the door. He's dressed in a blue serge suit with padded shoulders, a red print tie with a sailboat on it, and a golf-club tie clip. What's left of his hair is neatly combed: the wet look.

"What's the occasion, Harry? You a pallbearer in your spare time?"

"Very funny," he says. "I'm a professional. I'm here on business."

"I ought to throw you out on business."

Harry sits down on the couch when I walk to my desk. He looks around the room and shakes his head.

"What's the matter?"

"I've never been in a shrink's office before," he says, imitating a shiver with his shoulders. "It makes me feel a little crazy."

"So what's your business, Harry? I have a lot of work to do."

231

"First of all, I want you to know I'm dropping the suit against you. Don't look so puzzled," he says, pointing a finger at me. "You know exactly what I'm talking about. Assault and battery. Don't laugh, snotnose. I had a strong case. There were witnesses. People looking out the window."

"Harry, I'm very busy."

"Oh, yeah, I can hear 'em. They're beating your door down. Listen, Mikey, I didn't come here to make trouble for you." When I continue writing in my log, when I don't look up, he adds, "You're not making this easy on me. I'm concerned about your mother. She can't live in a motel for the rest of her life."

"I'm taking care of it, Harry. I've been looking for places."

"I'd like her to move in with me."

"All right, Harry, what's on your mind? Why don't you just this once come out and say what you're thinking. No bullshit."

"No, I mean it. No bullshit. Your mother and I have always been close. Long before you were born. More so, then. Look, I feel bad you think I was taking advantage. I meant to put that son of a bitch behind bars. It's still my intention. But mainly your mother and I have a lot in common. Our marriages didn't go terribly well, we're both alone in the world. I make a decent enough living, a lot of it under the table, so I don't have to pay taxes; she's a good cook. Between the two of us, my income and her Social Security, we could find a nice little place, who knows, on the Island."

"Now you want her Social Security."

"Well you let up for one fucking second? You can have her Social Security. I'll pay the rent. She can put it in the bank. I'm saying I want to take care of her. We can take care of each other, all right?"

I look at my uncle in total disbelief. He doesn't blink, he doesn't avoid my gaze. "I think you're serious. You haven't spoken to her about this?"

"Of course I've talked to her about it. She doesn't want to be a burden. We'd have to convince her. Your mother's rotting away, Michael." Harry sighs, rubbing his scalp with his hand.

"She needs somebody to care for her. She won't let you do it, you know that. She wants you to have a life of your own."

"So you've come to ask for my mother's hand in marriage."

"What kind of marriage? You wanted me to tell you what was on my mind and I did. If you don't approve, the matter's dropped. It'll be on your head."

"You know about the incest laws in this country, Harry? Your own sister? They could send you up the river ..."

"He's going to bust my balls. Go ahead, put me on the skewer. But think about it. Then just tell me yes or no."

"You know it's not up to me. I can't control my mother's life."

"Then you won't stand in the way."

"I want you to drop the case against my father, Harry. I don't want another penny wasted on it. I don't want my mother giving it another thought."

"You'd rather throw out eighty thousand."

"I want my mother to forget about it. To forget about him."

"That I can't control. But if that's the condition ..."

"It's not a condition, Harry, it's a premise."

"I'm not a lawyer. Whatever you say goes." Harry stands up, extends his hand. "Friends?" he says. I remain seated. "Look, I won't take a single penny for myself, not for a pack of cigarettes. I'm a lonely man. Someday you'll be like me and you'll understand."

"Fat chance."

"Then it's a deal," Harry says, taking my hand and shaking it. He walks over to the window and stares out. "It's going to be a nice day, I can tell. You know, when I was having trouble with Sylvia, when she wouldn't get off my back, we almost went to a family counselor. In those days, of course, it was unheard of."

"So what happened?"

"So what happened is she died, and I was rid of her. I cried at her funeral, then I was rid of her. I saved myself a lot of grief. Now you guys throw around a bunch of terms, you know, *ego, paranoid,* you analyze the meaning of a fork in a dream and some poor sucker hands you fifty bucks. It's quite a racket," Harry says, shaking his head. "I'm small-time compared to you."

"Don't overextend your welcome, Harry. We were getting along fine for a second there."

"I still dream about her sometimes. It's always on the Boardwalk, the sea is pounding, the gulls are there, she's wearing this dress that shows too much of her cleavage . . ."

"Good-bye, Harry," I say, rising, guiding him gently toward the door.

"I was just trying to get a little free advice, that's all."

"Take Nytol," I say. "Take care of my mother, Harry. I'll be watching you."

"Watch, watch. I'll look forward to it," he says, his hand on the doorknob, peering into the outer office. "We'll have you over to dinner soon. There's someone here to see you," he says, turning back to me, then winking, adds, "I feel much better, Doctor Jarriman. Who'd believe how much a fork could mean to me. All that pent-up emotion. I'm a new man. A new man."

Harry finally leaves. I close my eyes for a moment to relax before my first appointment. I open the door. Sitting next to Mr. and Mrs. Parrish is Evelyn, her hands folded in her lap, a suitcase between her knees. "Next," I say, and I walk toward her; I embrace her, I take her in.